The Truth Never Spoken

BAKER OAKS SERIES

AMBAR CORDOVA

*To all the girlies that love a Dirty-Talking Cinnamon Roll
who falls in love with his girl, even when she's imperfect.
The kind that would move mountains to see her smile.
The kind that puts her first, every time, no matter what.*

*..... and to Joey, because in you I found
exactly that and so much more.*

Author's Note

Hi friend,

I am so excited you picked up my book today. I hope you love it as much as I do, and that Allie and Jake will stay close to your heart forever. There is so much I could say about this book, but I just hope you give it a chance. Also, I would love to hear from you. Feel free to message me on social media, or shoot me an email. I love to chat!

The Truth Never Spoken is a contemporary romance with some on-page topics that may cause some difficulties for the reader. I will list them at the bottom of this page as they may be spoilers, and I want to allow those of you who don't care about Trigger Warnings to skip them if you want to. If you want to know what they are, just keep reading and you will see them soon.

This book is also a romance with on-page spice. However, there is an option to skip the explicit scenes. Some chapters have open door spice, so when this symbol ⊟ (signaling an open door) shows up, feel free to skip until the next chapter. It won't affect the timeline if you skip it so I wanted to let you know in case reading closed door is your jam, you could have an alternative.

This is a work of imagination and completely fictional. Some medical scenes may not showcase what would happen in real life. It is okay to not believe real doctors would do that. The characters in this book are not real and some scenarios may not happen in real life either. Same with some of the football scenes and logistics.

Now for the trigger warnings. If you read dark romance, these warnings are nothing for you; they are more for the rest of the population. There will be profanity, on-page violence towards a 17-year-old, a toxic parent relationship, and an on-page car accident. Some scenes feature an ambulance ride and a code blue situation at a hospital, as well as a football injury. There is some emotional abuse (neglect) in a marriage. There are on-page descriptions of drinks, drugs, and sex.

PASSPORT
The
Never
Spoken
AMBAR CORDOVA

Playlist

I LOVE MUSIC! I have been working on this playlist longer than I worked on plotting this book. There are no rules on how to listen to this but to enhance the experience, some chapters have song titles that match the overall feel of that chapter. Feel free to listen to them after you read the chapter (or during if your brain will let you do that<3)

Part 1: Bruises - Lewis Capaldi
Part 2: When The Sun Goes Down in Georgia - Corey Smith
Part 3: Unsteady - The Ambassadors
Part 4: Maybe Next Time - Jamie Miller

1 – Running with the Devil - Alexz Johnson

2 – Miss Americana and The Heartbreak Prince - Taylor Swift

3 – I Miss You, I'm Sorry - Gracie Abrams

4 – Tennessee Fan - Morgan Wallen

5 – Rockin' & Rollin' - Nashville Cast

6 – Bejeweled - Taylor Swift

7 – Meanwhile Back At Mama's - Tim Mcgraw Ft. Faith Hill

8 – Bicicleta - Carlos Vives Ft. Shakira

9 – Back To December (Taylor's Version) - Taylor Swift

10 – Robarte Un Beso - Carlos Vives Ft. Sebastian Yatra

11 – Coney Island - Taylor Swift Ft. The National

12 – Kiss Me - Ed Sheeran

13 – Cornelia Street (Live from Paris) - Taylor Swift

14 – Stay - Zedd Ft. Alessia Cara

15 – Steal The Show - Lauv

16 – You Are the Reason (Duet Version) - Callum Scott Ft. Leona Lewis

17 – Ho! Hey! - Nashville Cast

18 – Am I Wrong? - Nico & Vinz

19 – when the party's over - Billie Eilish

20 – Gold Rush - Taylor Swift

21 – If The World Was Ending - JP Saxe Ft. Eva Luna Montaner (Spanglish Version)

22 – Hey There Delilah - Plain White T's

23 – Without You - David Guetta Ft. Usher

24 – Hold On - Chord Overstreet

25 – Heal - Tom Odell

26 – This Love (Taylor's Version) - Taylor Swift

27 – Take Me - Alex & Sierra

28 – Dress - Taylor Swift

29 – Epiphany - Taylor Swift

30 – Back to You - Selena Gomez

31 – Chasing Cars - Snow Patrol

32 – Shivers - Ed Sheeran

33 – Fingers Crossed - Elijah Woods

34 – Champagne Problems - Taylor Swift

35 – Heart Like Yours - Willamette Stone

36 – The Last Time (Taylor's Version) - Taylor Swift ft. Gary Lightbody & Drunk Me - Mitchell Tenpenny

37 – Afterglow - Taylor Swift

38 – I Almost Do (Taylor's version) - Taylor Swift

39 – The Alcott - The National Ft. Taylor Swift

40 – Stick Season - Noah Kahan

41 – Little Did You Know - Alex & Sierra

42 – See You Later (in ten years) - Jenna Raine

43 – Tee Shirt - Birdy

44 – All I Want - Kodaline

45 – Big Girls Don't Cry - Fergie

46 – 21 - Gracie Abrams

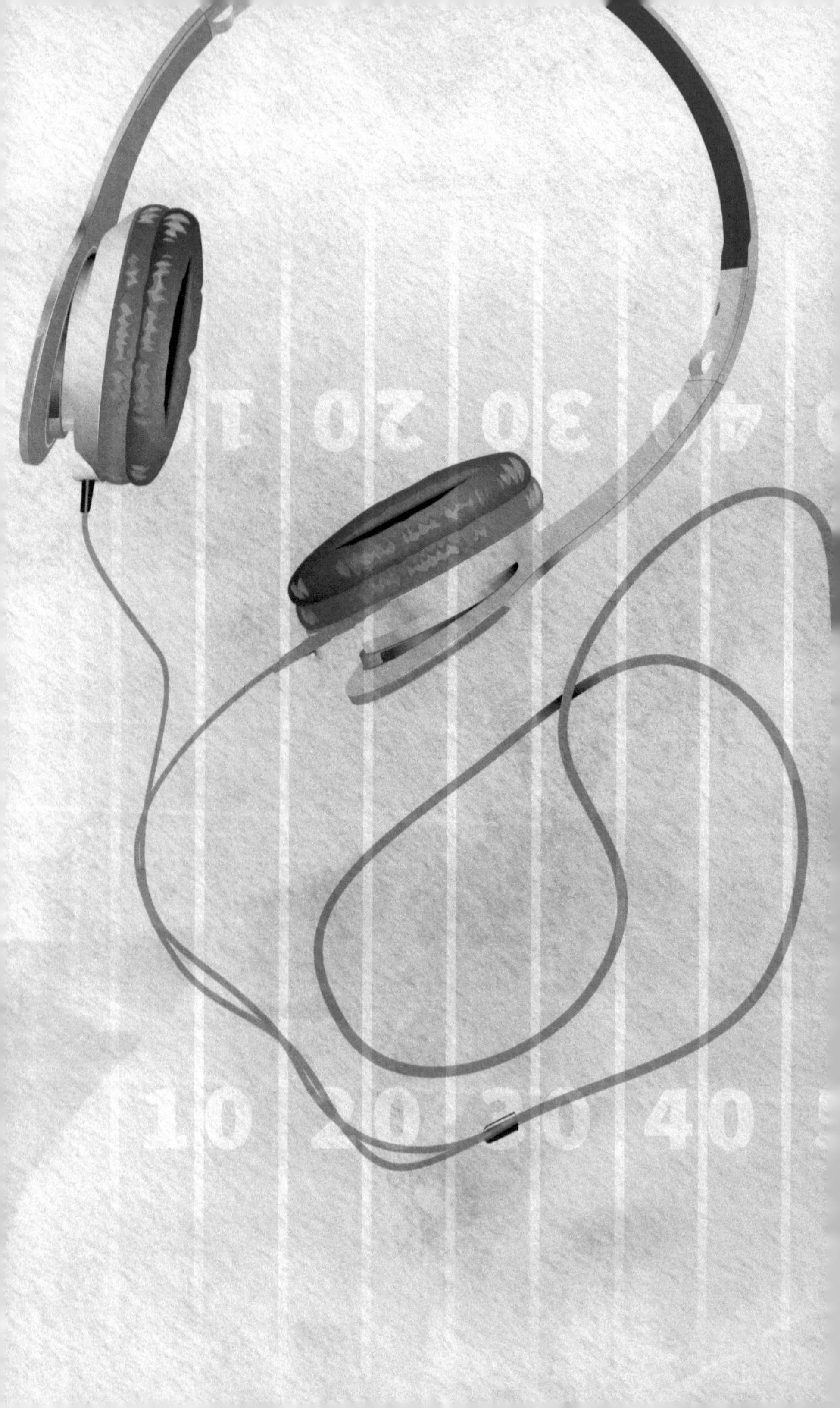

BRUISES, LEWIS CAPALDI

WITHOUT HER, MY WORLD
STOPS SPINNING.
MY HEART SLOWS ITS BEATING.
MY CONTROL FUMBLES
OUT OF MY HANDS.
I CEASE TO LIVE,
AND I JUST EXIST.

CHAPTER ONE

Running with the Devil, Alexz Johnson

I wish after years of traveling for work, flying would finally get easier, but it is just not in the cards for me. The moment I arrive at the airport I start thinking of all the things that could go wrong – all of the *what-if* scenarios - and all the things that already have gone wrong today.

As I'm rushing through the airport, going through my checklist for the hundredth time today, I feel my phone vibrate in my back pocket. I swear Cara is messaging me AGAIN about something irrelevant to get my mind off the flight. I can't deal with her right now as I'm speed-walking through TSA.

> **Cara:** Bro, I'm sure the whole plane will wait for you. Stop stressing 🙏

She knows I'm mad because I said so many times last night that I didn't want to go out. She never listens. She is so small you would think after a glass of wine she will be ready to go home.

ping

Cara: I called the airline and you are ON TIME.

But no, this girl can drink a bar dry and still wake up like nothing happened. But I guess every Yin needs their Yang because, after just two glasses of wine, I'm completely dead and can sleep through everything, including my alarm.

ping

Cara: you will not miss this flight

Cara: ✈ ✈ ✈ ✈ ✈ ✈

I can sense how angry she's getting that I'm not answering, but right now my focus is on getting through this TSA line and to Gate B to catch my plane to Florida.

Cara: for the love of Christ Allie, can you at least let a girl know you made it through?

Cara: or is this you telling me you are actually not going to Florida anymore?

Cara: You will not see him, OK? For all that you know, he doesn't even live there anymore. You need to relax ….

Cara: and let me know you are ok. Jesus Allie.

Cara: ⏰

Me: Would you please stop? I'm next in line. I'll text you while I'm on the plane. Stop blowing up my phone. Ok? Love you but chill the fuck out.

Cara: You know you love me. Xoxo, C

Ugh, I can't with her. We've been friends since we were kids because our dads used to work together. We were instantly meant to be friends when our moms were pregnant at the same time. We have somewhat grown up together since we lived in the same area until we were twelve. My dad's promotion required him to move often, and I guess he had to drag his family with him.

You could say that we look nothing alike, but we act like sisters. We are both short and curvy with hazel eyes. My skin is tanner than hers, giving me a soft caramel color, and she is a little more rosy-cheeked and pale. We couldn't be less alike, yet our friendship is one of the most beautiful things I have ever witnessed.

Cara is the definition of a free soul and the most loyal person you will ever meet. She would move heaven and earth for those she loves. My child-loving, animal rescuer, level-headed, blunt bestie is almost the complete opposite to me. We went to the School of Education together at Stanford University, but she will probably end her life as a special education teacher, and I ran away from the classroom as soon as I could.

It's my turn to go through the checkpoint and I pull out my ID from my black, cross-body purse that I took to the bar with me last night. I wouldn't be surprised if I were to find some crazy things in there, like the condom Cara slipped in 'just in case' I was 'feeling lucky' last night.

ping

Cara: remember even though you are going to work this week, your job ends at 5. Go out and have fun!

Cara: And by fun, I mean, act your age. Meet a guy and hang out. There doesn't have to be any strings attached but you need to get out there.

I give the agent my phone so he can scan my boarding pass when I hear the soft hum of my phone vibrating in his hand with a new text. His eyes grow open wide and he blushes instantly. He gives me my phone and ID back as he quietly says "I didn't need to see that, but be careful, that can get you into trouble." And gives me a wink.

WHAT. JUST. HAPPENED?

I go through the checkpoint, remove my shoes, and place them in the bin as I push them through the machine. I'm sweating everywhere at this point, trying to figure out what he meant by that but I'm already late so it can wait.

The security guard asks me to step through and when everything looks good, I grab my carry-on and phone from the belt, slip my shoes back on, and start walking to the gate.

ping

I decide to just quickly look down and see what her issue is, when I read the message the agent probably saw.

Cara: or even better, maybe find a hot stranger at the airport that can fuck you senseless before you hop on the plane.

Cara: God knows your grouchy ass needs to get laid ASAP.

SHE. DID. NOT.

Me: I just want you to know that this text popped up while the TSA guy was checking my boarding pass ON MY PHONE. Thanks for that.

Cara: SHUT UP. It did not

Me: Fml

Cara: Maybe he would like to volunteer? Was he cute?

As I'm trying to type a reply, I run smack right into a wall. Or, at least what I think is a wall, but it turns out to be a whole human standing there, also on his phone, so he didn't see me.

"Oh my gosh, I'm so sorry. I wasn't paying attention. I just-"

And suddenly, I'm speechless because this gigantic wall of muscle that I just ran into has dark chocolate eyes that can stare right into your soul. A woodsy but fresh scent that could destroy your brain cells and that I could recognize anywhere. Even after ten years.

"Allie," he says. Not a question, a statement. I'm suddenly at a loss, unable to form a straight thought as I look into his eyes.

Insert awkward silence.

After a few seconds that feel like an eternity, I'm still speechless and I don't know whether to cry or run. To scream or hug him. I opt for neither and just whisper his name, "Jake?". Not a statement, a question like this boy - no, not a boy anymore, a man now, for sure - didn't mean the world to me.

After I clear my throat, I try again "Hey Jake, so nice to see you." He keeps staring at me as I babble about *long time no see* and say how good he looks. Jesus, someone please kill me now. HOW GOOD HE LOOKS? He looks perfect. Like the same boy I loved ten years ago but grown. Taller and stronger somehow. With a thick beard and tattoos all over his arm that scream "fuck me now, please". I realize that I'm still yapping so I finally add "What brings you here? To this airport? On this day?" I take a deep breath and wait for his answer.

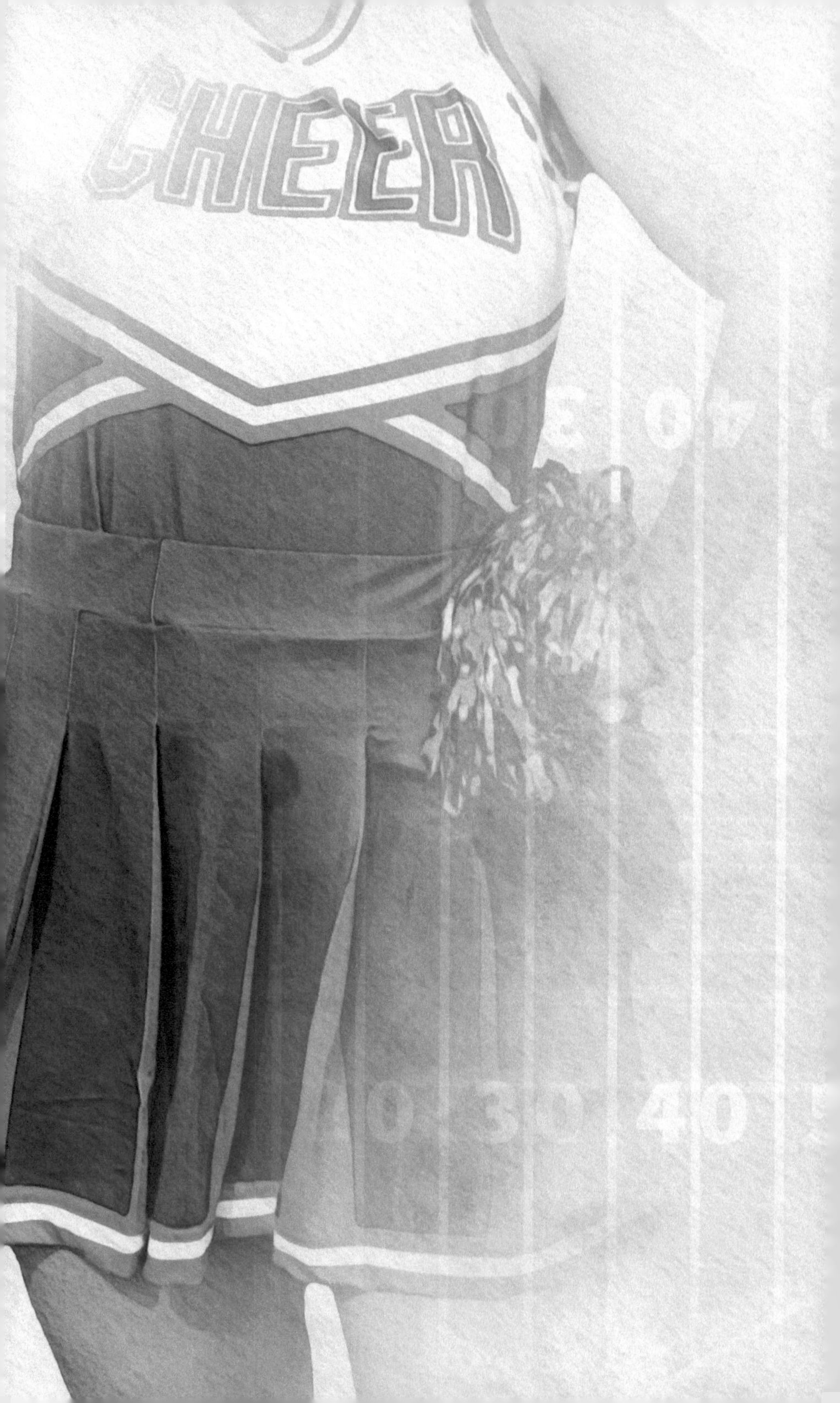

CHAPTER TWO

Allie

THEN

Miss Americana and The Heartbreak Prince, Taylor Swift

"Wait for me," I say, panting as I run off the field, dragging the bag of pom poms. I catch up to Cara, who is almost to my car, holding water bottles and our bags with the most expression I've seen on her in a while. "You don't have to look like you're going to puke. They just won a huge game, cheer up!" she tells me, while doing a little victory dance.

Shaking my head and staring at her like she's the last person I want to let down right now, I say, "I know, I know, but now we have to go and get ready for this last-minute victory party you decided to throw. AT MY HOUSE."

"Allie, you need to let loose. Nobody cares what your house will look like. They just care that there won't be any parents around and that tomorrow you have someone to clean up your mess. It is not my fault that your hot-ass daddy has you in the biggest house in Baker Oaks."

Cringing, I throw a water bottle at her and say, "STOP. CALLING. MY. DAD. HOT." This girl has an issue with older dudes, I swear, even though she has been dating the same guy for years, that doesn't stop her eyes from wandering every time an older man walks by.

She hasn't stopped raising her eyebrows at me as I sigh. "You know, we went to sleep so late last night reviewing the routine and then the game, and the boys, it's just a lot. I just want to go to bed for the next ten years."

I've known Cara since we were babies, and she has always been the ray of sunshine on my dark days. After the team won today, her boy Cole picked her up and started spinning while she shouted, "Party at Allie's!" for the whole field to hear. So even if I wanted to cancel, it is too late now. All the other girls are supposed to be at my house within the hour, but all I want to do is curl up and read.

"Allie, it'll be fine. Your parents are not even there, and I'll help you pick up afterwards."

"Fine, but you owe me," I tell her, getting in my car, starting the engine, and blasting the AC on high. It is hotter than hell outside, which means there is not much I could do to my hair without it becoming a lion's mane.

We drive to my house, and after three hours of getting dressed, tidying things up, making snacks, and answering a million texts, the house looks somewhat put together and the people that are here seem to be having a blast. Everyone is dressed like they're at an after-party at a club, even though none of us are old enough to drink. I'm wearing a black sequin miniskirt with a see-through white top that makes me look way older than I am. Cara looks straight out of a magazine with her long legs, mini dress, straight golden hair, and cherry lips. She is smiling so brightly, and I wish I was enjoying this as much as she is, but I really don't drink, and the rest of the girls are all over their boys, congratulating them for the win.

The Sharks won today against their biggest rival, so they are all buzzing with excitement. Some of the girls are doing handstands while drinking beer, while others are just talking and dancing. Cara is all over Cole like they have not seen each other in years. She is so happy when she is with him, and for that, I love him too.

"You know, it wouldn't hurt you to go mingle," someone says very close to my ear in a deep sulky voice that has my skin prickling immediately. I turn suddenly to see Jake Clarke standing next to me with two cups in his hands.

"Sorry, didn't mean to scare you," he says with a smirk, roaming his eyes all over me.

"Well, try again," I sass back. Jake is one of Cole's friends. He plays center on the offensive line and he is Baker's golden boy. He is friends with pretty much the entire school, including the underdogs. Tall, olive skin, dark hair, and chocolate eyes that make him look mysterious as shit. But then he smiles, and he looks every little bit the boy next door. He is in the same circle of friends I hang out with, but other than pleasant hellos, we don't really talk.

"Here, this is for you," he says, handing me one of the cups.

I grab it from his hand and take a sip while wincing. "Do you always drink nail polish remover or is this just a special occasion?" I ask, utterly disgusted by whatever this concoction is.

He chuckles and I suddenly find myself wanting to hear that sound forever.

"It's just Vodka and lime, Allison. You'll be fine."

"Only my parents call me Allison, *Jacob*. At least add some juice to it or something," I say as I stare back at him.

He is standing against the table with his legs crossed, wearing his Sharks shirt that hugs his arms in all the right places. His dark hazelnut eyes are gleaming at me as he sips on his drink.

"Why are you not mingling? I thought you were the queen bee around here?" he asks nonchalantly like he isn't standing there looking like a damn edible treat. *Get it together Allie.*

"I'm just tired, okay? I wasn't planning on you guys winning and I had a date planned already, so this," I say, pointing at the chaos in my house, "messed up my plans a bit."

He touches his heart like I stabbed him and dramatically says, "Oh my, you have so much faith in us, huh? Just kill me, why don't you?"

I smile and look at him, but I don't say anything. It's almost too much, the way he stares at me. He finally breaks the silence and says in a low whisper, "I didn't know you were seeing anyone." I don't even know what he's referring to, so I just keep looking at him. I smile and take another sip without wincing this time.

We both look away from each other as a loud noise comes from across the room. We see two of the players throwing their fists in the air and shouting, "Chug, chug, chug," at Cara and Tasha who drink a tall glass of beer. I chuckle while looking at them, when Jake gets closer and says, "You didn't answer my question."

"What question?" I ask without looking at him, my cup still on my lips.

"Whether or not you're seeing someone, Allison. You said you had a date."

I'm getting so flustered at his use of 'Allison' that I snap back and say, "First of all, it's Allie. Second, how is *that* any of your business? Third, not that you need an explanation, but I had a date with a book, okay?"

Why am I being such a bitch to Jake? Yes, it's true that he barely talks to me at school, or at all, which is weird since he is best friends with Cole, and he and Cara are basically attached at the hip. This guy can have any girl he wants, why is he wasting time talking to me? And why is my stomach fluttering at his question?

"So, you aren't seeing anyone. I thought so," he says confidently. Not a question but a statement.

I keep looking at him, waiting for him to say more, but he doesn't, he just looks all the way down to my toes and back up. Probably noticing the very small amount of fabric that's on my body, and between my outfit and my curves, there is probably very little left to the imagination. What is happening here? Why do I feel the air leaving my lungs? Why won't he stop looking at me?

"Why are you so interested in whether or not I am seeing someone?" I snap back.

As he lowers the empty cup that he has been sipping for the last seven minutes, he stands up straight, leaning close to my ear, and says, "I'm just glad I still have a chance to marry you one day. I seem to have been an idiot and not said something before." He is so close that I can smell him. He smells like a surfer boy who went to chop trees in the woods, and that's sexy as fuck.

"So, I am taking my chance now," he adds. I can't breathe. The room is closing in. I blink rapidly and chug my almost lethal drink to avoid looking at him.

He waits patiently, still close to me as I put my cup down. He gets closer—if that is even possible—and reaches behind me. Suddenly the room is so hot I'm burning up. His fingers feather my lower back as he grabs my phone from the back pocket of my skirt. He starts typing, opens the camera app, presses his cheek next to mine, and snaps a picture. We both look at the camera. He is smug and hot, and I am confused and flustered.

"Smile, Allison," he says, and I have no other choice but to obey. We smile, and after I hear a faint click, he reaches behind me again to put my phone back. Then he turns around and walks straight out of the house.

CHAPTER THREE

Allie

NOW

I miss you, I'm sorry, Gracie Abrams

"Allie, you really think that *what brings you to this airport* is what should be coming out of your mouth right now?" He says with a straight face, still holding my life in his hands like no time has passed.

Taking a deep breath I finally say, "Let me start over. Hey Jake, nice to see you again."

"Allie," he says simply, like my name is all he needs to convey his feelings. He doesn't need to tell me what I already know; that I fucked up and that he is annoyed to see me.

"Hi," I say with a smile, trying to cover my nerves.

"You owe me more than that."

"I know, I'm sorry."

As much as I want to continue these short exchanges, an announcement over the PA system interrupts my thoughts. "—now boarding Jacksonville Flight 904 at gate 34B." We both look up as if we're trying to find where the sound came from and hoping to grasp some sense of what's happening right now when I say, "I'm sorry Jake but I have to go."

I quickly turn around, grab my bag, and speed walk to the gate, trying to run away from him and everything he brings with him.

The future I thought I would have someday. All my buried hopes and dreams. All the love I had to give.

Get it together Allie, you were seventeen, nobody finds the love of their life in High School.

The line is gone by the time I get to the kiosk. The attendant scans my ID and guides me through the entrance. The minute I step foot on the plane, I am acutely aware of the sweat covering my body and the lump in my throat. It was bad enough that I had to fly today but I also ran into HIM. I find my seat and quickly sit down. There's nobody else sitting by me yet and I hope it stays that way. I already made a fool of myself and I don't need to do it again over my fear of flying. You would think with how much we traveled as kids, I would learn to just deal with airplanes but I never did. The feeling of being completely out of control, trapped in a huge tin machine, quite literally thousands of feet up in the air, gives me no comfort.

I grab my phone to read a text from Cara while people finish shoving their bags away and sitting down. The routine sounds of the compartments being closed and the high-heels of the flight attendants as they walk the aisle checking seat belts invade my senses. My palms are sweating so I lower my phone onto my lap and shove a piece of peppermint gum in my mouth. I close my eyes and lean against the window, hoping this will pass quickly. Praying it will be a smooth flight. Breathing so I don't shake. Counting so I don't cry. And we start moving down the runway.

In, one, two, three, hold.

Out one, two, three, hold.

In, one, two, three, hold.

Out, one, two, three, hold.

In, one, two, three, hold.

We must be in the air already because I feel a fast jerk that makes me open my eyes suddenly. The seat belt sign is still on and the pilot, with a raspy voice, announces that we are experiencing some turbulence and to remain seated with our seat belts fastened until the sign is turned off.

In and out Allie. You'll be fine. You can do anything. In and out.

Another bump and my hands instantly fly to the armrest. My knuckles are white from gripping so hard as the plane jerks up and down, and side to side. I close my eyes and breathe. *In and out. In and out. In and ...* I feel strong hands holding mine and I open my eyes to find Jake sitting next to me, lifting the armrest and holding my hand tighter.

I close and open my eyes to make sure I am not imagining this but nope, he's right there just looking at me.

"You are okay Allie, just breathe with me. Breathe in, one, two, three, four," he says, as he fans his hand, encouraging me to breathe in with him. "And out, one, two, three, four. Come on Allie, breathe for me." I let out a deep breath and continue to follow his directions, slowly relaxing my jaw, my shoulders, my whole body, and I lean into him like the last ten years were ephemeral.

When it finally seems like we're just cruising, I get the courage to whisper, "What are you doing here?" I'm afraid of any possible answer he might give me, and still looking at the hand that he is holding on to.

Rubbing the top of my hand with his thumb he says, "I'm flying home. I was in Chicago for a conference." Home? Wait, does he still live in Baker? Why couldn't I have googled this before I decided to take my next assignment in Jacksonville? I could have even gone on a social media hunt or let Cara do her thing and tell me any of the information she has tried to share with me these past years. Being without him wrecked me and I swore I needed to forget he even existed to move on. I asked her ten years ago to never share, and my very loyal friend never has.

"I could be asking you the same question, Allie. Last time I saw you, I thought you'd never step foot in Florida again." He looks at me with eyes that reflect what I'm feeling; *hurt.* I not only hurt him but I hurt myself when I decided to leave and never look back all those years ago.

Taking a deep breath, I finally say, "I'm going to Jax for work. I have a six-month assignment in a few of the school districts and the surrounding areas."

"You became a teacher after all?" He asks with pride in his words. "I always knew you'd be great with children."

I sigh, "Yes, but I'm not in the classroom anymore. I'm a professional development specialist for an educational company that services K-12 schools. I am sent to schools to help coach and train teachers. Then I get assigned to another district that needs me. You know me, always moving, never settling."

That hit him like a stab right in the heart and I can see it. "I didn't mean it that way, Jake," I say and after a few seconds I ask, "Where is home for you now?"

And he says, "I still live in Baker Oaks. I'm one of the team's coaches now."

"Like, the Sharks? Are you a teacher?" I sound so surprised because Jake Clarke never wanted to coach anything, not even his own teammates, let alone children. As I'm unraveling in my thoughts, I hear him say, "Yes, I teach social studies and I'm the offensive line coach. Still living in my small town, and I never want to leave." And with that, I remember the main reason why I have not seen him in a decade.

I have so many questions but I can see him fighting to keep something back. He still has tight lips and is holding my sweaty hand in his. I pull my hand away slowly, and grab it like I don't want to let him go, and ask, "Why did you come and sit here? How did you know I was struggling?"

"Because even though you left with my heart ten years ago, I know *you*, Allie. Probably better than you know yourself and definitely better than anyone else. At least I did." With that, we hear the pilot announce that we are getting ready to land. He grabs my hand again, looks forward, and closes his eyes. I close mine and slowly drift into my thoughts and into *how the fuck did I find myself in this position again*.

CHAPTER FOUR

THEN

Tennessee Fan, Morgan Wallen

Future Husband: Hey!

Me: since when?

Future Husband: since when what?

Me: since when did you decide you'll be my future husband, Jake?

Future Husband: How do you know this is Jake? I could be a secret admirer

Me: Because you used the picture you took tonight as your contact photo

Me: 🙄 Btw, I look like shit so I'm deleting it.

Future husband: you could never look like shit Allie. I forgot I took that though. To answer your question, let's have dinner and I'll tell you.

Me: dinner? It's 2:00 am Jake and I just got to bed after a day of hell.

Future Husband: So sassy. Not tonight, but soon.

Me: we have the football banquet soon. That's dinner.

Future Husband: are you always this literal? I'm trying to have dinner with you.

Me: why? You can just tell me who you're interested in and I can tell you if they're single. I know Tasha was talking to you at the game and she is always twirling her hair when you are near. She's single for sure.

Future Husband: 

I don't want to ask you questions about other girls.

Me: then what? I don't speak football and I'm sure your buddies are more entertaining at dinner than me.

Future Husband: Let's try this again. Allie, would you go out to dinner with me?

Me: like dinner dinner? On a date dinner?

Future Husband: yes.

Future Husband: I can see you typing Allison.

Me: sure

Future Husband: Can I pick you up tomorrow?

Me: 6:00 pm. Don't be late. See you tomorrow, Jake.

I lie in bed, hugging the phone to my chest, on top of my fast-beating heart. I whisper to no one, *What just happened?*

Did Jake Clarke just ask me out? Did he really save his name in my phone as *Future Husband*? Since when was he interested in me? He did say earlier that his chances of marrying me one day were not blown but I thought he was just fucking with me.

I've been in and out of Baker Oaks all my life, but this is the first year I've actually gone to school here. Of course I still know

Jake is practically Baker royalty after growing up here his whole life. Everyone knows him and his family.

Almost everyone at this school has been here their whole lives, and the only reason it was so easy for me to fit right in is because my parents and Cara's parents have been friends forever. We spent some time coming here to hang out with them through the years but when my dad got an opportunity to work at the Embassy in Jacksonville, my mom couldn't let us pass it up. Especially so she could spend her days living her best life with Cara's mom at the spa.

We knew we were moving here around April so I flew out here early to try out for cheer and I made the team. I was a gymnast until sophomore year when I hurt my knee and couldn't take the conditioning or the long hours of gymnastics anymore, so I switched to cheer. I've always loved to dance and that, plus my tumbling background, gave me the skills I needed.

I've seen Jake around, especially because of Cara's circle and I know his mom works for the daycare where I volunteer, reading to the kids. We hang out with the same group of people but he's Jake and I'm me, and we never orbit the same space. He's always around but never actually with me.

He is the king of the offensive line and even though he could be an arrogant jerk, he is truly the nicest. A true golden retriever. Friendly, nice, goofy, loyal. You can tell by his relationship with his friends, or even by how he treats the freshmen that are always melting over him. Everyone knows they don't stand a chance but he is still kind to them. Actually, he's pretty kind to everyone. From the cafeteria lady, to the band members, to the exchange students. It seems like everyone he meets, he is instantly friends with.

And he wants to take *me* out? How have I never noticed anything? Has he given me mixed signals or am I just too blind to see?

I keep looking back at every interaction we've had and I can't gather anything. He has always been nice to me but that is no different to how he treats everyone else.

As I continue thinking about it, I slowly close my eyes, take deep breaths, and drift off to sleep.

CHAPTER FIVE

Allie

NOW

Rockin' & Rollin', Nashville Cast

We walk off the plane in silence and wait by baggage claim. He helps me get my suitcase so it seems like the polite thing to do is to wait for him to get his too.

We start walking and he asks, "Do you need a ride? I'm parked here and I can take you to wherever it is you're staying. Maybe we can grab a coffee or a drink and talk."

"Jake," I sigh.

"Allie," he replies.

"I don't know if that's a good idea," I deadpan.

"Why Allie? You made it seem like we're just acquaintances so why not have a drink with me?" he says seriously, staring straight at me.

I won't tear my eyes from him. I refuse to back down but I do say, "You know why."

"I'm not eighteen anymore, Allison. I can handle a drink with you." He stares at me and I swear he can see right into my soul. There's nowhere to hide when he looks at me like that. He still has those beautiful eyes, perfect lips, and the thick dark eyebrows that mark his face. He has a full beard and some wrinkles by his eyes now but I can still see that beautiful boy - the one I loved so many years ago.

"One drink," I say.

"Yes, ma'am," he adds and grabs my suitcase as we start walking towards the parking garage.

The drive to the bar is awfully quiet. What once would've been a comfortable silence, is now thick and full of angst. I can feel all the things we haven't said floating around us, just like that day ten years ago. It feels like a lifetime ago, but also like no time has passed.

We get to R&P, a local restaurant and bar that has a rooftop overlooking the St. Johns river. He drives to the valet and pulls over where I get out of the truck. He meets me on the other side and says, "I guess old habits die hard, huh?" as he nods to the truck door.

"Sorry," I add. "Still a habit." He absolutely hated when I opened my own door. It took me a long time to get used to him opening them for me, and then, when there was no him anymore, I had to get used to opening doors for myself again.

"Still not dating? Or are you just dating jerks who won't open the door for you?" he smirks.

"Jake," I say.

"Allison," he replies, and it hurts because nobody calls me that anymore. He stares at me for a minute but then turns and guides me through the door.

We sit at the bar and he orders a beer on draft and I go for a Moscato and a shot of tequila. He lifts his eyebrow but doesn't say anything. While we are waiting for the drinks to come, he says "So are you going to answer the question?"

This man and his fucking questions, "Still not dating, Jake. Happy?"

He laughs and says, "Good one, Allie," like I told a fucking joke.

I feel the embarrassment creeping up so I ask for a change of topic. We talk for a few minutes about our lives and I learn that he loves teaching, but he never thought he would. He did open an auto shop with his dad, and he does rebuilds in the summer. During the school year, his Dad and a guy named Thiago handle the work. He asks me about my job and a few not-very-important things but he was always good at making conversation. Even the awkward ones.

The tequila shot is gone, but it gave me the courage I needed to whisper, "I'm sorry," as he looks at me with those big, puppy eyes. *I. Fucking. Can't.*

He breathes deeply and rubs his face, saying, "It looks like your life turned out okay, though," and he gives me a sad smile.

I look into his coffee eyes and after trying to fight it, I yawn. He pays for our drinks and we leave. We haven't talked about anything important but maybe that is what these drinks were about. Two old friends reconnecting and nothing more. No rehashing the past. No complicating things. He has moved on, clearly.

We step out and wait for the car. My skin prickles and I'm instantly aware of his hand on my lower back. His presence is intoxicating, just as it always has been. I don't want to make him uncomfortable so I don't say anything, but he moves his hand away and softly says, "Sorry, habit." I suddenly hate that word.

He tries to open the door for me, and this time I let him. I step in and he closes it behind me before walking around to the driver's side. I give him the directions to the B&B for his GPS and we start rolling. We're in silence for a while. Not even music is playing. It's a heavy silence too. The type when you can feel the pressure on your chest. The type that carries unspoken words.

"Jake, I'm sorry. I really don't know how many ways to say that," I say and it comes out shaky and breathy.

"What is it that you say all the time? Sorry doesn't fix it Allie." He holds the steering wheel tighter and not once does he look my way.

I stare at him, take a deep breath, and add "I think you are being a little dramatic, keeping a grudge all these years," and shit, maybe that was not the right thing to say but I am tired and it *has* been a decade.

"Dramatic? You said goodbye and never looked back. After everything we shared. Like I was disposable. Like we were replaceable," he says with a deeper voice.

"It was not like that and you know it. I said sorry then and I am saying sorry now. I can't change the past and I didn't think that you would even remember me by now."

He slows down rapidly, pulling to the side of the road. He puts the truck in park and looks at me. His eyes almost black and his jaw clenched. "Are you fucking kidding me right now Allie?" he says with a stern voice, and I can hear the hurt. He continues, "I'm not saying you need to fix everything right now because that can't be done, but God damn it, can you at least acknowledge that we still need to have a conversation? We might have been young, but you know that age doesn't matter when it comes to what we had. And if you think it meant nothing, then maybe I was just delusional." He starts driving again and adds, "Maybe I have been delusional all along."

I don't even know what to say, so I don't say anything at all. But as I am looking at him, I notice his scowl, so I say, "Alright. Yes, we can talk." He doesn't say anything else because we are getting closer to the house I am staying at, and he slows down.

It's a dark street and the houses are all small and squished in right next to each other. Not one light is on in any of them. Some have graffiti and damage on the outside and the house the GPS is taking us to has a homeless person lying on a sheet of cardboard right by the door.

He keeps driving right past the house and shakes his head.

"What are you doing? That was the house," I say, turning my head around looking back.

"You are not staying there, Allie," he says with an exasperated breath.

"Oh yes, I am. I have to report to work on Monday and I only have tomorrow to get groceries and get ready for the week. Turn around, Jake."

"You are not staying there. It's not safe."

"My company won't pay for a hotel for long-term assignments. Can you please just turn around? I'm sure it is just a misunderstanding, and I will call the head office tomorrow or Monday when they open again."

"I am not dropping you off there," he says, clearly irritated.

"So where are you planning on taking me then?" I ask, truly confused. I am tired and my feelings are all over the place. The last thing I need is to have to figure out a hotel right now.

"Home."

HOME? Whose home? I haven't had a place to call home in - I don't even know how long? To his house? Like, WHY? "I'm not staying at your house, Jake."

"I am not letting you stay in that place. You can call your company tomorrow and figure it out but it's getting late and you are tired and I have an extra room so I'm taking you to my house."

I forgot how bossy he can be and how protective he is when others are at risk. So I just nod and wait.

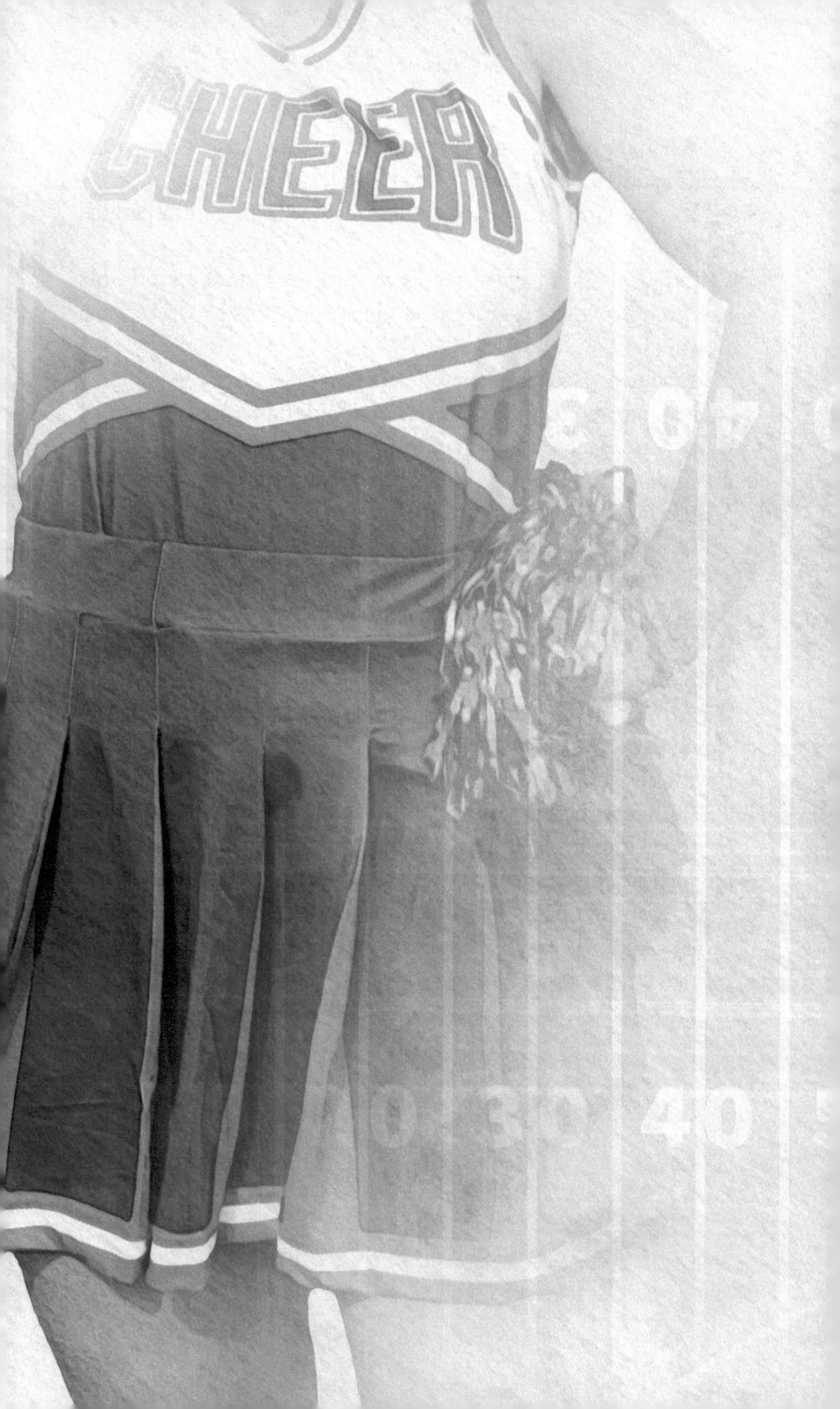

CHAPTER SIX

Allie

Bejeweled, Taylor Swift

The sun shines through the window that I forgot to pull the blinds over, warming my face and reminding me how much I drank last night. I reach for the water cup on my nightstand; I can't forget to fill it up every night due to the panic attacks that wake me up every so often. I've had anxiety for a long time but as I get older, and since my grandparents' accident last summer, it's getting worse. Especially at night. I started having panic attacks and waking up in the middle of the night, gasping for air, and other than my CPAP, having water readily available is the only thing that helps.

I take a sip and open my nightstand drawer to grab some Tylenol that will likely help nurse me back to life. Without getting up all the way, I grab my phone to check the time. *10:30 am.* Shit, I was supposed to be ready by 9:00 to go into Jax with my mom. I guess it's another ask-for-forgiveness kind of morning. My mom is usually pretty chill, especially because, most of the time, we give her very few headaches in comparison to other teens, so she counts her blessings when she can.

I have a few unread texts but only one catches my attention.

Future Husband: Good morning beautiful.

For a brief second, I scroll through our messages and quickly remember our conversation from only a few hours ago. I have a date with Jake Clarke tonight. I don't want to reply to his text immediately, so I go back to scrolling through the other texts.

Cara: Are you dead?

Cara: don't make me call your asshole brother to go check on you.

Cara: I realize I'm overreacting but can you just answer the damn phone.

I also have 5 missed calls from her. Does that girl ever sleep? I swear she is powered by a motor.

Me: barely alive

Cara: bitch, I was walking out the door ready to come and revive you.

Me: better bring coffee if you're coming this way.

Cara: k, be there in 20.

I get up from bed and walk to the bathroom. I hop in the shower, letting the hot water wash away the smell of sweat and booze clinging to my hair. Saturdays are for washing my mane of messy curls. It takes forever but I do it as quickly as I can since Cara will be here shortly.

I step out of the shower, throw on an oversized t-shirt and some shorts, and head to my bedroom. She's already lying on my bed, scrolling through her phone when I walk in there.

"You didn't tell me that you and Jake were talking," she says as she turns her phone to show me a picture. It's of her and Tasha with their cheeks pressed so close together that they are practically kissing. But if you look closely, you can see us talking in the back. Us, as in me and Jake. Jake is towering over me, and I am smiling like I am completely smitten with that boy.

"We talked for three minutes tops. Plus you were too busy smooching your man to talk to anyone."

"Jealous?" she says, as she pouts her lips and blows kisses at me.

A soft chuckle escapes my lips and I sit on my bed, grabbing the coffee on my table. I take a long sip, close my eyes, and taste the salty caramel deliciousness in the cup. I slowly open my eyes, blow a breath, and say, "Speaking of Jake," while looking at Cara. She turns her body to face me, the phone still in her hand, and looks at me, waiting for more.

"He asked me out on a date, tonight," I say, still unsure of what I'm actually saying.

"He what?!" she says, gasping.

"He kinda asked me out on a date tonight, after he saved his number on my phone under 'future husband'."

"I didn't even know you guys talked and now you are going on a DATE?!" Her surprised face is exactly what I was expecting because I was surprised too. She is also not wrong; we usually don't talk.

"I know. He was literally all like *I can still make you my future wife* and shit."

She opens her mouth and immediately grabs her phone to call someone. I assume Marie and Tasha, but I quickly stop her.

"I don't even know if I'm going. I mean, I said yes but it was completely out of the blue and now I don't know." I take a breath and continue, "I thought he was interested in Tasha."

"Allie," she says looking at me with tenderness, "Why would he ask you out if he was interested in someone else?"

I shrug my shoulders and look at her.

"If he went out of his way to ask *you* for your number, and then texted *you* to ask *you* out, I think he is plenty interested."

"I don't know. Why me?"

"Why not you? You're a catch, and guys have just been too blind to see it. Maybe he sees you."

I stare at her until a new message comes through and turns my attention to my phone.

> **Future Husband:** at the risk of sounding like a stalker, are we still on for tonight? I know you must be awake after seeing Cara's story.

I show the text to Cara and she chuckles as she clicks through her phone and turns it around for me to see her Insta story. It was me taking a sip of the Venti Salted Caramel Mocha she brought me with my eyes closed. My hair is wet and ringlets are falling around my face. I look calm and entirely too lost in the coffee. We both laugh and then I let out a sigh.

"Give him a chance. You need to put yourself out there. You guys are not moving any time soon and it's not like he's asking you to marry him. Entertain it for a bit," she says, pointing to my phone.

Rolling my eyes, I grab the phone to reply.

Me: Hey! Yes, I'm awake.

Future Husband: Good. Did you sleep ok?

Me: like trash

Future Husband: sorry

Me: not your fault.

I see the three dots pop up that show he's typing and then disappear. This happens a few times before I finally sigh and type.

Me: and yeah. I'm still good for tonight if you are.

Future Husband: is 7 okay?

Me: Sounds good. Where are we going?

Future Husband: Dinner and maybe for a walk?

Future husband: Or would you rather go to a movie?

Me: Either sounds good. Just wondering what to wear.

Future husband: Whatever you decide to wear will be perfect. See you tonight, Allison.

Cara is smiling at me and lifting her eyebrows as she opens up her hand, signaling to me to hand her my phone. I smack her on her hand and we both chuckle.

"Jerk," I say.

"You know you love me," she says while she winks.

She reads all the texts and gives me back my phone, smiling, and hopping off the bed quicker than lightning. She rushes to my closet opening both doors. She does a shimmy dance, and whispers, "It's showtime."

CHAPTER SEVEN

Allie

NOW

Meanwhile back at mama's, Tim McGraw

We arrive at Jake's house about forty minutes later and it is like stepping back through time. He still lives in the same house we used to spend all of our time in so long ago.

The house is a beautiful, southern-style, brick home, sitting in the middle of six acres of land. The front yard is surrounded by pine trees and beautiful canopies of oak trees that shade most of it. There's a gravel driveway that leads to the front porch that still looks exactly the same. Quaint and charming. Wind chimes are hanging up, a small fountain with fish sits to the right, and two white rocking chairs to the left. The wooden door has wear and tear marks from years of hosting busy boys and their friends, and the same "Welcome to Gma and Pop Pop's house" sign on the door that was there way back when.

Back when his Gma would host the best Friday night dinners. Back when we would all hang out in his huge backyard with chickens, cows, and goats walking around. He used to have a fire going most weekends, and people would just show up and hang out while we all talked about our hopes and dreams. Back when we used to sneak into his grandma's extra bedroom in the garage and he would touch me the only way no one else ever has.

"Allie," I hear him call from the front door out to the porch where I'm still standing, taking it all in, and I quickly snap out of it. With a *sorry* and a shake of my head, I step through and that's when my breath leaves my lungs. It looks exactly the same. I don't think anything other than the smart TV on the stand has changed in this house. Even Pop Pop's favorite recliner is still in the same spot facing the TV at the back end of the living room. I'm surrounded by emerald green carpet, pictures of Jake and Derek growing up, racing karts, trophies, football announcement clippings, and some porcelain dolls. The L-shaped couch right in front of me is covered with marks from people sitting on it for over a decade, but it's still holding its shape.

"Nothing has changed," I add.

"Except that she's gone now," he says as barely a whisper. "Come on, I'll show you where you can sleep."

Who's gone? Gma is gone? I can't even wrap my head around that statement as I follow him to one of the rooms that used to have all his pictures and things for when he decided to spend the night here. Except now it is a very standard guest bedroom without any personal touches. The bed still sits in the middle but the once-dark comforter with football prints is replaced by a plain gray one. The desk that used to hold all the shirts he always needed to fold and put away is replaced by a smaller one with a small chair and an empty flower vase. There's a couple of towels by the door on a small nightstand that he places my bags right next to.

"The bathroom is—" he starts but I interrupt him with *that way* as I point to the hallway that leads to what used to be the main bedroom.

"I remember," I add, giving him a guarded smile. He smiles back and tells me to make myself comfortable and that he will be taking a shower.

He closes the door behind him as I sit on the bed and take a deep breath. How did I find myself in this place again? I'm a little overwhelmed right now and low-key still shocked at the turn of events. I open my bag, grab some house clothes and go take a shower.

After the shower, I wander to the living room with my laptop in hand, where I find Jake sitting, watching TV. I look at him and wave my hand softly as I whisper a *thank you* for letting me crash here. I ask for the Wi-Fi password and start to walk back to the room when I hear him speak.

"You can come sit out here, Allie."

"I don't want to be a bother, I've already inconvenienced you enough."

"You are not a bother. Please, come sit out here, unless you want to be alone, which I'd understand."

"I don't love being alone, Jake. Never have and probably never will." I quietly walk to sit next to him in the spot that I have sat in so many times, long ago.

"I know," he says, while taking a sip of his beer.

"You know what?"

"That you don't like being alone."

After a moment in silence I nod at the beer while saying, "I see old habits die hard." He chuckles and asks if I want one. I shake my head and he offers me a glass of wine which I say *thank you* to. He gets up to grab it for me, walking to the kitchen and showing me his toned legs and perfect back. I open my computer and start typing an email to the help desk at my company to explain the situation about the B&B and ask how to proceed.

Jake comes back with a glass of white wine that is cold to the touch and as I take a sip, I can immediately tell it is a peachy Moscato. It is my favorite type of wine and I am in heaven. I don't take Jake as the type of guy that drinks Moscato but I'm not going to complain about it.

"I'm sorry about Gma," I say.

"Yeah, me too," he adds.

"I didn't know she passed. I know how much she meant to you. How did Pop Pop take it?"

"Brutally. It's still hard for him. He lives here part-time. The garage room is his now when he's here, but he's in Jupiter with my brother for a while."

Why is his brother living so far away? And why is Pop Pop not living with his parents? There are so many things that I want to know but I don't think it's my place to ask anymore.

"Do you know which school is your first assignment?" he adds, changing the topic.

"Yeah, I'm going to an elementary school on the west side of Jacksonville first, but I won't know the next school until I am almost done there. I'll be there for the whole of next week."

"What are you teaching them?"

"Small group intervention," and I smile.

"You always loved reading, so it doesn't surprise me."

"Correction: Love. Present tense. Books are still my lifeline."

"Noted," he says and turns his attention back to the TV.

My heart pings at what I am feeling right now. We fall into easy conversation immediately, like no time has passed, and it hurts because I am so undeserving of his kindness and his thoughtfulness. So I gather my stuff, put my glass down, and say good night to Jake as I walk to the room. I don't turn around to face him so he doesn't see the tears that are falling down my cheeks. The tears that have been threatening to fall since the moment I saw him at the airport this morning, and that I 100% deserve to shed alone, without any of his concern.

CHAPTER EIGHT

Allie

THEN

Bicicleta, Carlos Vives y Shakira

I spent the day styling my hair, painting my nails, and hanging out with Cara. No matter how much I see her now, I still feel like time is running away from me so I try to soak in all the minutes we have together. I am always afraid that I will never get the chance to do all the things I want to do with her, no matter how much time we spend together. I guess that's what happens when you grow up in different cities and countries than your best friend all your life. She leaves around 4:00 and I start reading a book to pass the time.

It is now 6:30 and I am dressed, lying in bed reading, when my mom comes in.

"Hola amorcito," she says as she steps through the door and sits on my bed, kissing my forehead and putting my hair behind my ear.

"What are you reading now?"

"Just _The Hunger Games_," I say and I look at her smirk as I add, "Again."

"Are you ever going to get tired of rereading that book?"

I touch my heart like she stabbed me and say, "Never."

We both laugh and chat books for a bit. My mom is amazing and a huge bookworm too. My love for reading grew even more because of her sharing so many things about the books she was reading. She read The Hunger Games once a couple of years ago so we could talk about it but dystopian is not her thing. We usually read the same book once a month and have our own little private book club.

"Are you going somewhere?" she asks, looking at my eyes once she notices the mascara I have on. I usually don't wear makeup unless it is a special event or game night so it makes sense why she is looking at me like that.

"I, um, yeah. If you are okay with that," I tell her.

She raises her eyebrows and says, "Cuéntame." *Tell me.*

I tell her about Jake asking me out to dinner tonight and maybe a movie. She knows who Jake is because in this small town, everybody knows everybody and I am cheering at almost every varsity game. I tell her that I'm a little nervous and that I don't even know where we are going. She reminds me that I am seventeen and a fun person and that no matter where we go, as long as I keep an open mind and a good spirit, I will have fun. As always, she reminds me of my curfew too.

I'm not shy by any means. Actually quite the opposite, but I have never had a boyfriend before. I kinda dated a guy named Ryder a couple of years ago but it didn't go anywhere because we moved. It's already hard enough to make new friends without the added stress of a long-distance boyfriend. So the idea of going on a date still terrifies me a little bit. She tells me to turn on my location and to call her once I know where we're going and whether we will be watching a movie or not. She kisses my head again and leaves me to read a little bit more.

I step outside around 6:55 and I see him driving towards me. He drives an old, black pickup truck that can't be newer than 95-96. He rides with the window down and his hand sticking out. He pulls up in front of the house and I go down the driveway and quickly climb up on the front seat. As soon as I do, I notice that his door is halfway open and his foot is already out of the truck.

"Hi!" I greet him with a smile.

He looks at me for a minute and pulls his foot inside. Closing the door, he says, "Hi, Allie."

He looks absolutely dreamy with a black fitted t-shirt that highlights his arms and shows the hint of a tattoo peeking out. He is also wearing dark jeans and I realize I don't think I've ever seen him in anything other than shorts before. I quickly look up at his face and find him looking at me with a showstopper smile, and he says, "You look beautiful."

I chuckle and look at my jeans and the flowy, teal top I decided to wear. I look casual; just as if I was going to school. "Likewise," I say, and quickly face forward.

We are both sitting there in silence so I look back at him while pointing at the road. "So, are we gonna get going?"

He smirks and nods without saying anything else. The truck starts slowly rolling forward and he turns the volume up just a little. Enough for me to tell that the song is *Son of a Song of a Sailor* but still low enough that it would be comfortable to have a conversation.

"For the record, you should let a guy open the door for you when he's picking you up for a date," he says in a low husky voice while he quickly looks at me then looks back at the road. Goosebumps rise on my arms as I am left almost speechless by his comment. I clear my throat and say, "Sorry, a habit I guess," shrugging and biting on my lip.

"You are in the habit of going out with jerks that won't even open the door for you?"

I almost choke as I cough and laugh at the same time. "I'm in the habit of getting my own door. I don't really date."

The light turns red and he slowly stops while raising an eyebrow and turning slightly to look at me. "Like in Baker?"

"No, like in general. We move so much that I don't think people even notice me. I meet new people all the time, but I think I'm more of the fascinating new girl than anything else." *Jeez, that sounds depressing*, so I continue, "It's fine. This is the life we live and it truly isn't a big deal. I love traveling and meeting new people, it just doesn't go hand in hand with relationships."

He stares for a second, then looks forward so he can keep driving. "Allie, if you really think that people don't notice you, you're wrong."

"Then maybe I come on too strong and scare guys away. Either way, I have only been on a handful of dates and this is my first time getting picked up for one, for sure."

"If they are too scared to ask you out, that's on them. Not you. You are just too strong for people who are too weak."

And with that, I die a little. What do you even say to that? I have no idea so I don't say anything and keep looking forward.

We pass the time talking about random things, food mostly, and some things we like. I tell him how much I love starchy food: all forms of potato, bread, pasta, and chips. He makes me laugh when he shares that he is not a favorite kind of person and that he enjoys it all. Food, music, hobbies. He says that the only thing he doesn't love is reading because he can't shut his brain off long enough to enjoy it, which opens the door for me to talk about all the things I love about reading, especially being able to shut my brain off and wander into new worlds with every book I pick up. We keep talking and all of a sudden I remember I don't even know where we are going. We are on the highway now so he might be taking me to Jax.

My heart starts beating fast, like palpitations, as I start imagining a worst-case scenario. I don't want to be rude and grab my phone but if I don't do something soon, we might need to pull over for me to go on a walk.

Breathe, Allie. Breathe.

I decide to just ask and stop freaking out when he takes the exit to Roosevelt and keeps driving. He looks at me and smiles and says, "We're almost there. I hope you're hungry."

Hungry? More like *starving,* but I need to calm down if I'm going to enjoy dinner at all. Until now, being with him has been so easy. He's easy to talk to and the ride has been smooth. He is friends with all of my friends so there's no reason for me not to trust him. This is not a psychological thriller and he is not a serial killer. Maybe if I was upfront with him about my anxiety issues he would have known that the unknown would drive me up the wall.

In the middle of my freakout, I completely zoned out and before I know it, he has parked, and is walking towards my door. I grab my purse and before I open the door, he beats me to it. He holds my hand as a step down his truck, and smiles at me, reaching over my head to close it. He guides me with his hand on my lower back while we walk. "I hope you like Mexican food," he says.

I could practically squeal with excitement when I say, "I fucking love Mexican."

We go in and get seated almost immediately in a booth by the back of the restaurant. It's a small mom-and-pop place with colorful decorations. There are booths and tall tables. Ranchera is playing in the background, and it smells incredible.

The waitress comes and asks in Spanish what we want to drink and to my surprise, he says, "Agua por favor."

I look at her, smile, and say the same thing. She leaves us to look at the menu and while I'm reading it, I ask him, "Do you speak Spanish, or do you just come here a lot?"

He smiles and says, "Both and neither. I speak a little bit but not as much as I would like. And I love this place but I also don't come here as often as I would like since it's outside of Baker Oaks."

"And here I was thinking you were trying to impress me with your Spanish," I sass while putting my hands under my chin and fluttering my eyelashes.

"What if I was?" he says smirking, not taking his eyes off me for one second.

We both laugh softly and go back to the menu. The waitress comes back with our water and takes our orders. A chimichanga, queso, and chips for me and fajitas for Jake.

We fall into comfortable conversation as I eat my weight in chips and queso, and not once does he say anything about it. He tells me about his plan to go to UF next fall to study history or business and continue playing football. I tell him that UF is my top choice too but I haven't gotten my acceptance letter yet. I talk about why I want to go into education and that I hope someday to share my passion for learning with children. I learn that his favorite color is green and that he loves being outside almost more than anything else. He loves animals and his Gma. He promises to take me over to have dinner with her so I can hear all the stories she has to tell.

We continue talking and eating as our food comes out. His plate is sizzling right in front of him and it smells amazing. Even better than my mouth-watering chimichanga. I don't want to stare but it smells fantastic; like someone's grandma cut the peppers and onions herself after picking them from the garden. He hands me a small plate with a fork and I look at him with a puzzled look.

"Do you want some?" I ask while taking the plate from him.

"No, that's for you to grab some fajitas," he says.

Shaking my head, I reply with, "No, no. I couldn't."

He smiles the biggest smile and says, "You know you want to. Go ahead. It would be an honor to share my fajitas with you." He hasn't even tried them yet and he is still letting me have some first. Looking at his eyes – I swear he is smiling with them too – I whisper a *thank you* and dig right in.

He laughs softly so I look up and say, "I know, I'm ridiculous," brushing him off.

"More like adorable," he adds and laughs some more as I lower my head.

I don't know how long we've been at the restaurant but it must be late because when he asks for the check I look around and notice we're the only people left. I offer to pay for half and he doesn't even entertain the thought.

We walk side by side to the truck. He opens the door for me and gives me his hand so I can hop up and slip right in. It's been such a nice night that I am in between not wanting it to end but also so full that I could take a nap.

He hops in on his side and asks, "Are you too tired from last night? I can take you home."

"Or?" I ask with a comfortable sigh as I take my sandals off.

"Or we can drive around and keep talking for a while," he says sheepishly.

"Option two, please."

"Atta girl." He winks at me and places the truck in reverse. We leave the parking lot and I wish this night would never end.

CHAPTER NINE

Allie

NOW

Back to December (Taylor's Version), Taylor Swift

I wake up to the smell of coffee and something deliciously fried so I know Jake is probably whipping up some of his mom's recipes. The first time he cooked for me, he made me my first ever country fried steak and I almost went to heaven just from the taste of it. It was fucking fantastic. He cooked for me often while we dated because he loved to see my face when I was trying and enjoying something new.

I slip into the bathroom to brush my teeth, wash my face, and make sure my curls have not completely fallen out of the top knot I put them in last night. I get out, grab my laptop and head to the kitchen.

"Good morning." My voice still sounds groggy because of the lack of caffeine in my system. I can be nice and cheerful, but not before my coffee. Everyone in my life knows that, even my coworkers.

"Hey," he says with a hoarse voice and a smile.

"It smells fantastic. What are you making?"

"Biscuits and gravy."

I just look at him but don't say anything. I love breakfast so much and his sausage gravy is incomparable to anything else I've ever had.

"Wanna help?" he asks, a little unsure.

"Sure. How can I help?"

He instructs me to crack some eggs and whip them, and to set the little table for two. He also offers coffee so I grab a mug that is sitting out.

"Thanks. Coffee is great." It is warm and creamy but not too creamy. It is just right. I wonder how many times he saw me adding the same amount of sugar and cream to make this so long ago; it is still as perfect as it could be.

"I'm glad," he says smiling at me and stirring the pot in front of him. "What are your plans for today?"

"I am waiting for the office to answer my email about the B&B but it might be tomorrow before I hear anything so I'm considering just getting a hotel in Jax until they can figure it out."

He doesn't say anything while he keeps mixing the gravy. He looks up and then to me and then back at his pot. He drags his hand over his face and says, "Or you can stay here until they figure it out."

"Jake, you couldn't even look me in the eyes when you said that. I'm not staying here. You have been so kind already and I appreciate it but I can't."

"Why are you being so difficult?"

"I'm not being difficult. I'm being respectful. You have a whole life that I am not a part of and I won't intrude." He winces at my words and instantly scowls. "I didn't mean it like that. You do have a life though and I don't want to be a burden."

"You will never be a burden, and I am offering," he says.

"I don't know anything about your life anymore, Jake. I don't even know if you are dating someone and the worst thing that could happen to me is having to explain to your girlfriend who I am, how we know each other, and why I am staying here."

He moves the pot of gravy off of the hot stove and places the mitten on the countertop. He turns around silently but I can feel the change in his demeanor immediately. He opens the fridge and, with one hand on the door, he bends down to grab something from inside. I can see his knuckles turning white from his grip on the door, and the tips of his ears are red. He's either completely mad or, at least, very annoyed right now. The ears were always his first tell.

He gets the orange juice out, places it on the countertop, and while leaning against it he looks at me and says, "Do you really think that if I was dating someone you would be here without me checking with her first?"

No, I don't think so. "I don't know, Jake."

"Allie, you know me better than that. Time has passed but values don't just go away."

His words are a stab to my heart and I immediately regret doubting him. What is the matter with me?

"And besides, every single person that I have been with since you, eventually gets to know who you are. Whether I want them to or not."

I stare at him, not knowing what he means and then he adds, "Either from me calling your name in my sleep, or when they realize that the *ghost of the girlfriend of the past* will haunt me forever no matter how hard I try to move on."

"Jake, we're either going to have this conversation right now, or you need to stop throwing little jabs my way. I can just leave," I say with the tears threatening to fall again. He is not the only one with a cage around his heart. Every time I look at him it's like I jumped in a time machine. But I can't keep overlooking his little comments.

He turns his body to face me completely, and in a soft whisper, says, "I don't want you to leave."

"Then let's talk. You want to talk? Go ahead," I snap back. I sound like the biggest bitch but I am on the verge of tears and I can't break down in front of him. *Get a grip.*

He doesn't say anything, or at least nothing that my regular ears can hear. He makes a low noise that sounds a lot like a mix between a mumble and a grunt, while he rubs his beard with his eyes closed.

"We were children, Jake," I add. "I said sorry then and I've said sorry now. I can't do anything to change the past and I can't sit around while you keep making comments like that. Like, I don't even know you anymore and I refuse to let you treat me like this." I can't tolerate this again so he can get it together or I can leave.

That catches his attention and he turns around slowly and looks me in the eyes. His eyes are glossy from either sadness or rage. *Maybe both.* "We were not kids. Nothing we felt was childish. Nothing we did was either," he sighs and continues "but I can agree to let it rest and try to have a fresh start. It will take time to get used to it though. To get used to seeing you back here."

"I'm not back, Jake. I'm here for work and honestly, I might be back in Jacksonville for six months and then on to the next place."

"A guy can dream."

We stare at each other for what feels like an eternity but also not long enough and then he says, "I miss you. No matter how much time has passed. I miss you so much but more than anything, I miss my friend. You were my favorite person, Allie, and I miss that."

Kill. Me. Now. Please. It was hard enough knowing I broke his heart, *and mine,* but also knowing that our friendship ended that night too, not only keeps breaking my heart; it shatters it. So I say the only thing I can think of. "We can definitely try to be friends again."

He smiles and says, "I'd like that."

CHEER

Robarte un beso, Carlos Vives & Sebastian Yatra

Future Husband: Good morning Allison

Me: Right back at you Jacob

Future Husband: nobody calls me that

Me: nobody calls me Allison either

Future Husband: but it suits you

Me: blah

Future Husband: I kinda like being the only one who calls you Allison.

Me: My parents do, so if you want me to relate you with them, then go ahead. Maybe I can call you Daddy.

Call you daddy? Who the fuck says that. Well, it's too late to take it back now but I can try to change the subject.

Me: I had fun last night, thank you!

Future husband: you don't have to thank me for taking you out on a date. But I had a good time too. Would love to hang out today too if you are free.

Me: Sundays are spent with my family.

Future Husband: no problem :)

Me: but you could come?

Future Husband: to your house?

Me: yeah, there's always people here and there will be food too.

Future husband: I don't want to impose

Me: you're not! My family are a lot though so be warned

Future Husband: what should I bring?

Squeeeeee. Did I really? Did I ask him to come over? What??

"Mami!" I shout, hoping she can hear me wherever she is in the house.

"Yes?" she says back, standing right by my door. She must have been close, which works for me because I don't want to get up.

"Can you tell Rosalia to add an extra plate for a friend please?"

"Sure thing mi niña. Anything else?"

"Nope, that's all. Gracias!" She closes the door, leaving me alone again. I grab my phone and shoot Jake another text.

Me: Nothing, just come prepared to deal with the loudest people you have ever met.

Future Husband: Not a problem.

We are sitting on the porch talking and snacking, enjoying our traditional Sunday shenanigans. My mom comes from a huge family of ten children from parents who lived their whole lives to make sure their children grew up to be friends more than family. It is very important for her that, although we live in so many places and move so much, we still stay in touch with this part of her. Hence why *Family Sunday* was born. We just eat and talk and dance. Sometimes my brothers' friends join, sometimes Cara and her family join and sometimes, it is just us. Cara is often a usual add-on here on Sundays. My brothers get along with her fine, well, at least one of them does. Manny seems to always pick on her but she takes no shit, which makes all of us laugh even more.

The weather, in typical Florida fashion, is hotter than hell and more humid than a steam room. However, the sun is out and the skies are clear, making it a beautiful day. There's a table set out full of snacks and drinks, and my mom's famous Sangria that we are allowed to indulge in as long as we stay home.

The bell rings and we all stop and look at each other when mom says, "Why is Cara ringing the bell? She knows the door stays open."

"I can go get the door," Manny adds quickly.

At the same time I say, "Cara? She's not coming today."

"Oh, I thought you said someone was coming."

"Yeah, my friend Jake." Everyone stops and looks at me like I have three heads.

"Wepa, un novio." *Oh, a boyfriend.* "Then you can go get the door yourself," Manny says.

"Stop it right now!" I say as I feel heat rising to my cheeks. I swear if I had fair skin I would 100% be blushing right now. If these people make a big deal out of it, I may just die of embarrassment today. I do, however, not blame them for wondering what is happening, considering this would be the first time I invite a guy friend here.

My mom clears her throat, looks at everyone else, and then looks at me. "Well, are you going to let Jake in?" she asks, pointing towards the front door.

I sigh and turn around. I can hear them giggling as I speed walk back into the house to open the door. I reach the door, close my eyes, and take a deep breath in. I open it and try to smile but my breath catches and it sounds more like a hiss at the sight of Jake.

He's wearing a dark t-shirt with cargo shorts and flip-flops. I'm pretty sure this is his typical attire but it is almost like I was blind and I can now suddenly notice every detail about him. How his t-shirt hugs his arms in all the right places. How tall he is as he towers over me, holding a dish and smiling. How his dark hazelnut eyes shine when he smiles and looks at me. How his lips are the perfect shade of kissable pink. He smirks and I know that I've been caught ogling him. I chuckle and try to brush it off. I clear my throat and say, "Hi, sorry about the wait."

"No need to apologize. I will happily wait for you." He winks. *¡Dios mio! Oh My God! I might die today.*

"Come on in. We have to walk out back, everyone's outside."

He steps in and turns around to look at the living area as he says, "I've never seen this part of your house before. I always come in through the back door. It's beautiful."

The first room after you walk into the house is dreamy. Beautiful, white marble floors with mahogany accents lead the way to an open-concept living room with floor to ceiling windows looking over the Spanish garden. There are two sets of staircases that wrap around on each side of the room and lead to the second floor of the house where our bedrooms are. There's a large beige sectional with plants on the corners and a coffee table full of photo albums. And across from it, there's an accent wall with forest green and safari illustrations from my mom's favorite artist. There's also a recliner chair that matches the accents on the staircases and it holds a burnt orange blanket and a copy of the book I'm currently reading. The room is light and airy but also minimalist. It says *stay a while but maybe not too long if you are planning on partying*, which is exactly why my mom had it decorated like this. It gives cozy vibes.

"Thank you. I love this room. It's my second favorite in the house."

"What's your first?" he asks, truly wondering.

"Maybe I'll show you one day," and then it's my turn to wink at him. He smiles at me and I giggle a little and start walking towards the backyard.

I try to warn him about my family teasing him and how everyone would be drinking and laughing and he just said he was fine and that he's got it. We walk to my mom and brothers, and their friend. I introduce them to Jake but they already know him so they shake hands and whatnot. My mom kisses him on the cheek and hugs him as if she already loves him, and I really want to crawl under the floor.

We sit next to each other and quickly fall into conversation with everyone else. I am learning more about him this afternoon than I did last night and it is great to see how easily he fits in with everyone. My mom is laughing at something he says. One of my brothers is dancing while the other one scrolls on his phone. It is almost like we have done this a thousand times before.

It starts to get dark and my mom sends us all on our way with a reminder that there's school tomorrow and we need to get in bed soon. We all say our goodbyes and I walk Jake back to the front door. "Thank you for hanging out with my family today. I'm sure you had better things to do," I say as I stand by the door.

He holds my eyes and says, "There's nothing better than getting to know you better, Allie, and that includes your family. Plus, I had fun." This boy is leaving me speechless and without air to breathe with his words.

"I like getting to know you too," I say because what else do you say after he comes out with something like that?

"Does your mom always kiss people on the cheeks? Or is that part of your culture?"

"Definitely part of the culture. Sorry if that was weird."

"It wasn't. I was just wondering if I should kiss your cheek right now too. You know, since we're saying goodbye and all."

I smile and nod. He dips down and kisses me on the right cheek. He then whispers in my ear, "Goodnight, Honey. See you at school tomorrow."

"Honey? That's new." I shiver after hearing the name come out of his lips in that raspy voice that makes my insides turn.

"I told you, I wanted a name for you that only I use." He walks backwards not dropping his eyes from mine, until he reaches his truck.

I see him drive away as my cheeks burn with heat. I turn around, go back inside, and close the door behind me. *Honey,* I whisper in the hallway, to no one in particular. I do a little leap and let a squeak out as I walk to my room holding my face like the dork I am.

Not washing my face ever again.

PASSPO

CHAPTER ELEVEN

Allie

NOW

Coney Island, Taylor Swift Ft. The National

"This is me calling you now, Cara," I tell her for the eighth time since I picked up the phone to Facetime her and explain the last twenty-four hours of hell.

"I just don't understand how you go from not even wanting to hear anything about Jake for ten years to staying at his house and not fucking telling me. A text would've been nice!" She is upset and I don't blame her. I can hear her heavy breathing and practically see her fuming.

"I needed to wrap my head around this too, girl. I'm still in shock and a lot is going on in my head. I'm sorry though." I sigh. I knew she would be upset but the last thing on my mind was Cara. "I should've called you last night. Maybe you would've slapped some sense into me through the phone."

It's suddenly quiet on both ends. I hate talking on the phone but with Cara, it has always been easy, especially when she lets me video call her and I can see her face. Her friendship means the world to me. Sometimes, just talking to her calms my nerves and she knows that too. I stopped pacing a while ago but I still don't say anything. I can see her walking somewhere and then I hear the sound of the ice cubes falling into a cup.

"What are you going to do?" she asks and then takes a sip from her cup. She must be annoyed if she is multitasking, talking to me right now and pouring herself some ice-cold water to drink. I know she only drinks it when she needs to settle her thoughts. That's what happens when you have known someone for as long as we have known each other, which is why I speak up and tell her the whole truth.

"I have no fucking clue. I'm still waiting for them to email me back. I have to show up at work tomorrow though so I guess I will be leaving from here."

"A ride share from there will cost half a kidney. Isn't your first job in Jax?"

"It is. It'll be fine. They can reimburse me."

"You know, you can also call your dad. He'll put you in the nicest hotel ever," she says. "You also have your trust fund, babe, if you wanted to you could use that to do whatever you want. To stay wherever you want."

I shake my head and stare at her.

She stares back and shrugs.

"I am not calling him. I don't even know where he's at now and I am not touching that money. I have made it this far without it, I can keep going."

My relationship with my dad got all kinds of messed up ten years ago and I promised myself I would never ask for anything else from him. I still talk to my mom and see her often but not him. His 'help' always comes with consequences and I have worked too hard to understand my value in life to let him make me feel like a failure.

"I can practically hear your thoughts. What else is going through that beautiful head of yours right now?" She smiles fondly at me. She's not mad anymore, she's worried.

I tsk and add, "I just don't want to mess this up."

"What 'this'? The job? Or Jake?" Her eyebrows raise as she smirks nonchalantly.

"The job." *Jake. Both.* I quickly look away so she can't see right through me and say, "I need to go."

"I need to go too. Meal prepping is calling my name. I'll talk to you later and please call me the next time something like this happens. I would rather not murder you next time I see you. Ok?" She sticks her tongue out and then smiles at me. She can be a pain in the butt, but Cara is seriously like the sister I never had but always needed.

"Love you, bye!"

I put the phone on the nightstand and start going through my suitcase to find something to wear now, and tomorrow. I get dressed quickly and start working on my plan for tomorrow on my laptop.

Taylor Swift is playing and I'm deep into my work when I hear a soft knock and the door opening. I look up through my lashes and whisper a soft, "Yes?" I need to finish doing this to be ready for tomorrow, so I really don't want to spend time arguing with Jake again.

"I'm just checking on you. I'm about to head to town and wanted to know if you needed anything or if you wanted to come?" he says.

He is looking at me with a shy smile while he stands there, leaning against the door frame. *God, he's gorgeous.* I feel my heart skip a beat just like it did back in high school and I really can't allow myself to go back there.

I close my computer and set it next to me. "I need to go grocery shopping but with where I'm staying still up in the air, I don't want to get too many things."

"Just come with and you can grab some snacks. For as long as you are here, you can eat anything that I have."

"I appreciate that but you are already doing enough." I look down because staring at his eyes for too long makes me think of things I want to do that I shouldn't. He is still leaning against the door frame, waiting for an answer so I say, "Do you mind if I go with you?"

He rubs his thick beard with his hand but simply says, "If I did, I wouldn't have asked you to come, Allie." He stops to look at me and quietly says, "Come on, let's go."

He walks out, giving me space to get ready. I already have on a black, beige, and soft pink maxi dress with tiny flowers. Flowers are my favorite print for dresses and maxi dresses have become a staple in my wardrobe because they can be dressed up or down, and they are so comfortable. I put my sandals on, wrap my hair in a messy bun, and grab my purse. I walk out the door and he's already waiting in his truck.

He has always loved trucks but this is nothing like the one he had before. He drives a black Silverado that is so shiny, almost like he just washed it. As soon as I step inside, I marvel at how beautiful it is. The inside is black leather and IT SMELLS JUST LIKE HIM. How did I miss all these details last night? *Oh right, you were freaking out last night, Allie.*

I snap my seat belt in place and look at him with a soft smile. He looks at me and asks if I'm ready. I nod and we start to roll.

The windows are down, the warm breeze blowing as we drive by. "Will this be awkward? You and me, at a store?"

"For who?" he replies while still looking forward.

"For us. For any people there. I don't know." I look back out the window.

"I think the more we hang out, the less awkward it will be for us. And as for people there, who in particular are you worried about?" He peers at me through his eyelashes. He has dark eyes but his lashes are practically black. They are full and long, framing his eyes and making them look even more beautiful. I know women who would kill to have lashes like his.

"I don't know, past girlfriends? Cashiers who are secretly in love with you? People who may remember me? Who may remember us?" I keep looking out the window because that was a ballsy thing to say. *Great job Allie. Keep making it weird.*

He chuckles, "Allie, people will talk regardless. I haven't dated anybody who works there nor are there any cashiers who are secretly in love with me. If it makes you feel better, we can go into Jacksonville or Live Oak."

"Nah, nope. No need. I'm fine."

He laughs and turns the music up. Joji is playing and he is singing the lyrics as if it was his favorite song and I start to relax. I can't continue to be this tense around him but it's so hard. I'm either so obsessed with him it makes my body tingle, or I hurt all over and I don't want to let my guard down. I'll find a hotel or another B&B tomorrow and call it a day.

We arrive at the grocery store and grab a basket. I turn to go our separate ways but he grabs me by the elbow and turns me towards him. "Let's walk this way," he says as he grabs my basket and sets it in the cart.

We wander in the store adding things to the cart. He grabs meats and vegetables but I opt for premade lunches, chips, and fruit. He chuckles next to me but then just shrugs when I look at him. He always thought that I had the cravings of a three-year-old and that's still the case. I could survive on deli meat, crackers, and fruit. It feels so natural to just walk the aisles and talk about random things with him. We catch up on the usual topics and joke about our snack choices some more. Being with him is refreshing, like second nature.

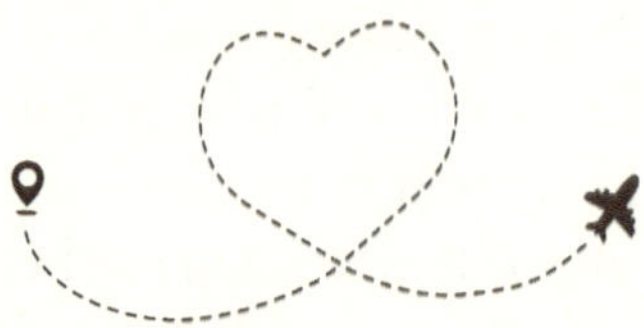

We make it back to his house, unload the truck, and put things where they go. We snack on some chips and fruit as we put everything away and I start packing things to bring with me tomorrow so it's ready to go.

I want to ask more about his life but I don't want to pry, and I also don't feel like I have the right to. I finish putting my things away and I'm about to walk away when he holds my hand and taps his hand on the counter. I LOVE sitting on kitchen counters. Back when we dated, he used to cook for me, and I would just sit there and keep him company. So when he keeps looking at me with his hand on the counter, that's exactly what I do.

I think about it for a second but honestly, what is there to lose? I hop up onto the counter and he says, "That's my girl."

Time freezes still. I don't think he wanted to say that but I also don't want to make him uncomfortable so I quickly say, "You have me on the counter, what are you cooking for me?" and smile at him. Hoping this will ease the tension, I open my palm up, move it across the counter space adding, "Chop chop, time's a wastin'." He laughs and turns around to grab things to put together.

He is cooking some sort of concoction that has the house smelling incredible. Country music is playing and I'm sipping on wine while I help him by passing him condiments when he needs them. It feels so good to be in his space like no time has passed; like we are living in this bubble of happiness where everything is possible.

Dinner's ready and he's bringing everything to the table. I start scooting forward to get down from the counter but he shakes his head as he holds my gaze. He walks towards me without looking away and comes to stand in front of me. Then he grabs me by the waist, whispering in a hoarse voice, "Let me help you down, don't need you getting hurt under my watch."

My skin prickles and I shiver while I slowly reply, "I weigh a lot Jake, you don't need to put strain on your knee by picking me up. I can hop down."

He leans closer, picks me up like I'm weightless, and places me on the ground but he doesn't move away. He is so close to me; his lips are almost touching my ear and my chest is practically flush against his. I can feel his chest moving quickly and his breath picking up so I don't move. I close my eyes and mentally count to try to keep my breathing even.

His warm breath caresses my neck as he says, "You are not heavy Allie, I can bench press 455 pounds. You are as light as a feather in comparison, I can pick you up no problem, no matter how many curves you get." He lets go of my waist and slowly walks back, giving me some space, but all of a sudden I feel like I might lose my footing and just melt into a puddle right here. *Puddle, I am a puddle.*

He is still looking, turmoil reflecting in his eyes. He lets out a breath and shakes his head. Looks back up and says, "And for the record, the curves suit you."

CHAPTER TWELVE

Allie

THEN

Kiss me, Ed Sheeran

There's a game tomorrow and we need to travel, so today we have been at practice all afternoon. It's almost 7 and I'm exhausted and ready to go home. I start walking out of the locker room and see that the football practice is not over. I head to the bleachers and watch them practice.

Jake and I have been talking nonstop since this weekend. He also finds me at school every chance he gets, even though we don't have any classes together. And every day he walks me to my car, even if he's not going home yet. He has been so attentive and overall the opposite of what I thought a football player would be. He hasn't kissed me yet and that's fine, if he wants to take this slow, but by the amount of time that we have spent together, or just talking this week, you would think we have been dating for months.

Practice is still going so I grab a book from my bag, get comfortable and start reading. The humidity in the air makes the pages feel almost wet, which is fitting, given the sinking feeling I'm getting while reading this chapter. The boys keep playing and I keep reading, wondering if I'm maybe overstepping waiting for him.

"Allie. Allie, wake up," I hear a voice in the distant. Suddenly, I feel like I'm falling so I jerk, but strong arms hold me in a tight hug and I start floating. I flutter my eyes open and see Jake smirking and when I try to move he softly adds, "Shh, it's ok. I got you."

Is he carrying me? What happened? I must have fallen asleep. Oh God, so embarrassing. "Jake, put me down." I AM MORTIFIED.

He smiles and says, "I already got you up, might as well let me finish this."

Why is this so sexy and mortifying at the same time? I squirm, trying to loosen the hold he has on me but he just shakes his head slightly. He's amused by this. At the fact that he is built of stones and not matter how curvy I am, I can't even make him flinch. "You are going to get hurt, put me down."

"Who's going to hurt me?" he says.

"My weight."

He scoffs and says, "You're not even heavy."

What?? I'm the biggest cheerleader on the squad because I'm built like a thick gymnast, as opposed to a petite cheerleader. It's not an issue. I have worked hard to love my body the way it is but love doesn't take away fact, and the fact is, I am heavy.

"Your eyebrows are speaking. I promise you, you are not heavy Allison. I warm up with twice your weight. Let me take care of you." He keeps walking like I am not dead weight.

We're almost to the parking lot when he asks if I drove today. I shake my head and he keeps walking to his truck. He puts me down briefly to open the door and places me in the passenger seat. He leans in to buckle me up and I can smell him even more now. He smells like wood, mixed with sweat, and a hint of something minty, and it should gross me out but instead, it sparks something in me. He closes the door and walks around to his side.

He starts driving as he asks if I'm hungry, to which I nod. We go back and forth with what to get but we end up going for smoothies and wraps. We're waiting at the drive-thru and I yawn, trying to curl up on his seat. I'm so tired from the week and practice, I could sleep for a week.

"Why did you wait for me? Don't get me wrong, I loved seeing you there when I got done but you're clearly exhausted." He starts to reach with his hand but pulls it back, probably unsure if he should even touch me. I look at his hand and then back at his face. He is sweaty and muddy from his practice. His shirt clings to his broad chest showing his shape almost as if he wasn't wearing one.

I smile at him, "Because I wanted to. Isn't that a good enough reason?"

"Yes, it is." He smiles back and places his hand on top of mine. It feels nice, like it belongs there. I can feel my skin flushing immediately and I have never been more thankful for having tanned skin than right now. *Seriously? My heart racing over a hand on mine?* Maybe it is not just the hand, but whose hand it is.

We make it to my house a while later and I don't think I'll ever get tired of his company. He's so funny, kind, and interesting. It seems like he has his shit together, too. "Do you want me to pick you up in the morning?" he asks as we reach the front door. He looks nervous, like he's unsure of what he wants to do, or like he wants to say more than what he's actually saying.

I look up at him and smile, trying to ease whatever nerves he has, "You don't have to but if you want to, I'm good with that," he smiles and reaches to grab my hand. He steps closer and holds it in his and my whole arm is suddenly aware of his touch. Like he ignited a fire within me with just a mere touch. "5:00 am good?"

"Great, just don't judge when I look like a raccoon."

He snickers and tucks a piece of hair behind my ear, "Not a morning person are we Honey?"

"Nope, not at all."

"I bet you are the cutest looking raccoon in all of Baker." He takes a step closer.

"Oh, is that so? Not in the whole country?" I close our distance a little bit more.

"Oh baby, in the whole universe." He is so close all of my senses are on alert. That woodsy, sweaty smell will be the death of me. It reminds me of camping and good memories. The hand he used to tuck my hair stays on my shoulder and his other hand still holds mine. He is so close that if I were to go up on my tippy toes and lean forward just a little bit, his lips would be on mine. *And I want that, oh so bad.*

"You can't take it back when you see me in the morning." I peer at him through my thin lashes.

"Don't you get it? Nothing can stand against you, Honey." He raises both hands to grab my face. We are sharing the same breath and the air is thick with intentions. He lowers his face to mine and our noses touch lightly, and right when I think he won't do anything he closes the inch between us and kisses me.

His kiss feels like my lips landed on a pillow made just for them. So soft and tender. He kisses me gently but with intention. He doesn't use his tongue, but it's not just a peck either. He is taking his time exploring my lips and I AM HERE FOR IT. I don't even know what to do with my hands so I just keep them next to me awkwardly because I am floating. He tastes like peppermint and good choices. My own little peppermint kiss that I never want to let go of. After what feels like ten minutes, but also not long enough, he breaks the kiss and traces my bottom lip with his thumb. "Sorry, but I had to," he says, a little out of breath. "I could not go one more day without tasting you."

And that my friends is how a girl dies a swooning death. "You don't have to apologize. I wanted it too," and he immediately kisses me again. He is still soft and gentle so I bite his lower lip and he smirks against my mouth. He pulls away but our noses are still touching, and his eyes are still closed, his hands holding my face to his. "Easy baby," he whispers, and if this man calls me baby one more time, I might change my name to that because I have never been more excited about being called anything other than Allie before. "Easy with my heart. If you do that, I won't be able to leave this porch and we both have a busy day tomorrow." He kisses me one more time and then walks back. Leaving me breathless and lost in him. "Good night, Allie," and he smiles walking back towards his truck.

"Good night, Jake."

I walk into my house, close the door, and lean against it. I feel like my heart is soaring and my legs are jello. What is happening to me? It's been less than a week but I feel like I've known him longer, and that kiss was just like if we had practiced for years. It was absolutely perfect. I have read books that describe this feeling of belonging to someone and I always thought it was fiction, but the way that one kiss made me feel, it's making me rethink everything I thought I knew.

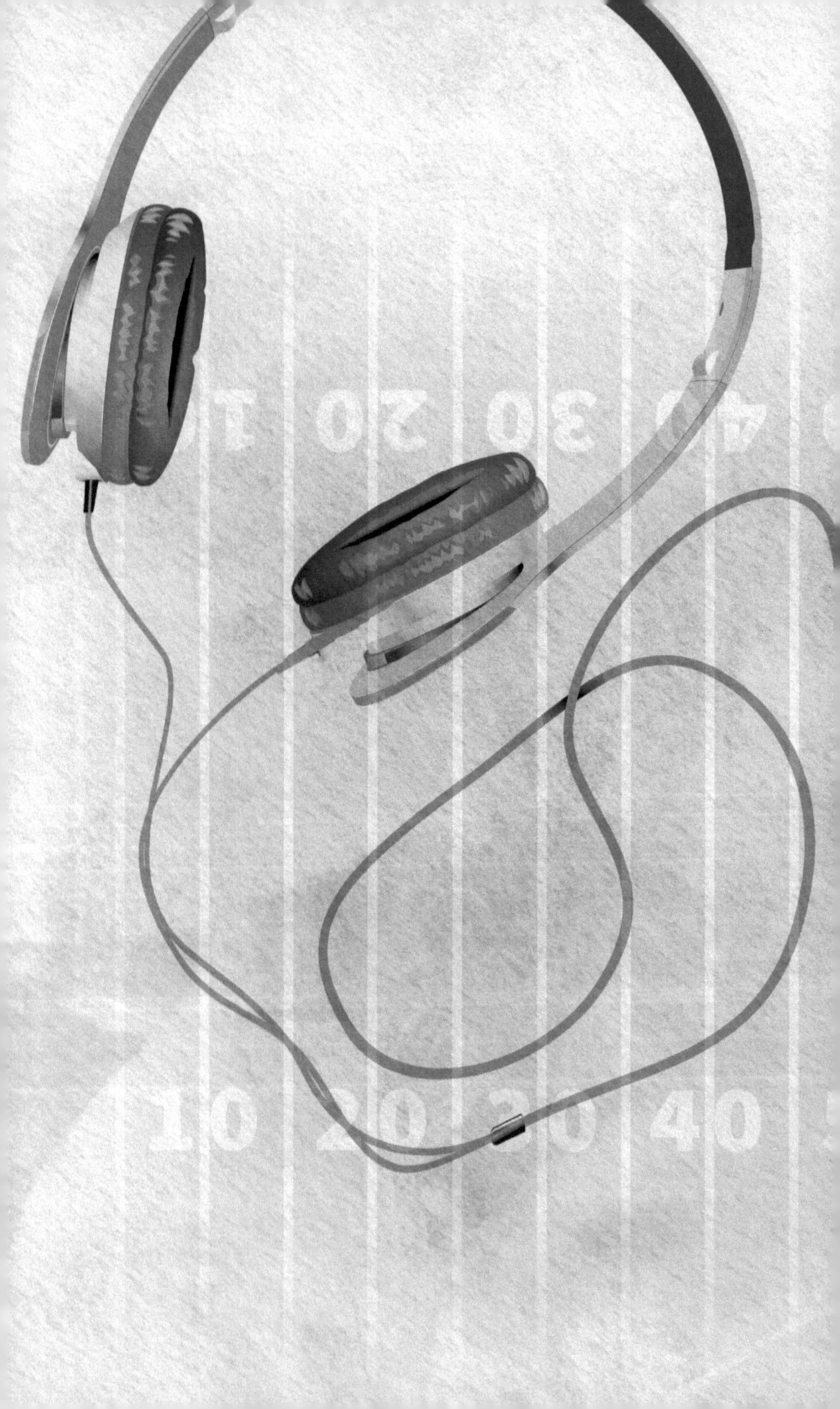

WHEN THE SUN GOES DOWN IN GEORGIA, COREY SMITH

FALLING IN LOVE WITH HER WAS
LIKE A RAPID WAVE TO THE SHORE;
NEEDED BUT CATASTROPHIC.
SHE LEFT ME STRANDED, WAITING
FOR THE TIDE TO COME BACK IN.
EITHER TO LET ME TASTE HER
OR TO TAKE ME WITH HER;
BUT NOT LETTING
EITHER HAPPEN AGAIN.

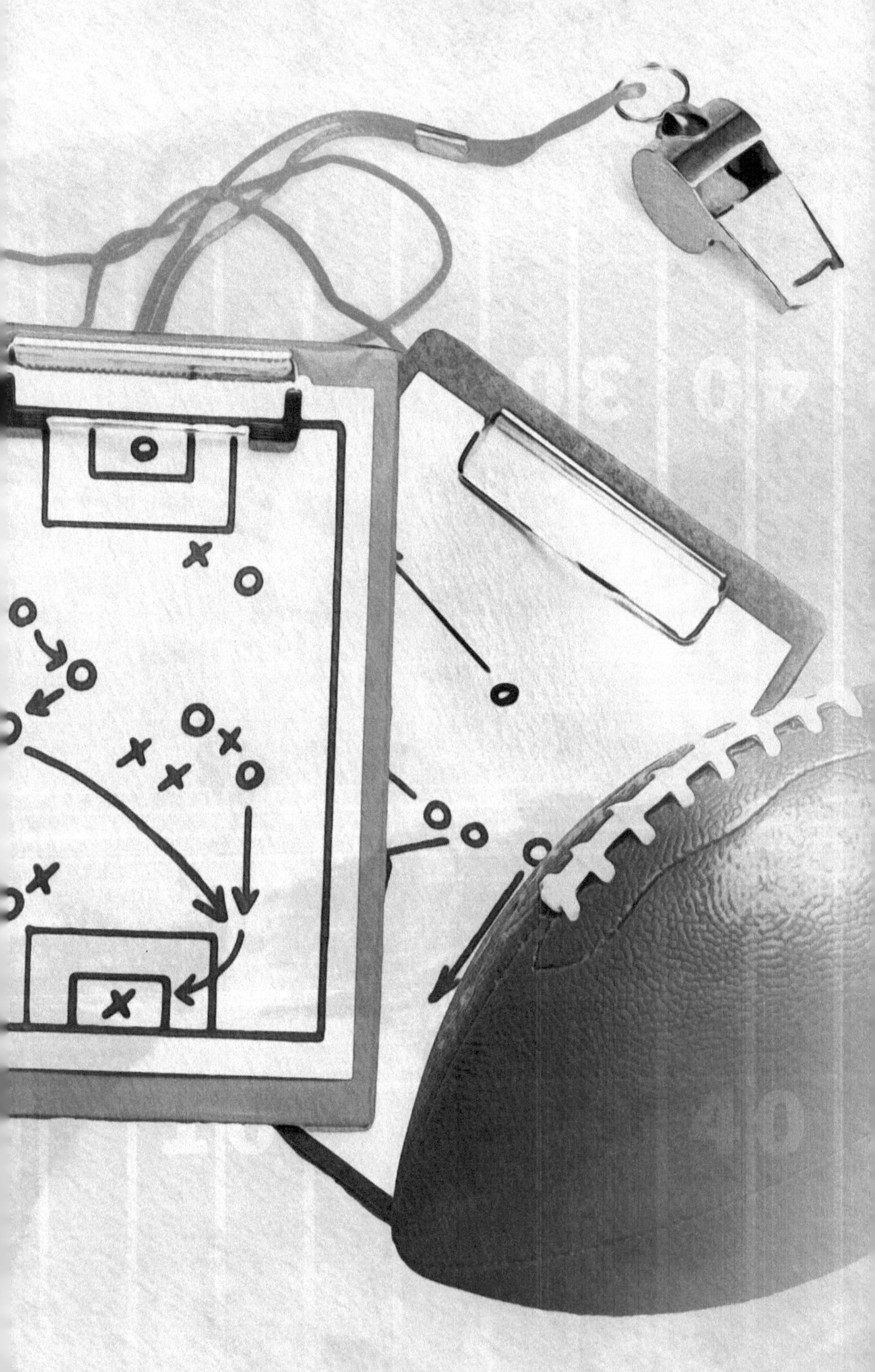

CHAPTER THIRTEEN

Jake

NOW

Cornelia Street (Live from Paris), Taylor Swift

It is 5:00 am and the noises coming from Allie's room sound like she's at war. *Allie's room.* She's been here a couple of days and my stupid heart is already claiming her. I know, logically, that this weekend was an alternate reality in which wishful thinking played a big part, but how could I not take anything she was willing to give me? Even if it was just letting me help her.

Pathetic. Anyone who sees this would see how I'm being a fool and acting like I am eighteen again. Allie came into my life ten years ago like a force of nature; touching everything in sight with magic and leaving devastation behind when she left.

I was finally in a place where I had come to terms that she was it for me. That we were a case of the right person, but the wrong place and time, and that I was just going to dedicate my life to teaching and coaching now. And then, she basically dropped into my arms. What if this is a gift? What if this is our chance at a redo? She seems as affected by me as I am by her, but you never know what's going on in that beautiful head of hers.

"Coño, why is it so hard to just find something the first time." I hear her through the door. She's clearly trying to get dressed and is annoyed at something. She always had that going on for her; thinking out loud. "Shit, shit, shit," she adds with the sound of more rumbling. I could go offer help, but help with what? It'll be better for both of us if I just stay out of it.

She used to be the worst morning person, and the crankiest one too. She needed coffee and fuel to even start her day, no matter what time she used to wake up.

This is why the coffee pot is on, and I'm at the stove getting ready to fry some eggs for her. Allie loves food and I loved feeding her. Still love, I guess, since it's all I've been wanting to do since I saw her at the airport.

Corey Smith plays in the background while bacon is sizzling in front of me, and the house smells like salt and grease mixed with coffee. I hear the door open and I turn, hoping to find a half-awake Allie since it's so early but instead, my breath catches in my throat and I'm frozen in time. Fucking shit. She is walking slowly towards me with a shy smile on her face, which is not like her. She's probably feeling guilty about her little Dominican outburst of energy this morning. *Which, apparently, I still find endearing.*

She is wearing what I assume is her business attire. She has on a blue dress that touches every single curve of her body down to her hips, where it gets wider. It stops right above the knees which shouldn't be that sexy but she makes everything look like it was made for her. She is wearing heels that hug her beautiful feet and give her a nice height. Her legs look incredible in that outfit. My eyes keep going up and I notice the top of her dress. It shows some cleavage but not too much; leaving a lot to the imagination but giving you enough material to wonder for hours what it would look like underneath the fabric. Her hair is half up and pulled behind her perfect ears, which are adorned by earrings that say "teacher" on them. She is perfect. She was perfect then, and she's perfect now.

Her lips move but I don't hear anything. "Mm sorry, what?" I say stupidly like I wasn't just caught ogling her.

"I said, you're up early."

"Oh, yeah. I have to be at school early. How did you sleep?" *Smooth Jake, smooth.*

"Great. The bed is great." Her cheeks darken. I always liked that about her. She always says that because she has dark skin, you can't see when she's blushing. Little does she know that her cheeks get a darker glow to them when she's embarrassed or when she says something she doesn't mean. It's adorable.

"I'm glad. There's coffee in the pot and creamer in the fridge." She thanks me and grabs a mug. Two teaspoons of sugar and a splash of creamer later, she sits at the breakfast table. She takes a sip of her coffee, closes her eyes and hums. The little sounds she makes will be my undoing, they always have been, and apparently, they always will be. The worst part? She doesn't even know she makes them.

Giving her the plate I made for her, her eyes widen. Two eggs over medium, a couple pieces of bread, some bacon, a piece of avocado and everything but the bagel. That used to be her breakfast of choice, and maybe I should have asked if she wanted anything because she's just staring at it in silence. *Fantastic Jake, way to go.* "You don't have to eat it. I can put it in a to-go box or something."

"It's... ummmm... it's perfect Jake. Thank you," she says in a tender tone. "How did you know?"

"How did I know what?" I ask, wiping the countertop to make sure things are clean before we head out. I try to keep my focus on her though, but it is so hard to look at her and not want to kiss that sweet pout off her face.

She looks at her plate and then at me. "That this is my comfort meal," she says quickly.

Because I know you Allie. "You used to say breakfast was the most important meal and I know you have a big day today. It's not a big deal."

"Thank you. This is so kind." Then she starts eating.

I grab a few things to put in my bag. We have practice after school today so I make sure to grab snacks for the long day. I set my bag on top of the table and see her standing, but I grab the plate from her hands. "Let me take this for you."

"Thanks. Did you eat before I got up?"

"Nah, I don't eat in the mornings. I have planning mid-morning so I usually eat then-" I point at my big duffle bag on the table, "-that's why my bag is so big. Full of snacks."

"You didn't have to cook for me, I'm already messing up your routine enough. I'll be out of your hair today."

Please don't leave is all I want to say, but instead I say, "I don't mind cooking at all, and you are not messing anything up. You can stay for as long as you need to." I'd take any time I can spend with her and get to know the woman she has grown into. I had a feeling that the reason I was never able to completely move on is because she holds my heart, but seeing her again confirmed it in ways I can't even begin to explain. I just wish it was the same for her. She looks so mature and grown up. And happy. So happy. Still a little erratic and skittish, but she wouldn't be her without that.

"How are you getting to work today?" I ask, knowing full well there's no way she'll get an Uber out here this early.

"Well, that's part of the reason for my screaming this morning," she huffs, "Sorry about that. The first Uber available won't get here until like 8:00 and I need to be at work at 7:45. I was going to ask if you could drop me off at the ride share stop on your way in."

She looks at me with a mix of embarrassment and guilt. It probably took everything in her to ask for that. She used to hate asking for help, and when things don't go according to plan. Right now, both of those things are happening. *I wish she knew that I would give her the world if she just asked.*

She swivels in the chair, slightly turning her legs as I walk towards her. There's a small wall right behind her with a metal basket that holds my keys and some mail. I stand in front of her and I see her eyes look up from under her eyelashes. She is wearing these oversize glasses that don't let you see her beautiful hazel eyes from far away but from right here, they look every bit the perfection that they are. Her eyes have a brown ring around them with speckles of green and gold inside of her honey-colored irises.

I reach behind her and her body stiffens. *So responsive to me still.* I grab the keys and put some space between us. I need it at least to think. She can deny it all she wants but her body doesn't lie, so I smile softly at her. I grab her hand and I feel her warm skin prickle under my touch. I open her palm gently and place the keys into it. "Here, you can take my truck." Over my dead body will she get a ride share when I have a vehicle she can use. "You can drop me off at school on your way out. I have practice, so I won't need to be back until later. If they solve your B&B issue, then I can take you tonight."

"Jake, I can't take this. You are already doing so much," she looks miserable as she shakes her head and her entire body says no.

"It's not a big deal. Please just take it. You'd be doing me a favor since I won't be worrying about you all day." She doesn't need to know that I have been worrying about her since the day I met her. "Come on, let's go. We need to leave so neither of us are late."

While she drives, she looks at the streets we pass as if she is seeing ghosts. Her knuckles are gripping the steering wheel so hard it is almost like she is holding on for dear life. I turn the music up to try and ease her jitters and Taylor Swift starts filling my truck with her voice. I know it is her because I can't listen to a single song of hers without it reminding me of Allie.

Allie scoffs and whispers, "Of course this would be the song to play." She is not really talking to me and I don't think she realizes it either. *God, she's adorable.* I stare at her little pouty lip as she tries so hard not to sing the lyrics but her memory betrays her as she mouths the words. Something about a heartbreak that time can't heal.

I swear I can hear her voice shake as she tries to stop herself from singing but then she whispers, *"Cornelia Street,"* as she stares at the road in front of us. Center Street is right in front of us. The same street where we sat so many times to eat, talk, and kiss. Something in the song says she wouldn't be able to walk the street again because it would remind her of something else.

Then everything clicks. This is her *Cornelia Street.* Her eyes are watering while the song keeps playing in the background. She blinks and keeps staring in front of her. Seeing her like this now, it breaks my heart. If she truly loved me, to the point that a street is bringing back all those memories and bringing tears to her eyes, why did she leave? Why did she leave me? If she truly didn't care about us, then why is she having this reaction?

We pull up in front of the high school and she is taking it all in. Her eyes are wide, full of emotion, "It still looks the same."

"Yeah" I sigh, "They have added some portables in the back and the rooms have been painted, but everything else is the same," I add. "Coach Blake is still the cheer coach and Principal Parker is still here."

She looks at me like I just brought her back in time. I squeeze her hand and smile at her.

"You'll have to come in and say hi to them before you leave." *She is leaving again.*

She nods as I open the door. I hand her a post-it note with my phone number, she looks at it and grabs it, touching her fingertips to my hand. Goosebumps spread through my arm but humid air slips into the cabin from the open door and it brings us back to reality.

"See you later, Allie."

CHAPTER FOURTEEN

Allie

Stay, Zedd & Alessia Cara

Today has been hell! I spent the day trapped in meetings to learn the needs of this school. I will be working there for the next two weeks and then I'm being transferred to another school. Their principal was so nice but they have a lot of new teachers in need of training and so little time to do so. I will be recording lessons, so they can watch, and doing professional development sessions with them. Those are my favorite! I call them Make and Take. They come in ready to learn but we also make things they can take and use in the classroom. I always leave those meetings giddy and proud of all their hard work and efforts to make learning more fun for their students. But the endless meetings are not my favorite part at all.

Also, my company is struggling to find me a decent B&B, so they suggested that I go to a hotel. I hate them though, so I am not entirely sure what to do. They make me feel lifeless, like I'm in a cardboard box. I have never liked them so staying in one for six months is not appealing at all. I will stay at Jake's tonight and then transfer to the hotel tomorrow. I have one more night with him and I really just want to get to know him more. Not the boy I loved once, but the man he has turned into. He still has the heart of gold that made me love him the first time. _The first time._ Like I ever stopped loving him. My mom once said that the most important people you are with in your life are the first and the last. The first one because they show you how to love, and the last one because they love you through it all. I truly think Jake was both, even if he won't love me forever, I know I will always love him.

They were able to provide a rental car for me, though, and they will have it available tomorrow morning. My plan is to drive to Baker now and hopefully catch Jake at practice and then head back to his house to pack. I already requested an Uber for tomorrow morning so the whole-taking-him-to-work deal won't happen again. I feel like the biggest chauffeur, no matter how much southern charm he shows. It can't be comfortable for him to have me staying at his house after everything that happened, especially without any notice; he is just too much of a gentleman to admit it or kick me out. Anyone else would have.

I make it to the school just in time to see the players walk off the field. It brings me back to all the Thursday nights we walked out of the field, hand in hand, after practice. Of the Friday Night Lights that we shared. Memories of happiness and comfort. I park the truck and grab my phone to text him to tell him I am here when I realize that I still have his number blocked on my phone but the name is still the same *Future Husband*. I sigh, unblock him and message him.

> **Me:** Hey, It's Allie. I'm here.

> **Me:** I mean, Allie Zabana, not sure how many more Allies you have saved.

> **Me:** Not that it is an issue! You can have all the Allies you want.

> **Me:** You don't need my permission or anything.

Jesus.

> **Me:** Anyways, I'm here.

I see the three dots dancing and disappearing, and dancing again. I am staring at the phone in my hand judging my own life choices when the driver side door opens, scaring me half to death.

"Por Dios!" I whisper, half in a gasp and in a scream, dropping the phone and covering my ears, as if not hearing whoever is at the door will save me. I slowly turn and see Jake standing there with a panty-dropping smile. *Kill me now, please.* Then I get a text, FROM HIM, while he's standing right there.

> **Future Husband:** Hey Allie, Allie Zabana, not my only Allie and not the one that needs to give me permission.

I look up from my phone to find him looking at me with the smuggest grin. *Tierra trágame enterita, ahora. Please earth, swallow me whole, now.* "I was rambling, you know," I say with a sigh.

"Yes Allie, I do know. Want me to drive? You're probably exhausted."

I climb through to the passenger side, struggling a little to get my butt over to the other side and finally making it in the least sexy way possible. He looks at me and smiles but it doesn't reach his eyes. His eyes are tired and heavy as he holds my gaze and puts his bag in the back. He doesn't say anything else as he swiftly gets behind the steering wheel, closes the door and blasts the AC on high. He has drops of sweat running down the side of his face and you can tell he is exhausted too. He is not wearing the same clothes he was wearing this morning, probably changed for practice. He has dry-fit shorts and a long-sleeved shirt that says Coach Clarke on the right side.

"Where are we going?" I ask.

"To get something to eat. I had a long day and I really don't want to deal with anything right now," he sighs, "and I think the feeling is mutual. So let's go eat."

"You don't have-" and I don't even finish my sentence when he gives me his I-mean-business stare. It's both terrifying and compelling, looking into his eyes when he's 100% serious about something.

We don't say anything for a bit until he adds, "Please don't fight me on this, I don't have the energy today to try to convince you to just be with me. Just - let's eat and then we can go home."

He turns his focus back to driving and we fall into an uncomfortable silence. It's never been like this between us but he just said *we can go home*. But it's not ours, it's his. I'm just crashing into his life and blurring all the lines. Ha, *lines*? More like years of walls built up by the pain I inflicted ten years ago. I look out the passenger side window and silently wipe away a tear from my eye.

"Chinese?" he asks.

"Always," I whisper.

We order our food, pick it up and head back to his place. We set the food on the table and start to eat, still in silence. There's soft country music playing in the background and the whole house is dimmed, casting low light around him, making his eyes look darker than they are.

"Do you want to talk about it?" I ask in between bites of my crab Rangoon.

He drinks some water, lays his elbows on the table and looks at me. You can tell he's thinking about speaking but it is almost as if something is holding him back. I can't blame him, not entirely. I may be sitting in his house but I'm practically a stranger so I say exactly that, "You don't have to talk to me Jake, I know I'm practically a stranger to you but you're upset and I hate to see you like that."

"You could never be a stranger, Allie," he sighs. "No matter the time that passes or distance between us. It was just a long day and some of the boys are struggling with a specific class and I feel like they're being punished for something they didn't do." He closes his eyes and shakes his head, "I'm just trying to figure it out and I didn't have the energy to worry about dinner, you know? It has nothing to do with not wanting to open up to you," he finishes and takes a sip of his beer.

"I understand. My offer still stands," and I reach to hold his hand. He lets me and I swear sparks fly where we touch. I squeeze his hand while holding his gaze for what feels like an eternity. The song changes and it is a more upbeat rhythm bringing me back to reality. I pull my hand back from him and clear my throat. "So, my company can't seem to find me a B&B so they are placing me in a hotel. I didn't want to take a taxi back to the city tonight, so I scheduled an Uber for tomorrow morning. I will head to school and then from there check into the hotel. If it's ok with you that I stay an extra night."

"Allie," he says softly.

I can see regret in his eyes so I interrupt him quickly. "It's ok, I can repack and be out tonight. I am so sorry for intruding. You've been nothing but generous and I took advantage of that." I start gathering what's left of my food to put in the container when I spill my cup of water, "Shit, I'm sorry," grabbing the paper towels and cleaning as fast as I can. I feel his warm and callous hand hold my forearm as he gently says, "Allie, stop for a second," but I don't. I can't stop. I'm making a mess; this whole situation is a mess and if I don't get out of his sight, I might start crying because it is suddenly too much to handle.

"I can't stop, Jake. I am ruining this table, and you have a life, and I didn't mean to crash into it at all."

"You are not."

"And I can't seem to get anything right, and this, this is all I can do. I can clean it up and be out of your hair in no time."

"Stop!" he says firmly with a deep voice that he only uses when he's frustrated, "Can you just stop for a second and let me talk?"

I stop suddenly and stare at him. His eyes look stormy and his usual chestnut color looks more like dark tea. I shiver at the intensity of his gaze. He looks troubled and I wish I could read his expression right now. I take a deep breath and place the wet paper towel on top of my bag.

"Can I be honest with you?" he asks, and I can hear the vulnerability in his voice. I nod my head and he continues, "I don't think you should go. If I remember correctly, you hate hotels because of how much you guys moved when you were growing up. Jacksonville is not that far from here and you can borrow my truck for as long as you need it. I have an extra room that has no use and I would love to have your company, even if it's only for six months. I meant what I said the other day about me losing my best friend when I lost you, and having you back is bringing back a lot of memories; not all happy I will admit but most of them are. I'd be willing to push the sad ones aside for a chance to make new, happy ones with you."

He stops and I think he's done talking but he keeps going, "I don't know much about you right now, but something tells me that you are still the amazing person that you were and I'd be honored to spend some time with you until you move again."

With tears in my eyes I say, "Jake, I don't think I can."

"I am sure you can. Now, if you don't want to, that's another thing. I never asked for anything from you and that's one of my biggest regrets in life, so this is me asking you to stay here. I am not asking you to stay forever, of course, God knows you wouldn't, but this is me asking you to stay for now."

I have no words, but I feel his, deep in my soul. Like the few pieces of my heart that were not shattered ten years ago fell. Knowing that, deep down, his biggest regret was not asking me to stay then and that he is asking me to stay now, even knowing that it won't be permanent, is breaking the rest of my heart.

I probably should not feel all these emotions, especially after not seeing him for so long but who am I kidding when I try to deny that my feelings for Jake never went away. No one but me, so I do the only thing that I can do right now, I nod and whisper, "Ok, I'll stay," and in one moment, he's pulling me into him and hugging me, like staying away from me for one more second was going to break him.

My arms are at my side and I am holding on tight to all my emotions when he whispers a broken *thank you* that makes me lose all my bearings. Tears fall down my face, I let out my breath, and hug him back. My arms wrap around him and for the first time in so long he feels like the one thing that I have never found before: *home*.

CHAPTER FIFTEEN

Jake

THEN

Steal The Show, Lauv

Touchdown!!

The crowd goes wild! We've won our first game in the playoffs. We all gather together clapping our hands, and smacking on each other's backs for a game well played. The Commanders didn't come to play fair tonight and for a minute there I thought we were not going to make it. The offensive line was on fire and I have never been more proud of being their captain. Our quarterback played his best game of the season and everyone knows it. His girl, Kate ran to him and all the cheerleaders turned to look at them while shaking their sparkling poms. I am sure they were all shouting something about winning but I can't focus on anything but *her*.

I have been secretly watching her for months. I don't get how nobody else is. Her caramel skin glows under the moonlight and droplets of sweat give her a shimmery look that shouldn't be legal. She has curves that make her skirt seem shorter than it probably is. Red is definitely her color, but I am sure that all colors would look so good on her because she is stunning. She has a high ponytail with one of those big obnoxious bows cheerleaders wear that makes her look like a doll, and she is shaking her poms in front of her but her eyes are on me. I have never felt like the luckiest man alive until now. I take my helmet off and run to her, slowing down when I am close to reaching her. Her smile grows wider when she sees that it was *her* that I was running to. I make it to her and whisper a *hi* between my toothy grin. With sparks in her eyes she tells me *congratulations*. Her poms stop shaking the same way my heart stops beating. I can tell that she doesn't know how to handle us in this moment, but I do the one thing I know will erase every doubt in her mind. I drop my helmet, close the distance between us, grab her face and kiss her like she has never been kissed before. I kiss her like she's mine and I don't care who sees it because if it was up to me, I would scream it at the top of my lungs. I can feel the poms on my chest, and I can't tell if she's pushing me away or holding on to me so I break the kiss and look at her beautiful honey eyes. *Honey.* If she only knew all the reasons I call her Honey. Her eyes, her skin, her hair. Sweet honey that has me sticky with lust and wanting to come back for more.

"Thanks," I say.

"For what?" she asks sheepishly.

"For letting me show everyone who wants to see, that you are taken."

"Oh, am I now? Since when?" she says with a smirk and biting her lower lip.

"Honey, since the moment your eyes met mine for the first time, I've been yours. It has just been a matter of you letting me show you that you can be mine too." And with that, she goes up onto the tips of her toes, drops her poms and tries to kiss me, but she can't reach me so she pulls down on my jersey, bringing me to her for another kiss. This one with more intention than the first and leaving no doubts in my mind that I will forever belong to her.

The ride back into town is smooth. The bus is loud with laughter, and everyone talks about the game. We usually meet on Saturdays to watch the replay and talk strategy, but the coach is letting us sleep in and meet on Sunday instead. I'm sitting alone when Nick sits next to me with a loud "bro" like he can't believe what just happened.

"So, Allie, huh?" he asks.

"Yeah, man," I say with a smile on my face.

"I thought you were not into being in a serious relationship, and she doesn't strike me as the one-night-stand type of girl."

"I know I said that but man, I don't know, there's something about her that I just couldn't stay away from. Have you ever even looked at her? Never mind, don't answer that." I sigh, "I think she might be the one."

"Bro, you've been seeing her for how long? A week? How can you even say that?"

"I know, but I think she is it."

"You're so fucked dude, I hope she feels the same way because this is a train wreck waiting to happen."

I look at him and punch him in the arm and nod.

"Later." He goes back to his seat in the back with the other guys, all talking about the party tonight and the girls they are gonna get with. In the meantime, there's only one girl on my mind and she has honey eyes and the perfect smile. God, her smile. I grab my phone from my bag and text her.

Me: Hola beautiful <3

Future Wife: Hey Handsome

Me: How's the bus ride? Full of glitter and screams?

Future Wife: more like full of make-up talk and gossip about you and me

Me: oh really?

Future Wife: yeah, I've been asked by so many of them when we became exclusive. I'm really close to making an announcement so they can leave me alone

Me: Oh, now I'm intrigued. What would said announcement be?

Future Wife: that we are not exclusive

What a way of breaking someone's heart.

Me: we're not? I didn't know you were seeing other guys. I know I'm not seeing anyone else.

Future Wife: what? no! I'm not seeing anyone else but we've never had the official talk so I just assumed

Me: Allison, we have been together every single day since our first date. I kissed you in front of everyone today, and for the record you kissed me back.

Me: I think that's pretty exclusive no?

I can see the three dots floating and disappearing, floating and disappearing.

Me: Do you want to see other people?

Future Wife: what? no! I just …. I don't know, I thought the guy was supposed to ask if I wanted to be his girlfriend, you know?

Me: oh! I mean, I can if that's what you want me to do.

Me: Would you do me the honor of being my girlfriend, Allison Zabana?

Me: Do you want me to ask your father too?

Future Wife: You are insufferable. Stop mocking me. I've never done this before so I didn't know. And stop calling me Allison.

Me: so, is that a yes?

Future Wife: yes, Jacob. I guess you could be my boyfriend.

Smiling, I look at the text and screenshot this conversation. I save it in my favorite pictures and go back to my texts.

Me: Luckiest man alive.

Future wife: goodbye Jake ⌧

Me: Goodbye Honey

I close my eyes with my phone in hand and a smile on my face. The way that I would give what I don't have to be sitting next to her right now. Maybe that makes me whipped or whatever but she is worth that and more. I can't believe she's giving us a chance, now officially too. I can't believe that I get to call her mine.

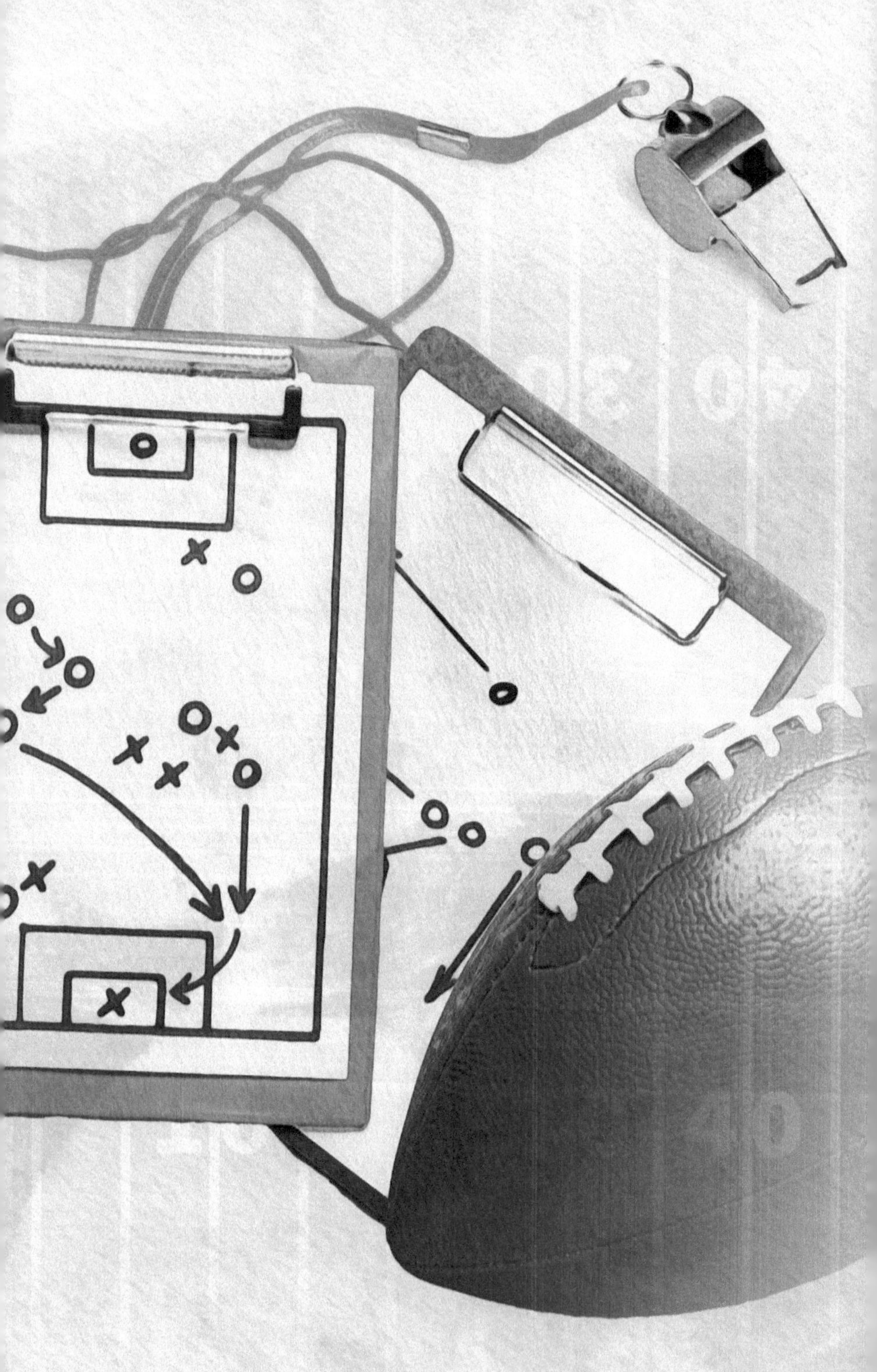

CHAPTER SIXTEEN

Jake

NOW

You Are the Reason (Duet Version), Calum Scott Ft. Leona Lewis

Allie's been here for a couple of weeks and we've fallen into this comfortable routine that has my brain in a fog. Other than not being able to touch her or kiss her whenever I want, it feels like we're in a relationship again. We come home every night after work, sometimes we cook together, sometimes we pick up takeout, but we always sit at the table to have dinner together. We laugh and tell each other about our day and it feels so good to have her here.

Today she finds out what her next assignment is and we have discussed that if it's on the other side of Jax, she might need to leave here and stay somewhere closer to her job. The logical part of my brain understands that but my mixed-up emotions don't. I selfishly want her to stay here. I am secretly hoping that she realizes the same thing that I did through the years; that we are IT and nothing will ever compare. I hope she realizes it soon since long ago, we were not enough. I see the way she looks at me though, and I keep hoping it sixtens the same thing that I have been wanting for it to mean for so long.

Walking towards my truck in the school parking lot, I get a text from Allie saying she's ordering pizza since I had practice tonight and it's already late. I smile while looking at my phone, frozen in place with the feeling of something dropping in my stomach at the thought of seeing her again. I'm so fucked.

"Jake, wait up," I hear Nick shout behind me. Nick has been my friend since middle school and is currently another football coach too. He teaches mechanics for the home economics department and like me, Baker is where his life is. He has lived here his whole life and he is not planning on going anywhere. Unlike me though, he married his high school sweetheart and they have a beautiful daughter together. He approaches me with a smack on the back and asks what I'm up to tonight since it's Friday. He knows I usually don't do much and often, he asks me to spend the night with them at his place. Fridays are his nights to hang out with Bella when there are no football games, so his wife Ashley can spend some time by herself. I haven't seen them in a while so I try my best to let him down gently.

"Just going home. Allie ordered some pizza and I'm sure we'll either watch a movie or play a game or something."

His face transforms from shock into something that resembles disbelief and disappointment, but he tries to hide it with a tight lip smile, and he nods.

"What?" I ask.

"Nothing man, have a good night." His mouth closes back into a straight line.

"Just say it, Nick," I say, crossing my arms.

"Are you sure this is a good idea man? Do I need to remind you what happened last time she left? Your whole life was fucked up. You're in a good place now. Is it worth it to mess with that?"

He was by my side when I had to venture into adult life without her after I thought we would share so many firsts together. First day of college. First day of football games. First graduation. First time moving in together. I could keep going but I just sigh, and rubbing my face, add, "She will always be worth it and you know it."

"Where do you two stand? Huh? Have you had that conversation or are you still just wishing that she realizes that you were the one for her?"

I stare at him but before I can say anything he continues, "Does she even know that you would give up your entire life for another chance with her? Does she know that you *did* lose yourself and your entire life because of her? Probably not, right?"

He isn't wrong but hearing someone else say it stings more than it should.

"I let her go once, I'm not doing it again. End of conversation."

He stares at me for a moment, shakes his head, and adjusts his red and blue baseball cap.

"Just be careful man. We're not eighteen anymore and at the very least you deserve explanations."

He walks towards his jeep, leaving me and my thoughts stranded. He is right but the thought of saying something to her and her not feeling the same, and fucking this up, is even worse than letting her go completely. I know she's not seeing anyone but could I even survive a fling with her, just for her to leave me again?

I drive home feeling uneasy. Nick's words replay in my head. My knuckles are white from holding the steering wheel so tight and sweat is running down my back. I pull into my driveway and see the little black sedan she's renting while she's here. She's home already which means I have no time to calm the fuck down, so I better get my shit together out here. Do I tell her that these last two weeks with her here have been better than ten years without her at all? Do I tell her that every time I see her and can't touch her, I feel like my blood is going to pour out of me? Or do I just walk up to her and kiss her senseless? Touch her like I know she hasn't been touched in years because nobody knows her like I do, even after all this time.

I walk into the house and do none of those things because when I see her, she is twirling around the house with her wild wet curls bouncing, her eyes closed and a broom in her hand acting as a microphone.

I knew at that moment that I would rather have her here as only a friend than be without her in any other way.

Closing the door, I lean against it quietly, setting my bag down and hanging my keys on their peg. Arms folded over my chest, I can feel my smile growing as I keep watching her dancing, oblivious to the fact that I am here.

She is absolutely precious; there is no other word to describe her. I used to think that she was perfect but nobody truly is, and that's okay. But she was perfect for me and seeing this twirling ball of energy in my living room, I think she might still be. She's mouthing the words to some song and I would bet money it is either Taylor Swift or some reggaeton but I can't pinpoint what it is. She never sings the right lyrics to anything and it sounds like a mixture of mumbled words and heavy breathing from the dancing and singing. I'm smiling, surely like an idiot, when she lifts her gaze and jumps back after she sees me.

"Dios mio, Jake, you scared the sparkles out of me," she says, holding her chest and grabbing her phone from the side pocket of her tiny shorts.

I snicker, "I didn't want to interrupt your little dance party."

She laughs and shakes her head, and that's the Allie that steals all of my breaths away. The 'unapologetically her' Allie.

"What are you doing with that broom? Do you even know how to use one?"

She squints her eyes, "Ha ha so funny. Of course I know how to use a broom, thank you very much and I am cleaning your house, that's what I'm doing."

"Why?"

"Because it needed to be done."

"But you're a guest here, I was going to clean tomorrow."

She takes a deep breath, while holding the broom in her right hand and stares at me with her ridiculously gorgeous hazel eyes,

"You can't expect me to live here and not help. You already don't want me to cook."

"I just don't want you burning the house down," I say smirking.

"Ha ha, again, very funny. I have grown up Jake and I am self-sufficient, so if I say I'm cleaning the house, I'm cleaning the house."

"Whoa, whoa, ceasefire," I say, lifting my hands in defeat. "I just hate seeing you doing so much after a week at work." Changing the topic I ask, "How was your Friday?"

"It was fine, I have one more week at this school and then I will be given a new assignment." She continues sweeping and uses the dustpan to collect whatever junk she got from the floor. She quickly walks past me to throw it in the trash can and the scent of warm vanilla with passion fruit hits me straight in my core. I clear my throat as she looks around at the space she still has to clean and looks back at me expectantly.

"Don't let me stop you then," I say, trying to control my smirk. The little sassy thing rolls her eyes, takes her earbud out of her ear, places it on the counter top and reaches to her back pocket for her phone. She does something on her phone and then Zac Brown Band starts blasting from her phone as she places it on the countertop next to her earbud.

She is bouncing up and down, swinging side to side, and carrying on like nobody's watching. But I'm watching alright. She looks so carefree and happy. So happy. My heart tugs as I reminisce about all the times that she looked just like that with me, blissfully lost in happiness.

I'm still standing by the door, lost in her presence when she says, "You know you can join me if you want. Stop being a grouchy pants."

"You know I don't dance, Allie."

"That never stopped you from dancing with me before," she says, opening her hazel eyes and it feels like she stares straight into my soul. She stops dancing and just keeps looking at me with a soft smile, challenging me to move to her. She sways her hips slowly, side to side, like a siren ready to enthrall a sailor and I am so utterly fucked if I think I'm getting out of this one unscathed.

She reaches behind her back and takes off the hair tie she had holding back half of her brown curls. She shakes her head like a puppy and the rest of her hair falls around her face.

Fucked, Jake, you are so fucked.

As if she knows what she's doing to me, she looks at me again as she sways, mouthing the lyrics, and she lifts her hand, palm up, and motions for me to join her. And I do because how can I ever say no to her?

I walk to her and she squeals and picks up the tempo of her dancing. She's still holding the broom like a microphone so I just stand across from her and move awkwardly. I have two left feet so I hate dancing, but for her, I always will.

Her smile is big and bright as she holds my hand and twirls under me. I take the broom from her hand and place it against the wall. I grab both her hands and dance with her. She closes her eyes and bounces while holding my hands and I try to keep up but fail miserably and end up almost stepping on her. She laughs and looks at me but keeps on moving as much as she can without dragging me to the ground. I am lost in her eyes, in her moves, in her scent, in her soft hands on mine. Completely lost in her.

She stops dancing and I look at her but I don't even notice the change in song until then. It's a slow song, something about being the reason for the heart beating and it's like the stars are aligning because, yes Allie, you will always be my reason.

Her breaths are picking up, even though she stopped moving, and she keeps looking at me. Her lips part slowly as she breathes through her mouth and she says, "Jake," barely as a whisper.

Holding her gaze I say, "Allison, no thinking, just dancing." I smile knowing how much she hates it when I call her that but it has always been our thing. She drops her gaze down immediately and bites those full lips that I am dying to taste, I want to know if they still taste like everything I have always wanted in life. I tuck my index finger under her chin and lift her face as I say, "Look at me." And she does.

I notice the tears falling down her face, and the turmoil hiding behind her eyes. I hold her face with both hands, letting my forehead drop to hers. I wipe her tears softly with my thumbs and drop my hands to her back, bringing her flush against my chest.

She's so nervous, I can almost feel her heartbeat about to match mine which is beating erratically fast. My hand is so close to her face so I do just what I've been wanting to do since the day she crashed into me in the airport, and cusp her cheek with my right hand. She leans against the touch as I say, "Hi."

Her hands that were loosely at her side slowly come up to lay flat against my chest, and she lifts her gaze back to me.

We stare at each other for a second. Then another one. It's taking everything in my power to hold up my end of the deal and be her friend. Just her friend. The music stops, breaking the spell we've been under and immediately grounding us again. Or maybe I am just transfixed by her eyes and her hands on my body that everything else ceases to exist.

I can't hold it in anymore, I release a breath as she catches hers, and growl, "Fuck it," while dipping my face and closing the space between us with a kiss. She releases the air she is holding as her lips dance with mine. Her lips still taste like fruity heaven. They still feel as soft as they used to and they still fit perfectly in mine. *Mine*, I repeat in my head as we get lost in this kiss. It's not urgent or rough but you can taste the desperation in us both.

I let go of her lips, foreheads still together. Our breathing is in sync, and our touch is electric. I am trying to find words to describe everything going through my mind right now when Allie beats me to it, whispering, "I've missed you." Completely shattering the only pieces that were left.

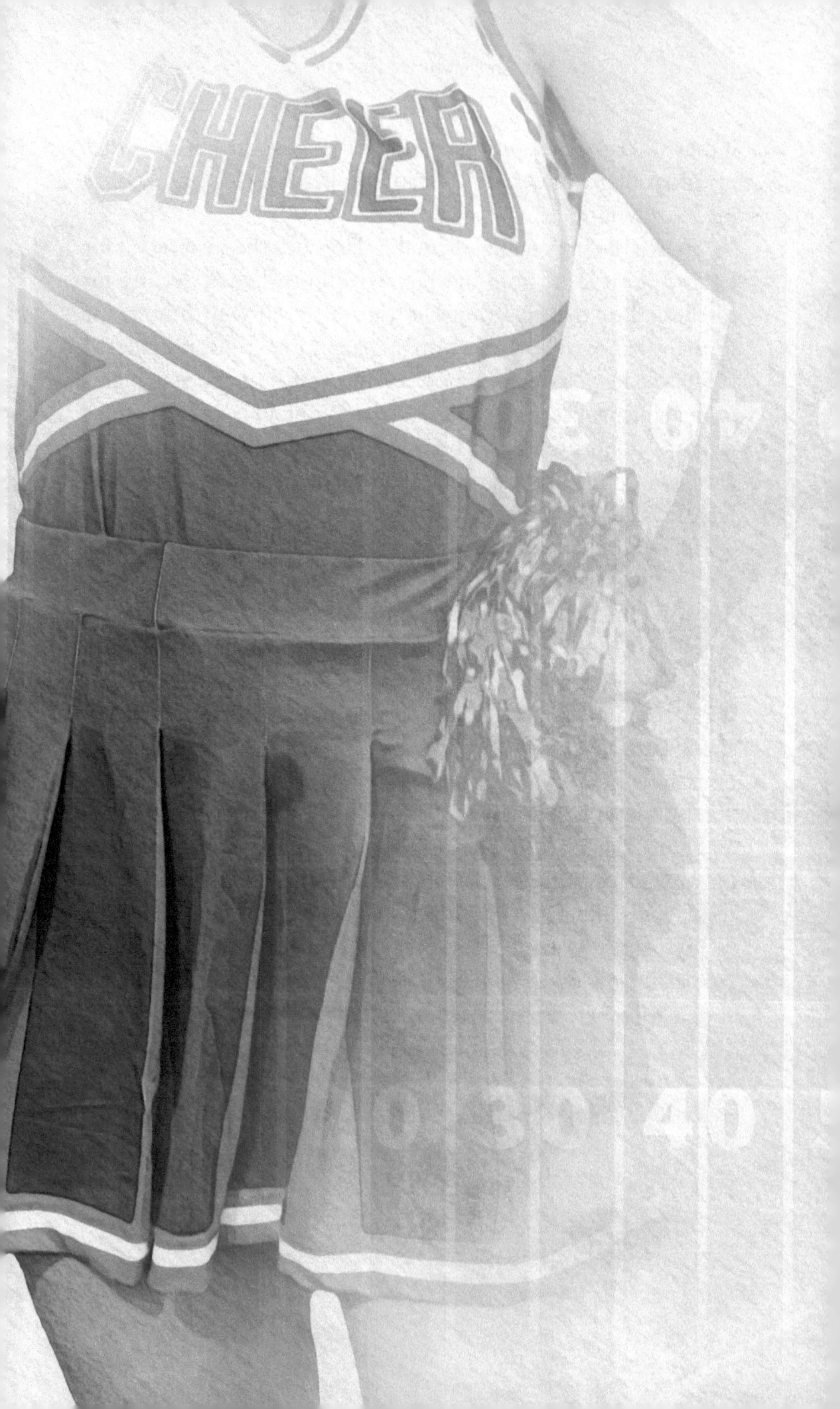

CHAPTER SEVENTEEN

Allie

THEN

Ho Hey, Nashville Cast

Jake and I are laying on my bed watching Friday Night Lights. It's been a whirlwind these past few weeks, what with us dating and our hectic schedules. With the team making it to the playoffs – which is next week – he has had crazy hours of practice which makes it harder to see him, but he still makes sure we spend time together every day. If they win this game, they go to State and our school's team has not been in ten years.

The people at school are still teasing us and Cara is always hounding me for details. Our relationship feels both too fast and not fast enough. Like my heart has been waiting for him all my life and now that he's finally here, I don't want to waste any time being apart from him. Which is crazy, right? Because it sounds a little crazy, considering that we're only in high school.

My parents are out of town for work and my brothers are camping with friends so I have the house to myself and decided to invite him over. We've been binge watching this show, cuddling and kissing for hours now. We ate pizza, popcorn and peanut m&ms while chatting about anything and everything. Some important and some just absolutely not. It's so easy to just be with him. And I hope it is as easy for him to just be with me too.

My head lays on his chest and his fingers trail across my arm. I yawn and he pulls the blanket higher to cover me more.

"I don't want to go to sleep yet," I say.

"You are tired Allie, it's ok if you do," he answers.

"I'm not ready for you to leave yet."

"Well, I don't have to if you don't want me to," he adds.

I lift myself up from my comfortable position to look at him. We have kissed plenty before and even felt each other up a little, but we haven't done anything else. Part of the reason is because of lack of privacy, but also partly because I have never done anything like that before, and I don't even know how to bring it up.

"Jake, I—" and he interrupts me, saying, "I can leave too, I just don't have to if you don't want me to. I just thought I'd offer. I don't have anywhere to be early tomorrow and honestly, being with you calms my nerves about the game next week."

"It's not that, it's just..." I trail off and he keeps looking at me, waiting to reply. "I've never slept with anyone before."

"I already know you snore baby, it's not a big deal. I kinda like it." He laughs a little.

"I mean, I've never had sex before," I flat out say, covering my face in embarrassment. I'm sure I would look very flushed if he was able to see my face right now.

"Allie," he says. "Allie, look at me please." He pulls my hands off my face. I look at him and take a deep breath before opening my mouth, but he covers my lips with his index finger and says, "When I said I could stay, I didn't mean we had to have sex for me to stay. I would never want you to feel pressured into doing anything you don't want to. I would be happy with just staying here and being your giant human pillow."

Before I can speak he continues, "If you want me to stay, I can even sleep on the floor if that'd make you feel more comfortable, but I can also go home. You tell me, baby."

I knew he was a gentleman, but I thought he wanted to have sex with me and that's why he said that he could stay here. This is all so confusing.

"You don't want to have sex with me?" I ask shyly.

"Oh, Honey," he says smirking as he puts a curl behind my ear. "It's not that I don't want to, trust me. I can't wait to be with you in every way I can. In any way, you'd let me. There's not a moment that goes by with you that I don't think about it. Not a single second that I don't think about your body underneath mine, and about the kind of sounds you'd make when I drive you crazy with my hands, my mouth, my whole body. Wanting you is not an issue but we have our whole lives, Allie. I'm not in a rush."

All of a sudden the room is twenty degrees hotter and my whole body feels like it's on fire. The mental image of him doing things to me with his hands and mouth has me tingling with anticipation and we're not even touching. He says he's not in a rush, but after hearing him say that, I might be.

"That was a good answer, Jake."

"I meant it."

And I believe him, and God if I wasn't already gone for this boy, I am now. But there's no denying my brain what my heart already knows. I am in love with Jake and I wouldn't love anything more than letting him take me completely. Take every part of me. I sit up all the way and straddle his lap coming face to face with him.

"Allie, I—" I put my finger on his lips.

"It's my turn to talk now." I start slowly grinding on him as I say, "I didn't think I was ready but hearing you say that, has my body all sorts of hot and I would very much like to find out some of the things that you have thought about with me under you." I bring my hands to each side of his face and kiss him like I've never kissed him before. We're all tongue and teeth. Moans and hands everywhere while I grind on top of him. He puts pressure on my back slowing me down so I break our kiss and look at him.

Our breaths were frantic and labored. I can see his chest rising and falling and I can feel my nipples hard against the fabric of my top.

"Allie, are you sure?" he asks with concern in his eyes, and this is the moment that I know for sure that I love him. The look in his eyes is one of pure adoration and his patient words and hands are making my heart skip a beat, even though I'm ready to devour him. I don't say anything and I'm just staring at him, biting my lips when he adds, "We can stop right now. I'm in no rush. Like I said, we have a lifetime baby." And with that I lay my whole body against him and hug him tight because I never want to let go. I inhale deeply and he says, "It's okay Allie, it truly is. I'm sorry if I rushed you or if you felt pressure in any way," and God can he be any more perfect?

"Jake," it comes out more like a moan than a whisper and he tightens his grip on my back. My chest is flush against his and our breaths are dancing against each others' lips.

"I want to, I'm just scared. Would you be gentle?" I don't even know why I ask because I know he will but I sense his hesitation. He is using every ounce of control he has not to touch me right now.

"Please Jake, I want to." I close the little distance between us and kiss him. I kiss him tenderly but with purpose. "Please, make love to me." I kiss him again. He responds to my kiss, immediately deepening it and bringing his hands to my hair.

I nip at his bottom lip and he tightens his grip even more so I chuckle, and in what feels like a second he has me flat against the bed with my hands above my head, and he's pinning my hips down with his.

He lifts himself up slowly and whispers, "I love you" right against my face. When I am going to reply, he says, "Shh, you don't have to say it back. It's ok. I just couldn't go another minute without letting you know," and he starts kissing me again. "I love you, sweet girl, and that won't change if we stop this now. I don't think it will ever change. Know that at any moment you can say stop, and we stop."

I respond with the only thing I can think of, "Please don't make me ask again." To be honest, I'm ready to beg.

I am lost by the kissing, the nipping, and the licking. He teases as he goes lower on my neck, on my chest. His hands go up under my shirt and when he feels the edge of my very thin bra, I arch against him with a soft moan and he hisses. He looks at me and says, "If at any point you want me to stop, you just say it, ok? No questions asked, I'll stop." I nod and he says, "I need words Allie, words."

"Yes, Jake. Yes."

And it is like that one word unleashed a beast. In a fraction of a minute, he pulls my shirt over my head. He's lowering the straps of my bra and nipping at my neck. It makes me wonder how experienced he is because there's no way he's a rookie when he kisses and touches me like this.

My feet are pushing against the mattress, trying to find some friction but he keeps teasing me. His hand grabs my breast and he touches my nipple with gentle fingers and it feels so good I moan. He lowers his mouth over it and licks it and I may just come from this alone. My back is arching, and he uses his other hand to pin me down while he's holding himself off of me with the other one.

His mouth is over my nipple, nipping, licking, twirling. My panties feel damp against me and I hope that's normal because this feels entirely too good.

I. Need. More.

I lift my leg up and pull his hip against mine and he lets out a sound like a groan. Keeping his eyes on me, he slowly pulls down my leggings, with tender hands, calming my nerves. He kisses my neck, and my chest, and keeps going, reaching my nipple, letting his hands explore down, right in between my folds. "You are soaked for me, Honey," he says.

And I whisper, "I'm sorry."

That has him looking up at me. "Baby, that's nothing to be sorry about. That's a good thing. It just means that you're responsive to my touch." He smirks and adds, "I love it." He drops back down to my nipple. With his hand still teasing, he works a finger in and it feels like heaven on earth when he curves it inside of me. He lifts my leg as he lowers his head right on top of my mound and he places my foot on his shoulder.

"This might feel too intense and you're going to want me to stop but trust the process," he adds confidently, and I feel myself tighten against his finger in anticipation. He lowers his mouth to my clit while slipping another finger in me. With my foot on his shoulder, I can't satisfy my urge to lift myself up every time he licks me. I feel like my belly is full of water and I get goosebumps all over my skin. He curls his fingers inside of me at the same time he sucks on my clit, and I see stars. My insides clench against him. My legs shiver. My toes curl and I scream his name.

He kisses my thigh, my hip, my belly and I flinch. "So beautiful. So perfect," he whispers in between kisses and I am on a high that I never want to get down from. He removes his shirt over his head in one smooth sweep. Seeing that move in movies and in real life are two very different things. Holy hotness. He pulls his pants down and I am sure he can see all over my face, exactly how I feel about the way his naked body looks right in front of me. I can't believe he is mine.

My body is still coming down from the orgasm, I instantly feel the tingle on my skin again as he climbs up my body. I'm squirming under him. He brings his hands next to my face and peppers kisses along my chin and my jaw.

"Hey, hey, it's okay. I've got you," he says in the sweetest tone. He holds my gaze as he lifts my leg again holding it under my knee. He looks straight at me, never dropping my gaze, wrapping me in this moment. He gently says, "Breathe," as he slowly thrusts inside. I hold my breath and close my eyes.

"Breathe, baby, breathe."

So I do, following his command and trying to relax.

"So pretty, so perfect," he coos and slowly I start to stretch around him. It's a burning sensation but with his praise and his slow gentleness, it starts turning into a good feeling.

His hands are everywhere but not in a frenetic manner. His moves are purposeful and tender. I feel him everywhere. On top of me, around me, and in me. It's too much and not enough at the same time.

His hand makes it to the top of my clit again and he circles it with slow motions as he pumps in and out of me. I feel that tingly wet pool again and then straight to fireworks everywhere. "So perfect," he whispers to my ear and then he shivers with his body tensing.

I can feel him still everywhere. His slick skin with sweat. His smell is slowly becoming my favorite thing in the world. His presence. His everything. I'm sure I'm never going to be the same again.

He falls next to me on the bed with his eyes closed and his hand on my leg. I turn my body to face him but I stay quiet because what do you say? I feel like telling him that I love him but it would be cliché so I don't. I just keep looking at his face as he smiles. He starts getting up and I try to stop him, when he says, "I have to go throw this away." I look down to see the condom that I didn't even notice he'd put on. And silly me because I didn't even think about that.

He comes back and we continue to snuggle until I surely drift to sleep because the next thing I know it's morning time and there's a note next to my pillow that says, "Getting coffee, be right back. One, Four, Three, J."

PASSPO

CHAPTER EIGHTEEN

Allie

NOW

Am I Wrong, Nico & Vinz

Jake kissed me. Holy shit he just kissed me.

The music keeps playing in the background and our bodies are still close but nothing is happening. My breathing is slowing, my tears are dried now and I don't even know why I was crying in the first place. A mix of longing and hope. Longing for what I lost and hope that I can find it again. I find the courage to finally look up at him and to my surprise, he is looking down, right at me. His eyes full of feeling, something I can't quite pin because it certainly can't be love.

Suddenly it's too much. I've let my guard down and we are both about to pay the price. I pull away from him saying, "I can't do this." I turn my body around trying to walk as far away from his as possible and lock myself behind the safety of the bedroom door.

I can hear his steps quickly behind me and then I feel his hand on my wrist, stopping me as he says, "Wait!" I stop dead in my tracks but don't dare to turn around to face him. He has man hands, I notice; not a boy anymore, a whole-ass man. His grip is strong, without hurting and he whispers for me to stop so softly I almost miss it.

I turn around to look at him but I can't, so I keep my gaze down. "Look at me, Honey," he says and I do because right now, I don't think I could deny this man anything. He loosens his grip on my wrist, pulling me closer to him. My chest is practically on his and I try to look up at him through my lashes.

He brings my hand to his chest and places it right on his left side. "Can you feel that?" he asks and then continues, "That's my fucking heart about to leap out of my chest. That happens every single time I look at you. Every. Single. Time. It happened then, and it keeps happening now. It never changed and I don't think it ever will."

I gasp and open my mouth to speak but he lets go of the hand on his chest and covers my mouth with his finger.

"Please, let me finish talking. Ten years ago, my whole world crumbled down and you were the last pebble that made the landslide final. I have done a lot to try to forget you. To erase you from my memories but fuck, Allie, you came into my life once like a wrecking ball and you have never left. No matter what I try, my heart knows it belongs with you. My mind knows it too. Whether that's what's best for me or not." He rubs his eyes and pulls me to him for a hug.

His hand drags over my head and I feel the tears starting to fall on my cheeks. "Nothing I do will ever erase you and to be honest, I was finally resigned to the fact that I was never going to be able to move on when you came into my life and hit me like a hurricane, again."

He kisses my forehead and pulls me tighter then says, "What if I'm ready to embrace you in my life again? What if I'm willing to take this natural disaster that is everything I feel for you and turn it into a natural wonder? Because that is exactly what you are. Pure, natural perfection."

I continue crying on his chest and I know he can feel it because he rubs gentle circles on my back. While saying soothing words that reach the deepest parts of my soul. "Shh, it's okay. I'm not mad you left, not anymore at least. If you let me, I would love to let you into my life completely again, even if it's for six months or however long you're here."

To that, I have nothing to say so my body stiffens. I pull back and look into his beautiful chocolate eyes. With his thick dark eyelashes and his eyes wet from tears, I realize that I am not the only one with the hundreds of what-ifs. I realize that this sweet man who has taken a huge part of my heart that will never be filled by anyone else might still love me. Even if it took ten years for me to come back.

That's when I realize that I might still love him too. I reach up to his lips on my tippy toes and kiss him. And we kiss until we are all hands, teeth, tongue, and moans. Oh God, moans! I stop before this goes too far for both of us. I take an abrupt step back and nod. I reach and grab the broom from the wall next to him and ask him if he wants to get cleaned up and we can watch a movie after he settles for the night. He nods and disappears into his room but before he turns I catch him rubbing his lip with a smile on his face.

We're watching some sort of Adam Sandler movie but I have not been paying attention; I can't stop thinking about his words, replaying them over and over again in my head.

Nothing I do will ever erase you.

We're sitting side by side, barely touching, and the air is thick with anticipation. Every now and then he looks my way and smiles, but turns back towards the T.V. again. I know he's being respectful and giving me space, but I have a knot in my throat and I feel the urge to say something.

"Hey, Jake?" I say softly.

"Allison," he replies with a smirk.

"Mm, how would this work? You know I'm only here for a short amount of time. I would hate for us to start something that would just end suddenly."

"We already started something and we hit pause abruptly. Can you look me in the eyes and say that it was ever truly over?"

Did he just say that? Okay, so I guess we're going with the absolute truth so I say, "I'm sure you've been around plenty in the last ten years. It's not like you have been here waiting for me."

"I'm sure you have too and yet, here we are again," he deadpans.

We stare at each other before he adds, "What are you afraid of? Of falling in love with me again?"

"Jake," I whisper.

"Honey," he says with conviction.

"Oh, don't *honey* me. That's playing dirty."

"I'm not going to push you to do something that you don't want to but the way your body reacts to me tells me more than your words ever will." As if on cue, I get goosebumps all over my arms. He is not wrong. We both know it.

"Tell me I'm wrong," he says as he pulls my feet off the ground and across his legs.

"Tell me you don't want me, don't want us, and I'll walk away. I'll just be your friend Allie." When I don't say anything, he grabs my hand and pulls me to him. Wrapping his hand behind my thigh he places me on top of him so I straddle him, and he raises his hand to cup my cheek. I lean into his touch and it is electric, magnetic, and the way my body wants to be as close to him as possible is absolutely unavoidable.

"Tell me I'm wrong baby," he adds.

He looks at my lips so I bite them slightly and then he looks straight into my eyes and says, "Or better yet, show me I'm right."

And with that, I lose all the control that I have left and let myself kiss him deeply as I melt into his body.

PASSPORT

CHAPTER NINETEEN

Allie

NOW

When the party's over, Billie Eilish

Jake and I have been *a thing* for two weeks now. We fell easily into a domestic routine that gives me a taste of what could've been if we had stayed together back then. He's still the sweet, kind, goofy, honest boy I fell in love with once, but now he has aged like fine wine into the man of everyone's dreams. And that's what he is, truly. He has all the qualities that a good man, boyfriend, or husband should have and somehow he is still hung up on me.

He wakes up an hour earlier than I do to tend to his garden and chickens, makes me coffee, and he always has something for me to eat even though he usually doesn't even have breakfast. He is patient with my morning grumpiness and comes back to the house with the biggest smile when he sees me. He is the easiest person to like and love and yet, he is still giving me his time. Regardless of what happened then.

Two weeks of sweet kisses, holding hands, and texts throughout the day. Two weeks of him respecting me to the point that he has not tried to do anything more than just kiss and hug me, because I pull back every time. Two weeks of him showing me his unending patience and understanding my feelings.

Two weeks of me daydreaming about spending more time with him but not wanting to share him so we stay in. Two weeks of him showing me how to do some things in the garden and letting me love on his chicks. Those are some salty ladies and it took them a bit to warm up to me, but just like Jake, they are so easy to love.

We walk hand in hand to gather eggs at night and share the kitchen to cook when possible. He has football practice almost every day so I do some work on my computer until he gets home every night. *Home.* A word that I didn't know the meaning of until I found him. A word that left my vocabulary for years and I never thought I'd find again. A word that pops into my mind when I think of him.

I'm driving back to his place thinking about what I'll wear tonight. He asked me last night if he could take me with him to the football game. He needs to be there early with the players but he is letting me come to the field and then we'll go out to dinner afterwards. A date. A date with Jake. My Jake. I never thought that would ever happen again. Yet here we are.

The road is wet from the rain earlier so I'm being extra careful and staying in the middle lane but the I-10 is still an interstate and the minimum speed is still pretty fast for these conditions. Taylor Swift is playing and I'm singing along when the car in front of me swerves into the other lane and I hit my brakes in response, just not fast or hard enough.

"Miss, miss, can you hear me?"

I cough and open my eyes to bright lights in front of me.

"There you are. Try not to move," the voice says.

"Can you follow the light?"

I squint my eyes but follow it as the voice behind it praises me for following directions.

"Can you tell us your name honey?"

"Allie," I try to say but it comes out as a whisper.

So I clear my throat and say it again, "Allie."

"Good, can you give me your full name?"

"Allison Marie Zabana, but please call me Allie," I say.

The guy moves away from the light and I can finally see him. He looks like he could be twenty-two years old. He is smiling at me kindly and it is then that I notice he's wearing an EMT uniform. EMT. *Oh shit, where am I?* I look around and see I'm in the car still but I'm on the side of the road. Oh God, I hit that car in front of me. I start to panic and look around when he adds gently, "You're okay. Can you tell me what happened?"

"I was driving and then the car in front of me moved suddenly to the other lane. I hit the breaks but I think I hit something else, too."

"Yeah, sounds about right. There was a truck stopped in the middle of the road and you managed to hit it. You hit it at the right angle that your car just flipped into the side of the road but nobody else was hurt."

I sigh with relief.

"You were unconscious for a while but you seem to be doing better. Do you know what year this is?"

"Yes, 2023."

"That's correct," he says. "The fire department will help us get you out so hang tight."

A few minutes later they stabilize my neck and get me out into a gurney. They put me in the back of an ambulance and we head to the hospital.

On the ride there they ask me more questions, take my vitals, and do another assessment. We make it there and I get wheeled into an exam room. After what feels like hours later I'm back in a room, waiting. They give me my phone and I text Jake to tell him I won't make it to the game and that I will text him when I get back. My mind is spinning, so I hit send without reading any of his previous texts or anything else on the phone.

The doctor comes in and basically says that everything looks great and that even though I am showing some signs of a concussion, I may be able to go home as long as I won't be by myself. I tell them I won't be and that someone will be by to pick me up, even if I haven't talked to Jake in a while. I don't even know what time it is. He tells me to take some Motrin and rest. I sign the release papers, put my clothes on and walk to the lobby. My phone is almost dead. I check to see if there are taxis or Ride Shares available but there are none so I grab my bag and start walking. I feel so stupid and I don't want to wait, so I walk.

The GPS says I'm about an hour walk away from his house so I choose to continue walking instead of waiting for an available taxi. My body aches, but I just want a shower and to lay down. It would be fine if it wasn't for the fact that it is starting to rain again and the sidewalks are still muddy from the rain earlier. I keep walking and after a while it is almost therapeutic, and tears start falling from my eyes. I don't even realize it until my lips taste the difference between the rain and the tears.

I feel a vehicle slow down behind me and when I look it is a dark Chevy Truck. The truck stops by me, the door opens and I hear a familiar voice say, "Get in the truck, Allie."

I hop in and continue crying. Jake says nothing and just lets me cry next to him. He takes his shirt off and passes it to me as he turns the heat on in his truck. He gives me gentle squeezes on my knee and asks, "Are you ready to talk about it?" When I don't say anything, he just turns the radio on and drives. The world around me kept moving while I was suspended in time between the accident, the hospital, and now.

We make it to his place and after walking in, I immediately hug him. I am covered in dirt and soaking wet but somehow he doesn't care and squeezes me tighter. "I don't want to talk about it," I whisper in between sobs. "I am okay but I don't want to think anymore. I just want to forget it all."

"Shh. Let me take care of you, Allie," he whispers in my ear as he holds my trembling body. He smells like mint, wood, and comfort. He caresses my hair and continues to whisper, alternating between soft shushes and gently asking me to let him take care of me. My sobs get lost between his tight hug and the rain pouring outside. I feel filthy and unworthy of his kindness, especially after not telling him the whole truth yet. How does this man continue to put me first? How does he choose to take care of me?

He pulls away from me and, while grabbing my face, he looks deeply into my eyes. I look down, unable to contain my tears and hating to see the pity in his eyes. "I am such a wreck, Jake. Please just let me go to bed. You don't have to take care of me."

"I want to." He kisses my forehead. Gently. Lovingly. Like I'm fragile and even the slightest push will break me.

"I don't deserve you. I don't want you to pity me. I can do it. Let me forget on my own." I break into sobs.

"It's not pity, it's sympathy. And if anything it's selfishness." He lifts my chin and holds my gaze. "Seeing you like this kills me. I'm looking out for myself here. Let me take care of you, honey."

Honey. I will never get tired of hearing that after I thought I never would again. Not from the only person I wanted to hear it from the most. From the only one who matters. *Him.*

I close the gap between us and crash my mouth against his with a kiss. He tastes like honey and mint. His lips are soft mounds against mine but nothing about the way he's kissing me is soft. It is ravenous. Like he has been in the desert and finally found water.

He bends down and grabs me by the butt as he lifts me. I gasp and shake my head rapidly and he groans against my throat, "Honey, so help me God if you make a comment on your weight right now. I don't care how crappy you feel, the only words coming out of your mouth about your body should be to say how fucking fantastic each inch of you is. Just wrap your legs around me." He guides me up with a squeeze. I look into his eyes that are darkening with desire and kiss him.

We are a mess of whimpers, kisses, and lust. Of years of words unspoken into this rush of desire without control. He keeps walking us into the bathroom without breaking the kiss. He turns the water on and shuts the door without even flinching. My hands are all over him and he finally puts me down. We break apart for a moment that feels like an eternity. Our chests are rising, and he looks at me asking for my approval before this goes any further. I nod and he smoothly takes his shirt off in one quick movement and charges towards me.

I am completely dirty after today but that doesn't stop me. He kisses my lips, traces my jaw with his tongue, and sucks on my neck. My entire body is tingling with anticipation. He unbuttons my dress as he continues to kiss me. I pull at his thick soft hair, slowly making my way to grab his neck. My dress falls to the ground around my feet and I remove my panties stepping out of each side, one leg at a time.

"Fuck. Get in the shower," he commands and he opens the curtains. I get in right under the hot stream of water, letting it run all over me. I don't want to cry but the weight of the day comes crashing down and my tears start falling once again. He steps into the shower too and grabs my ponytail gently. "May I?" he asks and I nod. I don't even know what he's asking, but for him it will always be yes.

He lets my hair down and pushes my head gently back. He massages my head under the water and I let a soft moan free. He tightens his hold on my head and I can't help but gasp and let out another moan.

"I want to do the right thing here and just help you get cleaned up. But if you keep making those sweet little noises, I won't be able to do that. I can't promise you I won't do all the things that I want to do to you."

His voice is hoarse and I shiver at the promise. He turns me around and starts rubbing soap on my back, pushing into my skin with his calloused fingers, giving me a delicious mix of softness and pain.

My head tilts back as he pushes me closer to the wall, massaging the knots around my neck and upper back. He grabs my hair and moves it out of the way and immediately my skin breaks into goosebumps. *Everywhere.* He gives me a quick kiss on the nape of my neck, and a shiver goes down my spine.

I can feel my nipples hardening against the cold tile and the more he massages my back, the more turned on I am. I can't help the sounds coming out of me as he intensifies the massage. The more he touches me, the more he pushes me against the wall and I am already a sloppy mess. I arch my back almost involuntarily and my ass touches the tip of his hard cock and he hisses.

"Is the wall too cold? I'm sorry if I'm pushing too hard." He lowers his mouth to my neck and places a gentle kiss.

I shiver again. "Oh yes. Please keep pushing." I try to sound normal but the words come out like a gasp. This is ridiculous, he's not even touching anything besides my back and my whole body is responding to him like this.

He gets closer and lowers his mouth right next to my ear. "Push you? Like this?" His voice is raspy and full of desire as he shoves my whole body against the wall to the point I have to tilt my head to the side. He grabs my hair and twists it in his hand without moving his mouth from my ear. "Against the wall like this?" He asks and when I shiver and gasp he growls and adds, "You want me to fuck you, don't you?"

"Please," I beg.

"My sweet girl grew up and she likes it a little rough now?" His voice has a hint of darkness and softness all mixed together.

I gather the strength that I need to say, "I wouldn't know how I like it now."

"Now don't be shy, Honey, tell me what you want. How do you want it?" He tugs at my hair making my head move back more.

With a soft moan, I add, "It's not shyness, it's just been ten years."

His whole body tenses and he moves backward. He slowly turns me around and lifts my face by the chin. "What do you mean?" His body went from *all fucking,* to *all business* in three seconds flat. *Jake, forever the gentleman.* He holds my gaze and I take a deep breath but I don't say anything. "Allie," he whispers, "Please, tell me what you mean."

"Exactly what it sounds like, there was you and then there was nobody else."

His breath catches; his wandering eyes roam over my face, looking for a tell, ready to call my bluff. I thought sharing this with him would make me feel pathetic but what it makes me feel is *seen.* He is looking at me with emotion that I don't see often. A mix of sadness and guilt. I can see his inner turmoil but he still asks the question that I was hoping he wouldn't as the steam from the shower keeps rising and water falls all around us. "Why? Why didn't you?"

This is it, now or never. I reach for his face, moving his hair from his face and softly touching his beard before I whisper, "How could I? Who would even compare? Who could even erase you?"

We stare at each other and I open my mouth to say, "I knew—" but his mouth is on mine instantly. His body, flushed against mine, pinning me against the cold tile wall again. His hands are in my hair and he's pulling and grabbing as he kisses me as if his life depends on it. He continues to kiss my jaw and my neck, his hands start roaming my back, then my arms, and my breasts. My breath catches and he lowers his mouth to catch one of my nipples. His tongue swirls, hardening it and immediately his other hand reaches for the other.

My hands find his hair and I pull him closer to me. I gasp. This feels so good. Too good. I might just come from this. *Get it together.* "Jake."

He takes his mouth off my nipple and looks up while still touching the other one. "Please don't ask me to stop, Honey, because I will, but fuck, I don't want to."

My chest is moving up and down. How do I even say anything but, "Yes, please."

He drops to one knee, leaving his left leg up. He grabs one of my ankles and sets my foot on his thigh. He traces kisses from my belly button to the top of my mound. He drags his nose against my folds. "God, you still smell the same." Opening me with his fingers, he flattens his tongue and strokes from my entrance to my clit. He doesn't just lick, he devours. Like he has been starving and this is his first meal.

He moves his hand from my leg and traces my thigh, climbing towards my pussy and the noises coming out of me are anything but decent. My skin prickles, the feeling of the water from the shower on my chest and the stiff wall behind me. His hands roaming and his tongue working me have my body on a high that I can't describe. And I don't ever want to come down.

He works a finger in and smirks against me. "So wet for me, baby." He's moving his finger in and out while licking me.

"More, please," I beg gasping for a release that I'm chasing but don't want to reach yet.

"There's nothing I wouldn't give you, Honey." He adds another finger. And as wet as I am, it should slide right in but he takes his time, and suddenly I feel so full.

"Fuck, you're so tight." He licks, sucks, and flicks his tongue around my clit.

"Oh God, I'm so close." His fingers pump in and out and I feel myself tightening around them. The flush against my skin feels as if I am in front of fire, and liquid pleasure fills my lower belly and then explodes.

He pumps his fingers to the rhythm of his tongue chasing my high with them. My pussy is tightening more and more around his fingers and I can feel everything throbbing. He slows down, letting me catch my breath. He moves back, taking his fingers out of me and rubs them against his lips. He licks his lips, holding my gaze and grunting, "So sweet." He sucks on his fingers still looking at me. "Just like passion fruit."

He smirks and stands up. His cock is so hard and precum glistens on the tip. "Come on, let me clean you up."

I grasp his dick and he hisses and adds, "Oh Honey, we'll have time for all of that but this moment is about you. I'm taking care of you, so hands off."

I do just that. Take my hands off and let him show me how well he can take care of me, again and again.

CHAPTER TWENTY

Jake

THEN

Gold Rush, Taylor Swift

> Me: Pick you up before school?

I wait a few minutes but she never replies. I wonder if she is even awake, and I would hate for her to be late to school because I know how much *she* hates it. Yesterday after I got back to her house, we spent half the morning in bed. Me, whispering sweet praises right into her ear while making her body shatter under my hands. I could have spent all day just making her feel good. The truth is that she is perfect and my heart and whole body realized it too. Eventually we got out of bed and then I spent more time caressing her and showing her how much I love her in the shower. I helped her wash her beautiful hair, even though she had to guide me little by little on how to brush and detangle those wild curls I love so much.

We left the house briefly around lunch time and when we got back, her parents were back just in time for Family Sunday. I met her dad this time and chat guy is a scary motherfucker. He towers over me by a few inches and he is so broad that I asked if he ever played football himself. The guy is solid, and he kept looking at me like I was an unwelcome sight in his home. I don't blame him, I don't fit in her beautiful three-story home full of marble floors and hardwood accents. Complete with a garden tended to every day by professionals and where her Titi Rosalia, who I found out is not her aunt but more like a governess, makes sure the house is running smoothly. I have never experienced so much luxury before in a home and I think everyone could tell.

I stayed next to Allie through the afternoon but eventually, I felt way too out of place with him looking at me like that, speaking mostly in Spanish and annoyed when Allie would translate for me, so I excused myself and left. Her mom is the complete opposite and so are her brothers, but I have a feeling that her dad doesn't approve of his princess dating a country boy like me. She messaged me last night checking on me but I let her know that I needed some rest and she needed to spend time with her family.

Now that she's not replying to my text, I'm worried that she might still be asleep so I head to her door to ask someone to go get her. I park in the front of her driveway, careful not to block any of the vehicles parked, and walk to the side door where the kitchen is. I can hear people talking so I start to walk towards the door but then stop when I hear the conversation.

Allie is talking to someone mostly in Spanish. She sounds annoyed and there's no hiding that, but I can't tell what they're saying. *Oh, how I wish I had paid more attention in Spanish class.* I can't hear the other voice but Allie is getting more and more agitated. Her tone is clipped and her usual confidence is not there. I shouldn't be eavesdropping, but I don't know what to do. Suddenly, I hear something being smacked on the table and her dad saying, "I told you to take the damn jersey off Allison, now." *Allison.* She said nobody calls her by her full name, and if that's how her dad talks to her when he does, then I don't want her to associate me with *that.*

"Papi, Jake *IS* my boyfriend so whether you like it or not, I am wearing the jersey to school," she says with the sassiest tone I have ever heard coming out of her mouth. I am starting to worry and my instincts are screaming for me to go be with her. To get her out of whatever is making her this uncomfortable.

What happens next stops time. It feels like an eternity is happening in a split second. I hear a slap and a soft sob asking him to stop. That is the exact moment all my senses go on high alert. Like every cell in my body is screaming at me, "Go to her!" Completely unraveled by the thought of someone, *anyone*, hurting her, I push through the door and ask what the hell is going on.

Her dad is standing tall right in front of her and she looks scared as shit. I walk to stand in front of her and he raises his hand motioning for me to stop.

"This is between me and my disrespectful daughter," he says without looking at me. "You can go back to the farm you came from."

I walk around his hand and add, "Respectfully sir, I am not comfortable with you laying hands on Allie. Your daughter or not."

"If you don't walk away from my house, I will have you escorted out in five seconds flat." His tone is dry and harsh, but all I can focus on is the small sobs behind my back and Allie asking me to go. I turn around to face her, grab her bag from the floor, and hold her hand. Not looking at her dad once, I pull Allie out of the house and keep walking. Her dad says something like this *isn't over* but I can't stand there and let him degrade her like that. Nobody lays a finger on her, especially not her dad.

We speed walk to the truck without saying a word. I help her climb into the front seat, walk around to the driver's seat, and turn on the truck. It is a beautiful sunny day outside, even with the light fog, I can see that it will be perfect. I start driving away from the house, the opposite way from school. Allie is not crying anymore but she is just looking out the window, with her back turned to me.

"Sorry if I was out of line," I say with concern in my voice.

"It's complicated," she says without looking my way.

"Allie, nobody should lay a hand on you. It's that simple."

She sighs and says, "In my family, and how my Dad grew up, the way I talked to him was not acceptable. The slap was his way of reminding me who he is and who I am. That I'm his child and I should have not raised my voice at him."

"It doesn't matter. He shouldn't have done that. I'm sorry. Does this happen often?" My knuckles are white from holding the steering wheel so tight. I could hurt him for just talking to her like that, let alone hurting her.

"Long story short, no, it doesn't. He travels a lot, so we don't see each other often and I usually don't talk back to him, like ever. The last time I said 'no' to him, I was twelve and he wanted me to continue music classes but the schedule was killing me so I said no. That was the last time I got in trouble."

She'd rather not talk to him or express her opinions than risk him being offended and doing something like that. Call me old-fashioned if you want, but I don't think that should be the relationship you have with a parent. Your parents should be the people that believe in you the most. Even if you are not close to them, you should not fear them. They should be your safe space.

I'm sure her mom is exactly that for her, but is that enough? Aside from Cara, does she have anyone that she can be unapologetically herself with? Or is she constantly walking on eggshells around the people she loves?

"Where are we going by the way?" she asks.

"I figured you needed some time and school didn't sound like the place for that. So we're going to the river."

"The river? For what?"

"To relax, baby. We don't have to swim, but some fresh air will do you good. This may be as good for me as it will be for you."

Moments later, we make it to a grassy area where we park and I guide her down the path to the river. This is one of my favorite spots because of how quiet it is. The St Mary's River is not very big but it is peaceful and full of little critters. Some parts are deep and perfect for swimming but not where we are right now. This is just a good thinking spot. She walks beside me but I can see she doesn't love the sand on her feet so with one quick sweep I pick her up and carry her.

She yelps and wiggles in my arms but I just kiss her forehead and keep walking. Her eyes are so light right now. Like they are reflecting the light and the shades of green, yellow, and brown dance in them. Now that I look at it, her hair also has golden, brown, and reddish tones to it. It is beautiful, just like her. "You are stunning, Honey."

She looks down after the compliment, surely a little embarrassed having my eyes all over her. How did this beautiful and magical girl ever begin to feel like she didn't deserve all the attention in the world?

Once we make it to the river bank, I put her down. I take my shoes off and she does the same. Then we walk hand in hand to the water. I stick my feet in, but she is hesitant. I raise an eyebrow at her.

"Doesn't it scare you? This water is so brown."

Laughing I say, "It's clean, I promise. Look." I squat down to scoop some water on my hands and she can see how clear it is so I explain, "Tannins make it look this dark. The roots from the trees around here release that color and it acts as a dye on the water. Almost like when you steep tea."

Her eyes widen and she nods. She walks closer and lets her feet touch the water. She closes her eyes and takes a deep breath. She whispers something so softly that if I wasn't focusing solely on her, I would have missed it. Smirking, I say, "Can you say that louder so my brain knows that I didn't make that up?"

She opens her golden eyes and looks up at me with a soft smile. She has my jersey on and some tiny shorts that show her thick legs and she looks like an absolute mirage with her toes in the water and her wild hair in the air.

"Allie, can you say that again, baby?" I press.

She turns her body towards me, places both hands next to my face, and says as clear as day, "I love you, Jake Clarke." Then she kisses me. This is it. This is the kiss that ruins me for everyone else. And at eighteen, I know at this moment, that this girl holds my whole future in her hands.

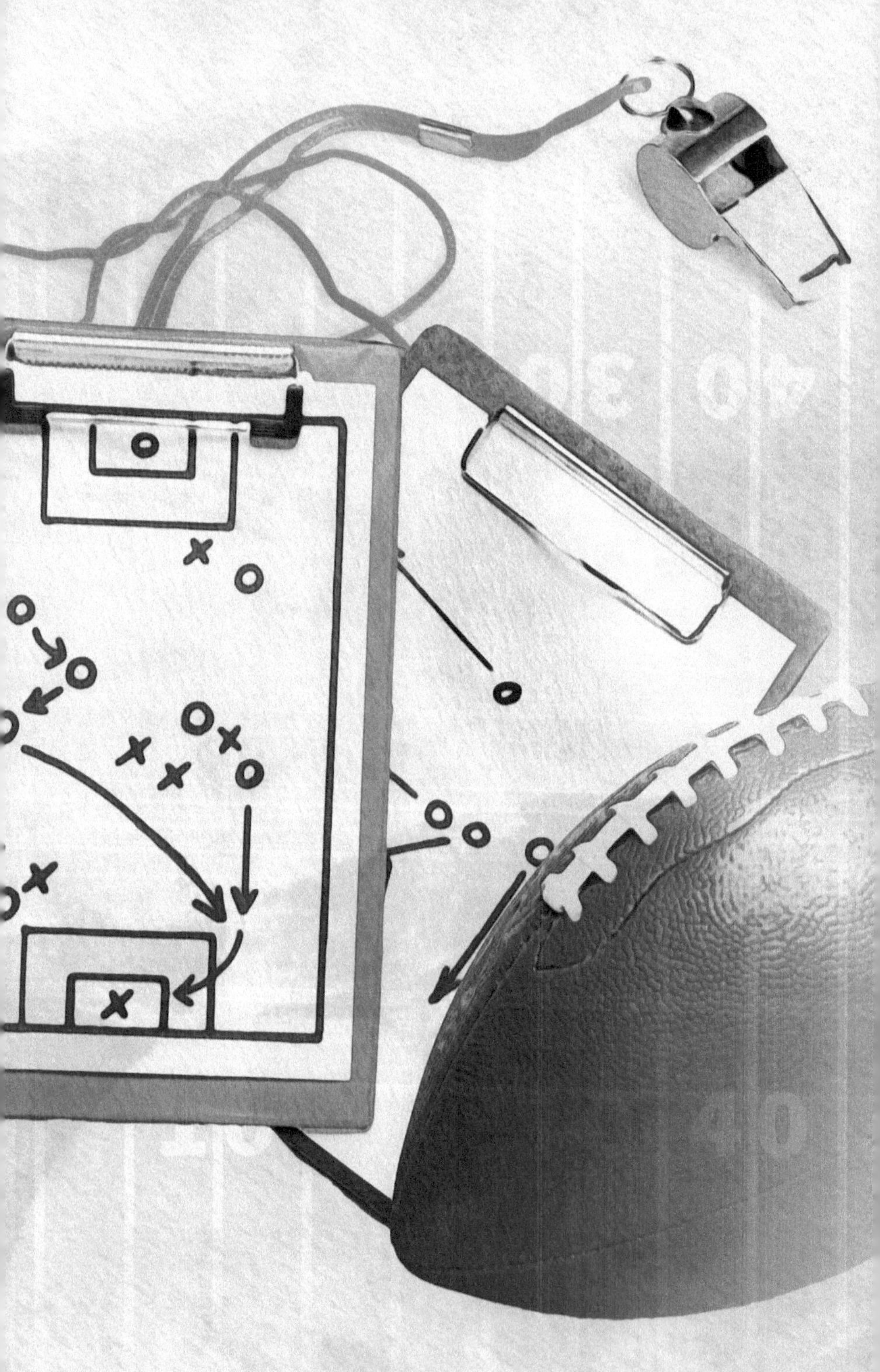

CHAPTER TWENTY-ONE

Jake

NOW

If the World Was Ending, JP Saxe and Eva Luna Montaner

After the shower, I take Allie to my room. Get her all dried off and into one of my shirts. She's still in shock. I can tell because she hasn't said much after the shower. She is sitting on the couch right now watching the rain fall outside while I am making her some tea.

When I got her message that she wasn't going to make it to the game, I knew something was wrong. It's not like her to not give details. The game had ended when I heard about the crash on the highway and started to panic when she wouldn't answer my calls. I was on my way home when I saw her walking on the side of the road and if it wasn't for her explaining that she was in a crash, I would have never guessed that she was in that one.

I thought my heart was being ripped out of my chest seeing her walking and crying in the rain. I could recognize her body from feet away but it took self-control not to jump out of my truck the second I knew it was her. She was defeated and physically spent. Her shoulders sagging and her swollen eyes told me more than words could ever say. She needed me, that was clear. I don't want to pressure her into telling me more about what happened because I swear, I will kill whoever did this to her. The kettle whistles, pulling me from my daze. I add a bag of chamomile tea, a splash of cream, and two teaspoons of sugar. Just like she likes her coffee.

I walk back to the couch and hand her the cup. I sit right behind her and she crawls up to sit right between my legs with her head on my chest. She sighs and takes a sip before she turns her head around and asks for some painkillers. I push her forward a little to get out from under her, grab her some medicine, and sit back down. She takes the pills, swallows them, closes her eyes, and places her head back on my chest.

"I'm sorry I made you get up after you were already comfortable," she says. The sadness in her voice is making me feel like the world's biggest asshole for being intimate with her after the day she had. "I am sorry to be such a burden."

I notice how she uses her hands to wipe her eyes. "Shh," I say. "You are not a burden." She takes a sip of her tea but sobs impede her from drinking more as she continues to cry.

"Please don't cry, Honey. I promise you I like taking care of you. You were never a burden and you never will be, but I do need you to talk to me and tell me what happened."

She takes another sip of her tea, puts the mug down, and turns her body so she can look at me. She starts talking about her day and ends with the recollection of the events and I feel like an even bigger asshole after she tells me that she lost consciousness. All I could think about was making her feel good without even knowing the magnitude of the crash. I hug her tight and apologize for that. She just giggles and reassures me that it was exactly what she needed. She finishes telling me how she told the doctors she wouldn't be alone but then she wouldn't even call me to tell me to pick her up.

"Why didn't you call, baby? You shouldn't have left the hospital walking after a concussion. That was reckless."

"I didn't even know what time it was and I knew you had a game tonight. I didn't want you to worry—" she says nonchalantly like she is not the thing that matters most to me right now "—and I didn't want to see you at the hospital again."

"I am always worrying about you, especially now. I can definitely be at a hospital. I am a grown man." I don't need her worrying about me to the point where she is putting herself in danger. I am supposed to be the one protecting her. I can take care of myself.

"I didn't want you to leave the game," she says, sounding completely hurt. Like the thought of asking me to be with her, at the fucking hospital nonetheless, would cause issues for me. Little does she know that I would leave it all just to be what she needs.

"I would have left my wedding to find you," I add.

"The roads were dangerous," she rebuttals.

"Even if the world was ending, I would have gone out to find you. Also, you are sleeping in my room tonight." I look straight into her eyes and hold her stare so she doesn't think for a second that I was asking her a question.

"That's your space, Jake, I don't want to intrude," she says.

Silly, silly girl. This whole place means nothing without her. Having her here proved what I knew all along. I want her here with me, always. I always did and I am sure I always will. I am tired of living with the ghost of her here.

"Please invade my space. I want you everywhere. I want to see every corner of this house and remember how you looked sitting, standing, or lying there. Go ahead and take over. You already live in my thoughts all the time, might as well be a physical part of me too." I kiss her forehead before continuing. "I am not letting you out of my sight so if you don't sleep in my room, I will sleep right on that chair watching you sleep in your room."

"You will be sore."

"Happily sore," I add, still comforting her with my touch.

"Why are you so good to me?" she asks with a soft sigh. I can tell she is completely done. Emotionally, and mentally done. She needs a break, she needs to be taken care of.

Because I love you, I want to say but it seems frivolous; too soon. Instead, I say, "You deserve it." I rub her arms. Right here, with her head on my chest in the dim light of my room, is where I want to be for the rest of my life. I knew it at eighteen and I sure as hell know it now too.

"I have to call the company tomorrow and figure out the car situation too. This is just a nightmare," she sighs with hopelessness in her voice.

"The most important thing is that you are alive and you are okay. I think you should give yourself grace and a few days to rest. The world can wait."

"I need to send an email at least." She tries to grab her phone from the table but I grab it first and open her email app and start composing an email instead. I am very familiar with concussion protocol and she should not be looking at screens right now.

"Who should I send this email to?" I say showing her that I am typing.

She frowns and adds, "To Lindsey, she is my direct supervisor."

"Sent." I place the phone back down on the table and return my hands to her arms.

"Thank you," she says, resting her head back down.

I caress her arms and place gentle kisses on her head until I feel her breathing slow and hear soft snores. She cuddles deeper into my chest, the palm of her hand next to her face, continuing to sleep peacefully. *This right here is heaven*, I think as I stare at the most beautiful girl I have ever seen, sleeping soundly on me.

CHAPTER TWENTY-TWO

Allie

THEN

Hey There Delilah, Plain White T's

I stand in front of my locker trying to get the things that I need while waiting for Jake to show up, as he does every morning before class. Even though we have been spending more time together this week and he has picked me up or dropped me off practically every day, I drove today because I have to run a few errands after cheer practice and can't wait for him to get out of his.

We have been together every free minute these past few days but I try to avoid the *my dad slapped me in front of you* topic. Things at home are not great, even though I haven't seen my dad since that day. My mom is trying to play peacekeeper. My brothers are trying to get me to chill and maybe apologize but I refuse. I am almost eighteen and in less than a year I will be moving away for college so why should I apologize for loving this boy? Jake has done nothing wrong, and the thing he has done right from the start is putting me first. Even when we got caught skipping class on Monday he took the blame. I only got detention but he got community service, too.

I am placing things back inside my locker when I hear a squeal coming from who I am sure is Cara. She starts bouncing next to me and hands me her college acceptance letter. I know what it is before I even open it because I also received mine this morning. Deep red letters on an envelope with the name Stanford University front and center confirm what I already knew; she got in too. I hug her and whisper a congratulations. I kiss her cheek and I can't help but also jump with her. For years we have been talking about going to Stanford together, even when we were miles apart, and now that we get to spend our senior year together AND go to college together, I don't blame her excitement. I would be feeling the same way if it wasn't for the tall, handsome, sweet boy with chestnut eyes staring right at me with furrowed brows.

He walks towards us and as I stop bouncing, he says, "Don't stop on my account, beautiful," placing a quick kiss on my head.

"You are looking at two girls who got accepted into their top choice of college, boys," Cara says, referring to Jake and Cole who are both standing next to us.

"Congrats, babe," Cole says and picks Cara up from the ground. They walk in a tight embrace back to class without even looking back.

I close the distance between Jake and me and give him a tight hug without uttering a word about college. I turn back and close the locker as I ask him about the game tomorrow. "Are you nervous about playing the Commanders?"

"No, but don't change the subject, baby. You got into your top choice?" he asks with pride in his eyes, but if only he knew that my top choice was not UF like I had told him. What if he won't be as supportive? When we had the college conversation, I always talked about UF because it was my second choice, and the chances of me getting into Stanford were slim.

"I did."

"Congratulations! I am so proud of you!" he adds with a huge smile.

"Thank you," I say in a clipped tone. I am trying to keep this conversation moving quickly so I don't make a scene this early in the morning, which I know is about to happen at any moment.

"I guess now we won't have to find out what long-distance relationships are like, huh?" he says pulling me closer to him and grabbing my backpack.

I guess we *will* have the conversation now. *Tierra trágame.* "Yeah, about that," I say, and he stops abruptly, turning his body to face me and losing all the light that he had in his eyes before. As soon as he looks in my eyes he knows there is something wrong and I don't know how to approach this with the five minutes we have before the bell rings. I take a deep breath and keep talking, "I haven't heard from UF. This acceptance letter was from somewhere else."

"Oh, I thought UF was your top choice. I must have remembered wrong. Where were you accepted?"

I stare at him and bite my lip slightly. Concern floats in his eyes as he says "Allie, where did you get in?"

"Stanford," I say.

"Like California, Stanford?"

"Yep, that's the one."

"What's up, Jake?" I hear someone shout from behind us, but Jake pays no attention to them. His eyes are only on me when he drops our bags, picks me up by the back of my legs, and spins me around like I am made of feathers and not flesh and bones.

"Aah, put me down," I squeal.

"FREAKING STANFORD BABY! My girl is going to Stanford!" he shouts and people around us stop and clap.

He finally sets me down but won't let me go. Noticing my inner turmoil he whispers in my ear, "We will figure it out, Honey. You and me. I have no doubt, but please let me celebrate with you right now." Then the bell rings.

"Saved by the bell," I whisper hoping he won't hear me but he gives me that look. The one that asks me to trust him and to breathe and to not let all my negative thoughts swarm me quicker than lightning.

"One Four Three, Allie," he says and walks into class leaving me in the hallway both speechless and breathless.

Tomorrow is the big game. If they win they will be going to state, and you can feel the air charged with electricity. Lunch is utter chaos in the cafeteria. All the players are being pulled in multiple directions, the band is playing nonstop, and some cheerleaders are screaming and shouting everywhere. It is so overwhelming. The tin trays are being smacked on the table. The instruments play. There's clapping, stomping, and shouting. A sea of red, white, and black. Everyone is up on their feet participating in some way or another and I am just standing in awe of how this small town is coming together for its own. Even the quiet kids are smiling and looking around. Some cheerleaders are practically being thrown in the air and the cafeteria monitors are just looking down as if nothing is happening.

I see Jake surrounded by his offensive linemen and you can tell that they are one close group. They have their inside jokes. They have each others' backs.

They are gathering together in what looks like a huddle and these huge 6-foot-tall-over seniors are all trying to pick up Alex, their quarterback and captain. He's fighting them but eventually, he loses the battle and they lift him. "Cap! Cap! Cap!" and "Hoo, Hoo, Hoo!" are being shouted as they move him around. Finally, they place him on top of a table and this is when one of the teachers looks up. The whole room goes quiet and looks back at Mr. Porter. It feels like the longest three seconds. Mr. Porter and the crowd are in a staring contest with Alex standing on top of the table then Mr.

Porter smiles at everyone and turns his body around like nothing is happening.

The crowd goes wild and in no time you can hear them shouting, "SPEECH! SPEECH! SPEECH!" I know tomorrow they will be more focused and reserved, so they are allowing all the silliness and chaos to happen today and it is intoxicating.

I feel an electric pull somewhere near so I look around and I find Jake looking at me from across the cafeteria. As soon as our eyes meet, he smiles. And gosh if that smile doesn't make me feel like both putty and the shittiest person alive for not telling him about Stanford.

The room is quiet and Alex starts giving the people what they want; a speech. He talks about sportsmanship, but more than that he talks about brotherhood and how this might be the last chance they all get to play together. He talks about how proud he is of all of them, that whatever happens tomorrow won't change how he feels about them, and that everyone can just enjoy the game. He talks about being a Shark no matter where they go and no matter what tomorrow brings. The crowd goes wild.

Everyone is clapping, cheering, screaming. Some of the freshman girls are swooning over this soon-to-be man and I don't blame them because that was pretty impressive. In the meantime, I can't focus on anything really because Jake keeps his intense gaze on me and I feel like a million bucks. Alex keeps talking but everything is fading on the outside because Jake is walking towards me. I smile at him and give him my attention like I have a choice. Like if him looking at me that way is making me question EVERYTHING.

"Hola, beautiful," he says.

"Hey, handsome, I love when you talk Spanish to me," I add with a smile, wrapping my arms around his neck and stretching on my tiptoes to reach him.

"I am trying to use some words in Spanish every day. I figured starting with greetings would be ideal."

His sweet smile, his hands around my hips, and his fresh mint scent invade all my senses and I have no other choice than to close the space between us and kiss him. The kiss starts soft and tentative, like all of our school kisses but it turns quickly into a heavy and passionate kiss. The type of kiss that erases all previous memories and ruins you for the future. I am pretty sure there was a before Jake but there won't be an after. I can feel it in my bones.

Someone coughs and we stop immediately. I feel like we were just caught. When I turn my face, Alex, Nick, and Cole are all whistling, clapping, and grabbing Jake. I just want to kill them all. "You are all insufferable," I say.

"But you love us," Cole says with a wink as they walk back, dragging Jake with them.

"See you later, love bug," Alex adds, blowing pretend kisses my way.

I roll my eyes and catch up to them so I am not left behind.

I went straight home instead of waiting for Jake today because the football team had practice after school. I am avoiding my dad like the plague, so I have been reading in my room since school ended. This week has felt like it was a whole month in between spending the weekend with Jake, dealing with my dad's outburst, end of the quarter tests, and getting ready for the game tomorrow.

I hear a soft knock on my door and when I look up I find my mom and Jake both standing there. I look at them astonished, but before I can say anything, my mom opens the door wider saying, "Don't make me regret this. In bed by ten, Allie." She lets Jake inside and closes the door behind him.

"What are you doing here?" I ask sheepishly. He grabs my hands and lifts me up from the bed, straight into his arms.

His arms are an immediate comfort, giving me reassurance that whatever funk I thought we were in may not be it but I really do have to talk to him about my dreams so he doesn't freak out about us. I say nothing though and he knows something is up, because Jake knows me to my core. We are in tune. One heart beating in two bodies.

"Words, Allie, I need words. What is going on in that beautiful head of yours?" I let out a sigh and sit on the edge of my bed with him following beside me. I breathe again and then let it all out.

"When we first started dating, I told you my top school was UF, and before you ask, no, not because you were going there but because their education program is fantastic and I never thought in a million years I would have a chance at Stanford. So imagine my surprise when that letter came in the mail. I was worried about how you would react and a thousand scenarios went through my head so I hid it from you." I stop, breathe, and swallow. I look into his eyes and see nothing but warmth so I continue, "I know we have talked about dating through college and then coming back here and I still think that's a great plan, Jake. I love you so much and even though we are young, I think that there will never be anything as special as this ever again."

"But?" he asks and I swear I can see the light dim in his eyes.

Ah, I hate this, "I know when we talked about this we were both going to be in the same college or at the very least, close by since my other choices were less than five hours away. But Jake, now I am going to be 2,000 miles away in different time zones and I don't want to be the reason you miss out on living your best college life. I know how men are and I would rather let this go than worry about you being miserable or regretting making a promise to me when you didn't have all the facts."

He looks at me with eyes wide open and grabs my hands. He takes a deep breath almost like he is mustering the courage to tell me we are about to be over so I beat him to it and put him out of his misery.

"Jake, it's okay, I understand. I'm not going to lie to you, I will be heartbroken but it will be okay."

"Allie stop," he says and I hear the pain in his words as he continues, "Is this what you want or is this what you think *I* want?" He waits and when I don't say anything he continues, "Because if this is what you want, I will fight it. I will prove to you how much I *don't need* to be single to enjoy my college life. I won't ever look at another woman after you regardless of how many miles exist between us. I would wait a decade for you if that meant I get to have you. You are it. I mean it and I won't let this go." He smiles at me and keeps going, "And if this is what you think *I* want, let me show you right now how wrong you are." With that, he closes the distance between us with a kiss.

His hand is in my hair and the other one is on the lower of my back pulling me flush against him. The kiss is nothing but frantic. It is rushed, deep, and slightly rough. His tongue invades my space with purpose without one doubt in the world. *Mine* is what it feels like he's telling me with his lips, his hands, and his breaths. I moan into his lips and he swallows the sound by deepening the kiss and when my hands go up to pull on his hair, he lets go of my lips, and whispers exactly what I need to hear. "You are mine, Honey. I only want you and I will only ever want you." We are a mess of heavy breathing, fast heart rates, and pent-up want, but with my parents in the house we won't take this further.

He brings both hands to hold my face and says into my lips, "Two thousand mi or twenty thousand, if that's where your dreams are, you go chase them. I will wait for you. And we can do long-distance. You love flying so you can come to me as much as you want. There will be a spot on the right side of the bed for you."

Tears fall and I smile saying, "I actually hate flying. I just love traveling and flying comes with the territory. I love you Jake and if you truly mean that, I would love nothing more than to continue this."

As he hugs me he whispers, "It was never an option, Honey. I'm never letting you go."

CHAPTER TWENTY-THREE

Jake

THEN

Without You, David Guetta Ft. Usher

This is the game that we have all been waiting for since last year. *Last year* we lost right before State, and it won't happen again . I can't keep my head focused because of the whiplash I am getting from Allie. She says she will be fine going to Stanford and coming back to this small town, but for some reason, I don't believe her. She seemed almost torn to even tell me she got accepted and I think it's because she is thinking of letting me go.

She said she wanted to still be together and come back here to continue our lives together. But she said that when she thought she had no chance at going to Stanford. And now that she got accepted, who am I to clip her wings? Will I miss her? Absofuckinglutely. Will I pout and make a big deal out of this? No. She deserves to be celebrated even if I am scared shitless that she will leave here and never look back. She will leave us and never look back.

There is some chatter on the bus but mostly, we are all quiet. Some of us are listening to music, others are snoring. I can hear Alex and Coach talking about the game, and Nick is sitting next to me, completely out. We play the Commanders tonight and although we have won games against them, we lost against them at this same game last year. We really need to work together and try not to be predictable if we are going to be able to win and go to state. I am pretty sure everyone in Baker is going to this game tonight. Businesses closed, the school had an early release schedule, and the parents were carpooling so they could make the hour drive to their field.

We are pulling up to the Commanders' parking lot when the coach tells us to grab our gear, get off the bus, and get set up. As we quietly walk down to the locker room in a line we look around and see all the families and fans from the Commanders. Green and tan fill the space everywhere and we have to walk through the masses to make it to the locker room. You could hear a pin drop with how quiet the crowd got when we got there. Everyone staring at us and us keeping our heads forward. The only sound is of the pads bumping against our bags or helmets and the cleats click-clacking on the sidewalk.

The cheerleaders, band, and flag team should be here soon and that sense of dread comes back to my stomach just thinking about Allie. I wish she would just talk to me. Instead of hiding whatever she is trying her damnedest not to tell me. But I need to get my head in the game and push that aside, as hard as it is.

We get in the locker room to get dressed. We can hear the people outside and there is music playing too but we are focused on getting ready. Coach gets up and we face him waiting to hear what he has to say.

"Today we are here not only to play a game but to win it. Last year we almost had them and then we crumbled at the end and lost. I could tell you that we play football for the fun of it, but we all know that in a game, you play to win even if sometimes it doesn't pay off. Last year we lost big, against this same team, on our field. It was hard but we learned from it. I look around this locker room and I see players that took that loss and worked on their weaknesses from that game to the point where I now find strengths. I see players that worked twice as hard to be better. To make it to this game y'all are about to play tonight and you better show it. I want this win more than anything but I can't be the one to get it for you. You have to want it badly enough to go out there and show them WHO. YOU. ARE. I know who you are but sometimes you forget. So before we go out there, let me remind you. You are the kings of this game. You are the best team I have ever coached and probably ever will. You work together as a team COME WHAT MAY and it shows. You are leaders. You are beasts. Don't go out there and act like fragile ballerinas. Go out there and dominate the field. Show them that you are the mighty Sharks and nobody goes up against a shark and comes out without battle scars. Let's show them what we are made of."

We are all clapping, stomping our feet, hitting the lockers, and ready to go. Alex gets up and shouts, "Sharks on three," and we all get up and follow along. "One! Two! Three! SHARKS!"

Claps sound all around until Coach settles us down before we get out onto the field.

Lights are bright and burning. We are tied in the last quarter, the ball is in our hands and we just made our first down. We are on yard 50 with a ways to go but we are making it count. Coach calls a time-out to bring us all in and he looks furious. The offensive line has played like shit today; letting too many players pass us by, making it harder to score when we should have been ahead by the way their offense is playing. Our defense is solid but theirs is a different beast.

"What on earth are y'all doing out there?" he screams at us. "I have never been more disappointed IN MY LIFE of my offensive line like I am right now."

We all stare at him in the dead silence, nobody willing to speak up or anything. Those questions were rhetorical and even though we are tired as shit, our self-preservation stays strong and we just say *yes sir* as he speaks. "Blake, stop fucking up out there. Clarke, I don't know where your head is tonight, but I need it BACK IN HERE RIGHT FUCKING NOW. Go play like you want to go to state NOW!"

"Yes, sir," we all shout, military style, and get back on the field. The cheerleaders are doing some chants and my eyes go quickly to try to find curves for days and tan legs to see if she'll look at me and give me some reassurance. She doesn't and I still kind of like that because she is so immersed in what she does that not much can make her lose focus.

I take my position and Alex calls the play. I take a step back immediately after we break and cover him with my whole body so he can run the ball. James and I are basically his human shields and where he goes, we go. This is the one play in the game in which I have to run and I am ready. The play starts and we follow in position quickly. They are coming at us but the rest of the line is pushing and shoving them away as we advance with our QB. A big Commander is running this way so I get ready to block him when I feel something big and hard hit me from the right, into the ground, and everything goes black.

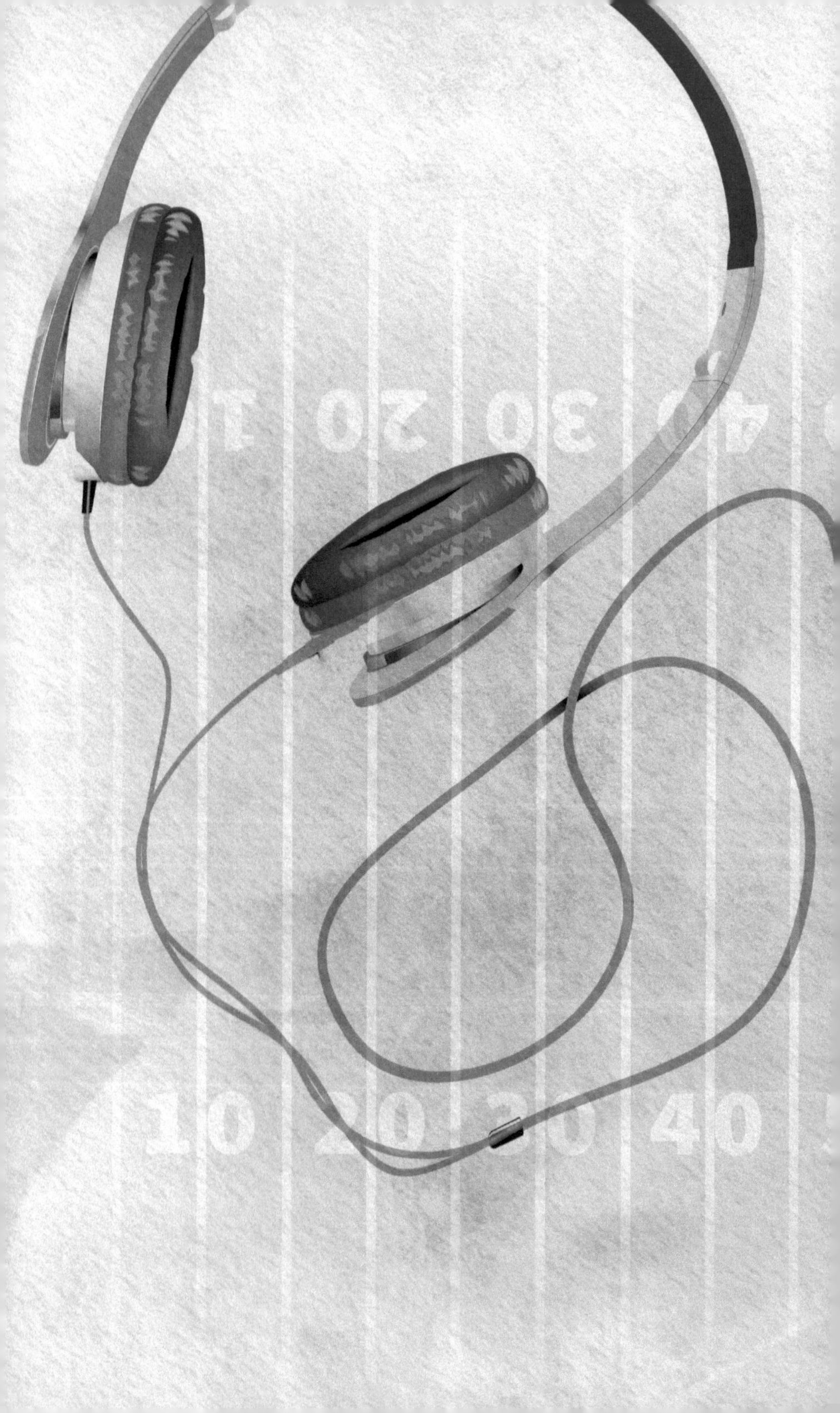

UNSTEADY, X AMBASSADORS

HOLD ON
HOLD ON TO ME
DON'T LET ME GO
BE THE THREAD OF GOLD
I NEED TO HOLD ON TO.

CHEER

CHAPTER TWENTY-FOUR

Allie

THEN

Hold On, Chord Overstreet

The crowd is bouncing and screaming about whatever play is happening. Then a big gasp can be heard. Instantly, everything goes quiet so I turn around to see a player on the ground. I frantically scan the field looking for Jake but I can't see him. I keep looking trying to remain calm but I can't see his broad frame. I can't find his eyes on me like they usually are, or the shiny number fifty from his jersey. The medics are running to whoever is on the ground and when they clear the area, I can see what I have been worried about since we started dating. Jake is on the ground surrounded by the medics and he is not moving.

I drop my poms, and run to him ignoring everyone shouting my name. Telling me to come back or stop. Fuck that and fuck them, I need to see what is happening. I finally make it there and he is unconscious. Eyes closed, helmet still on, they are checking so many things at the same time.

"Jake," I let out a sob covering my mouth. Nick comes toward me quickly. I'm crying, seeing what is happening, it feels like everything is in slow motion but going so fast at the same time. And I am completely useless. I just stand here sobbing and silently praying. *Open your eyes, baby, just open them.* I can hear the ambulance pulling up and in seconds two EMTs run in.

They check his vitals, remove his helmet after securing the neck brace, and tilt him to put him on the gurney. He opens his eyes and screams. An earth-shattering scream. It is then that I pay attention to more than just his face, and see what is making him scream like this and I notice he is grabbing his leg. He keeps trying to get up to look at it before the EMTs force him down.

He won't stop twitching and pulling on the neck brace. He won't stop moving and he is not letting them do what they need to do. I try to get close to see if I can get through to him, but they won't let me so I just watch as he is desperately trying to figure out what happened and is completely overwhelmed by pain. The female EMT, a little blonde that couldn't be more than 100 pounds, basically climbs on top of him to keep him from moving while the male EMT gives him a shot of something and finally, he is back down with his eyes closed and calm. *Did they sedate him? Holy shit.*

They are wheeling him out and I run behind them begging them to please let me go with them. Coach looks at me with pity in his eyes but when the EMTs say that is his call, he nods and says, "I'm calling his parents and I will be right behind you."

I run behind them trying to keep up. Tasha runs towards me and brings me my bag and my phone before running back to formation. She looks destroyed too, just like how I feel. And that is when it hits me that Jake is so loved by everyone, and nobody knows what is happening. I catch up with the paramedics and as soon as they put him in the ambulance, I hop in too and try to stay out of their way to the best of my ability.

It smells sterile here, just like a hospital would, and I hate it. There are very bright white lights over where Jake is lying down and the male paramedic, *Smith,* according to his badge, hooks Jake up to an IV. Suddenly we are moving and he keeps working on Jake. He puts some medicine in the IV and then he moves on to stabilize Jake's leg, prepping as best as they can. That has to hurt like hell but I keep my comments to myself and try to calm my breathing. I shoot my mom a text letting her know what happened but I don't have Jake's family's number to message them and say anything. *God, please be okay.* I keep repeating on a loop in my mind.

"Could you answer some questions for us about his medical history?" he says.

"Sure, I can try to answer as much as I can. I don't have his mom's phone number," I say.

"Can you give me his full name, date of birth, and his address?"

I answer his questions to the best of my ability. He asks how old I am and I lie and say that I am eighteen because I don't wanna be in trouble for being in here with him as a minor. However, there was no way in hell I was going to let him ride by himself. He explained that he gave him a sedative as well as some pretty strong painkillers. He says the doctors will have to confirm but he thinks Jake tore something in his knee, which is why his leg looks like that. He also has some bruising in his abdomen. The EMT is worried about internal bleeding and he's going to keep Jake sedated until we get to the hospital and they can triage him properly, especially since he freaked out before .

In the blink of an eye we make it to the hospital and he is taken inside. If this does not look like a scene from Grey's Anatomy, I don't know what does. He's brought in quickly and I'm trying to follow along with them, but they are faster than I am. The hospital feels even colder than usual and the chaos that usually surrounds an emergency room is even worse. I feel as if I am twirling inside a tornado from hell.

They bring Jake into an exam room and are running all sorts of tests on him. They are talking about how they need to wake him up to test his brain functions and assess his ability to answer questions. Nobody is talking to me, they're just going around, passing along information and I have never felt more alone than this moment. I want answers but above all, I want to wake up from this fucking nightmare and see Jake smile again.

I speak up and explain what I was told happened since I didn't see the hit. I tell them that he was not hit in the head, he was slammed into the ground. They explain to me that sometimes you can get head trauma from hitting the ground.

They step away for a second, and I sit right next to him and hold his hand. I start whispering how much I love him and that he can't leave me. "You are the love of my life, and I can tell there will only always be you. Please hold onto that. I will be so lost without you. Please." I repeat my pleas over and over while trying not to cry more than I have. I can feel my heart beating faster. My hands are sweating, and I swear to God if I am about to have a panic attack, I will lose it.

Nothing happens for a while. He is still asleep. They bring different specialists to check on him but none of the terms they are talking about make any sense. I am so tired that I can barely function but I try to ask as many questions as I can. They said they called his mom and she's on the way but she's still not here.

I step away to go to the bathroom and call my mom so I can explain to her what is happening when I see Coach and some of the players in the waiting room. Coach is talking to one of the doctors, so I let them be.

I run into the bathroom quickly and I come out to see a lot of nurses and doctors running around. There is an alarm going off; it's blasting, "Code blue! Code blue!"

When I rush to try to get to Jake, I see all of them are crammed in the room with him. He is the code blue patient.

No, no, no, no, no, please don't let this be it for him. Please let him survive this. I pray to someone that I don't even know. I pray to God, maybe the universe, but if there's something out there, please don't take him. I stay there in shock from what is happening and all I hear is "Charge to 100! Clear!" Pads are being brought up to his chest. *Hold tight baby, I still need you.*

"Again!" says the doctor, "Clear!" All hands are off. He's being shocked again, and this is when the first sobbed scream comes out of me. It takes me a minute to realize that I'm saying my thoughts out loud, loud enough for them to turn their heads to me, and for someone to shout to get me out of there.

There is a nurse who rushes over to me. But before I can be taken out of the room I scream at the top of my lungs, "Please don't leave me. Please come back to me!" My tears keep falling and I am sure you can hear the desperation in my voice.

"Ma'am, ma'am, you have to calm down," the tiny nurse says and I swear it takes three of the football players and the nurse to drag me out of there. If it were up to me, I would be sitting right next to him, holding his hand and whispering in his ear that I'm still here. That I will love him forever, and I need him to fight and stay with me.

One of the boys pulls me into his arms, and I am so distracted that I can't even tell who it is holding me. All I know is that the door opens up and Jake is being rolled out with a team of doctors following along with him. There is one nurse who stays behind to talk to us, but she says she can only talk to next of kin. I am still sobbing and shaking, waiting to hear what just happened and nobody will speak because his family is not here. I am losing my mind.

Coach talks to them and shows them that he has the release waiver from the parents saying that medical information can be shared with him. They walk away from the rest of us to talk. Coach nods and rubs his face. He looks concerned but he's not crying so I take that as a win.

He walks towards us and tells us that they found internal bleeding and they are taking Jake to surgery now. They were able to get his heart beating again but right now it's touch and go. We should know more in the next few hours about how bad things are. He said the best thing to do right now is wait and pray.

I collapse sobbing into the ground. *Please don't leave me.* It's the only thing that is on my mind. Everything else fades to the background. Nothing makes sense. Nothing will ever make sense until he is out of there and his beautiful eyes look at me again.

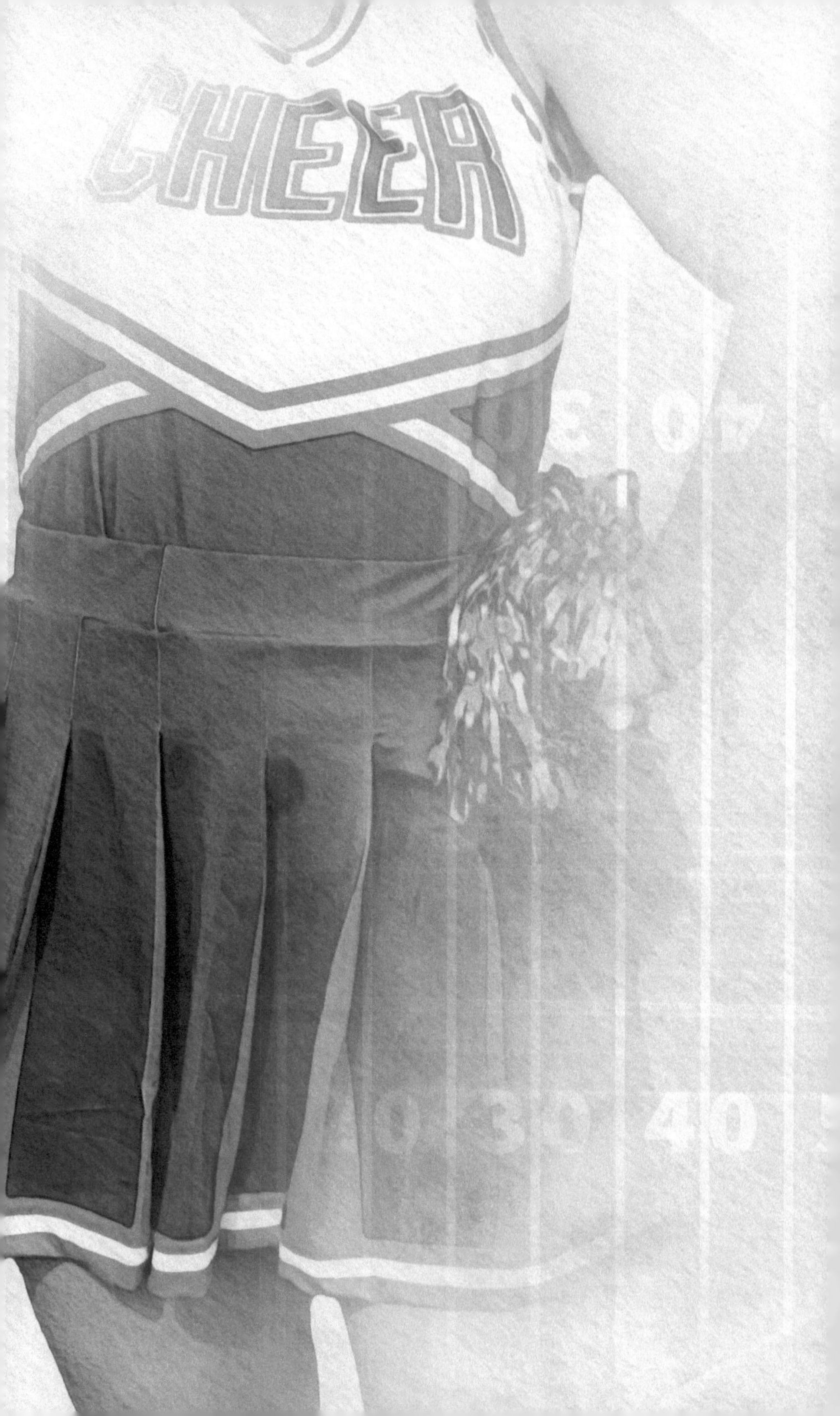

CHAPTER TWENTY-FIVE

Allie

THEN

Heal, Tom Odell

I climb on the bed with Jake, taking advantage of the fact that the nurses are not hovering right now. I skipped school today to visit him now that he is finally out of the ICU and his visiting hours are longer. His mom is at work so I don't have to share him with anyone right now. It sounds selfish but I just want to be alone with him, even if he can't talk to me. Even if he can't look at me.

On Friday, they were able to control the bleeding. He had a lacerated spleen and they repaired it without having to remove anything. He tore his ACL and they did a reconstruction on Saturday. They used a part of the muscle and tissue from the other leg to restore it so both his legs are in different types of bandages and braces. Unfortunately, he is still not waking up but they have high hopes. They say that the trauma to his body was enough for his brain to need a longer rest and they are hopeful that he will wake up soon. Of course, they can't promise that there is no damage to the brain. I am choosing to stay positive though and praying for the best.

I sit right next to him on the bed and slide down slightly to lay my head against his chest. I start telling him about the weekend. How the team was so distraught this happened, they lost the game. About how nobody is upset they lost but upset about what happened to him. How the hospital has had to turn people away because the waiting room is always full of people here to support him. I talk to him and I tell him everything, secretly wishing that he will say *anything* back to me.

When I am not talking to him, it is so quiet. Not the type of comfortable silence that you can have with someone you love, but the kind that shatters your heart every second that passes. I try not to cry but it is impossible to stop the tears from falling down my cheeks. I just want him back and I want him back now. Patience has never been my virtue but right now it is practically impossible to just wait. I stay lying there with my head on his chest and my heart on the floor as tears stream down my face, quietly drifting off to sleep in this eerie room.

My phone is ringing which wakes me up from the deep sleep I was in. This is the only place I have been able to sleep since Friday but it is never for very long because of the nurses coming in, or my mom begging me to come home. The ringing was thanks to a series of text messages from several people including my mom and Cara. My mom just wants to know if I will be there for dinner, which I respond yes to because the nurses will kick me out before then and she sends a heart emoji. My dad is not in town this week so I am planning on seeing my mom more.

I take a deep breath, rub my face, and get my ass up from the hospital bed. Stretching my arms I hear footsteps behind me and turn to see Cara and Cole standing there. Cara has a soft smile on her face that is complemented by her beautiful yellow dress. She always feels like a ray of sunshine. Even though people sometimes say the same about me, I think she is the true representation of that statement. Just looking at her right now makes me feel happier.

"Hey, babe," I say, smiling at her. They both look at me the same way that everyone has in the past week; with pity. I hate it but I guess there's no way around it.

"Am I chopped liver?" asks Cole as he walks in and sits on the chair opposite me. He has a smirk on his face that goes away when his eyes wander to Jake. There's no change in his status so he is just lying there, half here, half somewhere else. His eyes drift quickly back to me, surely trying to hide his hopelessness. Seeing his best friend like that cannot be easy.

"How do you know I wasn't calling *you* babe?" I say lifting my eyebrows hoping to relax the situation a little. I am tired of people walking on eggshells around me and if I can't be myself with these two, even when I am sad, who can I be myself around? They also don't deserve to just be miserable. We all miss him, but we are hurting ourselves by continuing to drown in the hollowness.

"Because we all know that the only person other than me that you are allowed to call babe"- she says kissing my cheek and sitting next to me -" is lying on that bed." She wraps her arms around me, comforting me instantly.

Cole scoffs a small laugh and adds, "And Jake is a scary motherfucker even lying down, so I am glad it wasn't me you called babe."

All three of us laugh and it feels almost normal. I didn't know how much I needed to just talk to friends without talking about Friday or Jake. Cara and Cole know the same that I do, and I bet if I were to ask, they would tell me they are here for me and not Jake right now. The four of us stay there for the next hour as I try to catch up on whatever happened at school today. We also take turns telling Jake something we don't like about him, hoping that he will wake up and yell at us for making fun of him while he is in a hospital bed, but nothing changes.

Visiting hours are over and we don't have any choice but to leave. We pick up our stuff and start heading out. I turn back around and quickly give Jake a kiss and whisper, I love you," in his ear before running back out and heading back home. "I will be back tomorrow, mi amor, "I say softly. "Please come back to me."

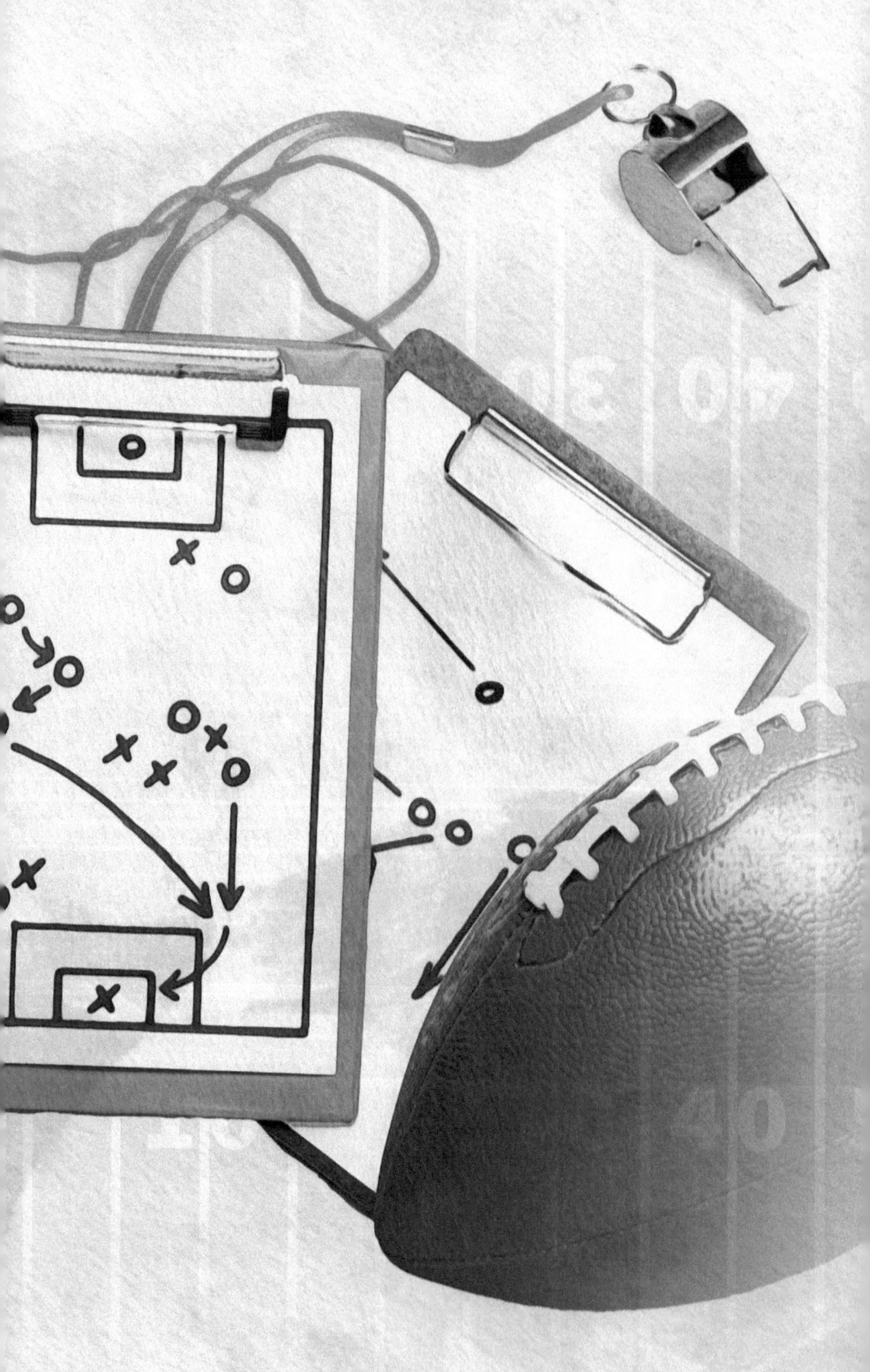

CHAPTER TWENTY-SIX

Jake

NOW

This Love (Taylor's Version), Taylor Swift

The past few days have been torture trying to stay focused at work. I try to be my best self regardless of how worried I am about Allie, alone at the house. I know she is capable of taking care of herself but knowing how close she was to being seriously hurt makes me go full neanderthal.

"Mr. Clarke?" I hear someone say. Looking up, startled and confused, the whole class laughs.

"Where is your head at, Coach?" Tyler – one of the juniors on the team – asks, with a know-it-all smirk on his face.

Was I ever this cocky in high school? Rubbing my face and annoyed at the question I reply, "Want extra work sixty two?" The class riots in laughter.

There is nothing wrong about apologizing when you are in the wrong so I own up to my mistake, "I apologize if I have seemed off or unfocused these past few classes. Someone close to me was in a bad crash last week and I am just worried that's all. Now get back to work."

"Ooh Mr. Clarke has a girlfriend," Brynlee sasses from the back. I give her a death stare but the bell rings and I have never been happier that it is 2:00 pm in my life.

I open the door to my house, in utter exhaustion, after working all day and a long-ass practice because the offensive line couldn't get their shit together and I had to deal with more than just running plays. I've been looking forward to the day being over so I could rest right next to the beauty waiting for me inside.

I walk in and find Allie sitting on the couch with her computer on her lap and a cup in her hand. I would bet money it's espresso bean coffee, two splashes of half and half, and two teaspoons of sugar. That girl could have a coffee IV and *still* go to sleep. What I seem to almost miss is the smell. It smells fucking delicious in here. She looks up from her computer and gives me her megawatt smile. I look around and see that the table is set up and in the kitchen, there are some pans with covers on. It smells like my Dominican food mixed with some vanilla scent. *Probably the coffee* I think. Setting my bag down, I walk to Allie and close her computer on her lap. She keeps smiling at me as she says, "Hey Jake," shyly.

"What is this?" She says nothing as she smiles and gets up from the couch. She places her coffee on the table and stands to the tips of her toes in a futile attempt to reach higher so she can meet me face to face. I drop lower to meet her where she is and tenderly kiss her sweet little nose. She closes her eyes, fluttering her lashes and then, as if she loses all the control she has, she throws herself at me in a tight hug. Her arms are around my neck and her body is flush to mine. Somehow she is still not close enough so I pull her as close as I can.

Her lips whisper right in my ear another sweet hello. I want to leave again just to come back and be welcomed like this. "Did you go all homemaker on me and cook dinner, Allie?" I ask her gently and she giggles.

"Maybe not a homemaker but I did cook some dinner." She tries to let go of my neck but I pull her tighter against me, not letting her go. Never letting her go. She laughs again and says, "It's nothing fancy, just a little thank you for everything you have done for me. I feel a lot better today and I wanted to surprise you."

"Oh, I'm surprised alright. You managed to do it with the house intact too." We both laugh a little more. She kisses my neck and then my cheek on a spot between my beard and my eye that I always thought of as her spot. I didn't think she'd remember that she used to kiss me right there when she was trying to cover up that she wanted to kiss me on the lips. Embarrassed that Gma would see her, she would kiss me in that same spot. Apparently, she remembers it all too well too.

She lets her head fall against my chest, lowering her feet back to the ground and hugging me around my back. Her warm vanilla scent invades my senses and my head. My thoughts go round and round on how much I love her and how much I love her *here*, with me. "Thanks, Honey, it means the world to me."

She tightens the hug when I call her 'Honey' and that is all it takes for me to stop dancing around the fact that I want her, *right now*. I dip my face and kiss her. I kiss her how I often kiss her, always worrying that she might slip through my fingers again, gently at first and then without reservations. I kiss her like I know that this might be our last kiss for right now or even forever. I kiss her like I'm losing my breath and she is pure oxygen.

She moans into my lips and I lower my hands down her body gripping her ass and lift her to me. She wraps her legs around me without any hesitation or comments about her body or her weight like a fucking Goddess. "Good girl," I tap her ass with a growl. That makes her shiver and she goes back to my lips. Wild and sweet.

"Jake," a breathy whisper. A silent plea. My hands grab her ass tighter and she arches against my chest.

I walk to my room without letting her go as she kisses my neck, my ear, and my lips. I bite her lower lip which earns me a whimper and a smile against my lips. I lay her down on my bed- *our bed* -and kiss her lips again. Holding my weight with my hands, I cage her face. I kiss her neck, tasting and licking. She tastes the same, tangy and sweet. A mix of passion fruit, guava, and vanilla. I could drink her up all my fucking life. I continue down her body, lifting her oversized tee which I notice is my shirt. I hold it in my fist and look at her with an unspoken question.

Biting her lip she says, "I found it in your closet and it is so damn comfortable. I always loved wearing your shirts, and I was so happy to find that even after gaining weight they still fit me. I can take it off if you want." She holds my stare, waiting for an answer or my comment.

I give her a devilish smile and say, "Let *me.*"

I pull my shirt off her and she's not wearing a bra. I growl at the view and she smiles like she knows exactly what she is doing to me. I touch her breast and pinch both her nipples, earning me a little whimper and her legs shimmying under me. "Please," she says, breathy and raspy.

"Please what, Honey?" My voice is also raspy and low, full of lust and want. My dick is hard but I want to hear her tell me exactly what she wants. I want to hear her say she wants *me.*

"More, I want more." If I were a better man I would give her just that but, I'm not and I don't. I give her *just enough*. I lap at her clit and suck it lightly between my teeth. She writhes and wiggles. I lick and suck enough to get her moaning my name.

When she brings her hand to my hair I stop. I look at her and ask again, "More of what, Honey?" I slide two fingers in her pussy and feel how tight she is and how fucking wet she is for me. Her body is already telling me what she wants but I need *her* to tell me as well.

I don't want her to go shy on me so I say those words that often will make her shiver under my gaze, "Words, Allie, I need words."

That sentence makes whatever she is holding back snap and she says, "You, Jake, I want more of you. No, not want, *need*. I need you." I think she will stop at that but she continues, "I need you over me, under me, all around me, and inside me. I need you now. Please don't make me beg anymore and show me that *you* want me too."

That's when I snap, too. I go to the end of the bed and pull her by her ankles to the edge. I keep pulling until her ass is practically hanging and I place her feet on my shoulders. "Open up for me babe," I say and she does on my first command. "Such a good girl," I add before going back down on her pussy, showing her exactly how much I want her. How much I need *her*, too.

I kiss and lick her clit. My beard is covered in her arousal and I don't give a fuck. I add one more finger to the two that were already inside her and she lifts her body off the bed. I lift my other hand and push her back down, holding her in place, my eyes locked on her.

"Too much, Jake, This. Is. Too. Much," she says between gasps and moans.

I stop and raise one eyebrow at her, she shakes her head no, and with a smirk I go back down on her. I flatten my tongue against her clit and when I feel her tense a little bit more, I bite and tug gently. She drops her feet from my shoulders and her knees take their place. Trapping my head against her delicious pussy. If this is how I die, I will die a happy man. I pump my fingers in and out and then curl them, touching the spot that drives her wild. That touch is what it takes to drive her over the edge. She scrapes my scalp and pulls my hair as she screams my name. In this moment I decide that is my new favorite sound. I keep going until her legs go loose around me and I get up to grab a condom from my nightstand that I got a couple of days ago, hoping that this would happen again.

She follows my every movement and when she sees what I'm doing, she stops me, grabbing my wrist. I look down at her raising my brow in question and she speaks a little breathlessly, "Jake, I'm on birth control. I have not been with anyone since you. Have you gotten tested lately?"

This girl is going to kill me tonight, I'm sure of it. "I get tested every year and always come back free of STDs." I know I should tell her that I haven't been with anyone in a while either but I don't want to open that door. It would lead to too many questions about how long *a while* is and who the last person I was intimate with, without protection, was.

She smiles at me and says, "Then drop it. I want to feel *you*. All of you."

I get back on the bed and kiss her. My hands roaming every inch of her skin. Every part of her. I hike her leg up by her knee as my dick goes to her entrance. She hisses when I am halfway there but I kiss her deeper and she relaxes around me.

She pulls me flush against her and I am terrified to smother her to death but she says, "I want to feel all of you. Let me feel your weight on me."

I go down as much as I can but I refuse to let go completely. I keep diving deeper and deeper, praising this beautiful girl as I go. "God, Honey, you take me so well." She moans my name. I dive a little more. "Fuck, you are so tight. So good. You feel so good." She moves under me in gentle circles making me groan and I drop my forehead against hers. "Stop for a second, baby. If you keep making those sweet little noises and moving like that, this won't last long."

She laughs at my confession and I really just want to flip her over and smack her sassy ass but that won't help my cause either. I am so hard it hurts but she does stop moving for a while, giving me time to settle all the way in and gather some form of control. I lower my head right onto her nipple and suck, earning me another moan as I drive into her, setting a fast pace. She squirms, moves, and moans under me. Her nails drag on my back as I lick and suck and fuck her how I want to. Like she is mine.

I hike her leg higher, forgetting how flexible she is, and place it on my shoulder freeing my hand to bring to her clit. I tease and pinch her clit as I push inside of her, and she shatters again. Her legs tense around me. Her head comes off the bed. Her nails slide across my back. Her pussy clenches around my bare dick as she screams my name. And that sends me over the edge, whispering her name against her skin.

I collapse right next to her as we both pant. Sweaty and spent but sated. I turn my face to look at her and she looks back at me with glossy eyes. I look at her full lips, and skin shiny with sweat. At that moment I realize how impossible it is not to tell her how I feel about her. In a soft, intimate breathless whisper I say, "I love you."

She opens her eyes wide and opens her mouth to speak but I beat her to it, "Please don't say anything right now. It's okay. I just couldn't go one more minute without letting you know." I pull her against me and kiss her softly. I keep kissing her until we are all moans and hands all over again. I won't stop until she is undone under me, coming and saying my name again and again.

CHAPTER TWENTY-SEVEN

Allie

THEN

Take Me, Alex & Sierra

"Adios, Ma, te amo." *Goodbye mom, I love you.* I shout as I try to run out the back door unseen. I have been able to avoid my parents all week and today should not be the exception. Except that when I turn to go out the door, my mom is sitting right by it, newspaper in hand and coffee next to her. I stop as if I had a bucket of ice-cold water thrown at me but try to play it cool.

"Oh, hola, Ma!" I say, trying to hide my rush and my nerves. I am sure the school has called her to tell her I have not been in all week. However, I don't have the energy to argue with her right now. I have always been a straight-A student so this won't affect my grades tremendously but I know they would have a coronary if I started skipping school.

She looks up at me and points to the chair across from her. I wait a moment or two before saying, "If I sit, I will be late for school."

"Te crees que soy estupida?" *Do you think I'm stupid?* she says and I have no other choice but to sit down right there and then. I sigh but she interrupts me, "Allie, what is going on? Why have you not been at school for a whole week?"

"Ma, Jake is still in the hospital. I am not going to keep going with my life like he is not laying in a hospital bed without waking up."

"Allie," she sighs, "You said it yourself, he is not awake. You can't throw your future away, sitting next to someone when you don't even know if he will ever wake up again."

"He will and I will be there to see it. I would hate for him to be left there alone like he is not human, Ma," I all but yell at her and she flinches at my outburst. I am treading in deep waters with this reaction but I will not let her treat this like an inconvenience, like it is not his life on the line here.

"I'm completing my assignments and I'll be back at school as soon as he wakes up. In the meantime, I want to be there for him," I say, as calmly as I can manage.

"I know you love him, mi niña, but you also need to remember to love yourself and that means taking care of yourself. Are you eating? Are you sleeping?" her soft gasp takes me over the edge and tears start falling down my cheeks.

"Ma, how can I when I feel like my whole body is on fire, just trying not to collapse, right beside him?" I say between sobs before continuing, "I feel like my heart is being ripped out of my chest with every minute that passes by without him opening his eyes. It is like he is so close but also so far away and I can barely take it," I gasp. "So no, I am not eating or sleeping. I am not worried about my future because my whole future is lying in a hospital bed, lifeless."

She gets up and walks towards me. Sitting next to me, she pulls me close to her and drags my head to her lap like she always used to when I was younger. She will always be my safe place so I let it all out. I cry and sob asking someone to please heal him all the way. Maybe God or maybe a high lord, I don't care as long as he is completely healed. "Sh, sh, sh. Esta bien mi niña. Todo va a estar bien." *It's okay my girl. Everything will be fine.*

We stay like that for a good while until my breathing is more settled and the tears stop falling. I am a mess of snot and hiccups when she lets me sit back up and hands me some tissues. "Allie, I didn't know you loved him this much, sweetie. This is exactly how I would react if your father was in the position Jake is in. But darling, you do need to take care of yourself. I will call the school today to get your absences excused, but you need to promise me you will eat something and you will get home before 9:00 pm tonight."

I nod at her and after the warmest hug I've had in a long time, we get up and walk to the kitchen where an array of breakfast awaits for me, for us.

I finally make it to the hospital and I am practically running to see Jake. I like to be there when his dad or brother are there because they lighten the mood as opposed to his mom who cries probably just as much as I want to, bringing everyone down. I don't blame her though. I can't even imagine what it is like for her to see her first baby lying there like that. Last night, I was there when the nurses were moving him around and they were explaining that the biggest complication they have with patients like him are infections due to sores from lying down for so long. They move his body to let his back rest from laying on it all the time. So imagine my surprise when I walk into his room and the hospital bed is empty.

I look around but I don't see anything so I drop to my knees practically screaming *no, no, no.* My face in my hands on the cold hospital floor. The contents of my bag are spilling everywhere as I sob hysterically, screaming for him to come back to me. *Take me with you babe.* I feel cold hands on my shoulder and a soft voice whispering something I can't make out. The world is closing in and I feel like I am going to be sick. I get up and run to the bathroom, emptying everything in my stomach into the toilet bowl. I am sitting on the ground, not even caring about how many germs may live here, because what is living if Jake is gone?

The same voice that was talking earlier calls for me again, but this time it's saying my name. I look up towards the door and find Brooke, one of the nurses who has been working with Jake, looking at me with pity in her eyes. I run to her crying some more and she hugs me tight but tells me to stop crying. How could I? I hug her tight until I hear a raspy deep voice that I have been doing nothing but begging to hear say, "You are scaring the poor nurse, Honey."

Letting go of Brooke I run towards him and stop right in front of him, hands on my chest, begging my heart to not give out on me right now. He is in a wheelchair, with his leg in the cast propped up, giving me the biggest smile I have seen from him. I swear my breath is leaving my body taking all the air from my lungs. My Jake is completely awake looking at me with the same love in his eyes as last week.

"Stop freaking out and come give me a hug, baby. I hear you've been waiting for me to come back to you," he says, opening his arms to me and that is all it takes for my control to escape me and I leap right into his arms. Fuck hospital protocols.

PASSPO

CHAPTER TWENTY-EIGHT

Allie

NOW

Dress, Taylor Swift

It is finally the weekend again. Although, it feels like it has been a week-long weekend for me since I took some time off and then worked from home for the rest of the week after the accident. It was exactly what I needed to heal my body and my mental health. Being alone in his house though, not so much. I already cleaned, cooked, read, slept, and tidied as much as humanly possible. I went outside and played with the chickens and helped with the garden as much as I knew how without killing any of the plants. I have the blackest thumb so I don't want to send my bad mojo to his beautiful garden.

Jake worked long days and with me not leaving this place at all, and the fact that I have no friends or anything to do here is making me be bored beyond existence. Cara and I talked every single day on the phone and the obvious *I-told-you-so* smirk in her voice is uncontrollable.

Jake said last night, in between lasagna bites and sexy sessions, that he had plans for us today, and I have been beyond excited since. He is already up and about around the house and I am still lying in bed contemplating what I will wear. *In his bed*. Since the night of the accident, he has not let me go back to the spare room and I basically moved into Jake's bedroom. We keep ignoring the fact that there is a ticking time bomb with me eventually getting assigned to another city or state. So far, we are just enjoying every day we can and for once in my lifetime, I am giving myself permission to do so.

I hear footsteps so I look up from the book that I have open on my chest, but I have not been able to read, just thinking about all the little things. I see Jake, walking in with a tray that has a cup of coffee, a plate with what looks like mashed potatoes, eggs, and sausage, *shirtless*. All his tattoos are on display and his arms look damn edible as they hold onto the tray full of homemade deliciousness. My eyes rake down him from head to toe and he gives me a cocky grin, knowingly, as he says, "Hola, beautiful, like what you see?"

"Good morning, handsome. And yes, you holding coffee and breakfast is a true vision." He lays the tray of food on my lap, and *holy shit is this Dominican Breakfast?* "Jake, is this mangú?"

He kisses me on my forehead and nods. "I missed eating this when you left and after a few years I googled how to make it."

He smiles and walks away toward the bathroom. I hear the shower running and thoughts of the other night invade my senses, but I need to focus and eat this before it gets cold. This man can fucking cook and it has always been my biggest weakness. This breakfast is what people would pay good money for and he just made it for *me*. On top of that, he made my absolute favorite. Mashed plantains, mangú, Dominican sausage, and fried eggs. I bet he didn't even eat. It is a crime that someone who can cook breakfast this good hates eating early in the morning.

By the time I finish breakfast, Jake is out of the shower, walking around naked without a single care in the world. He oozes confidence as he strolls around gathering his clothes for the day and my eyes can't stop tracking him. I sip on my coffee and look at him from under my eyelashes trying to hide how much I am ogling him. *This man could've been mine for a decade now,* is all I can think about.

He starts pulling up his boxers when he says, "Stop looking at me like that, Honey. If you don't want me to do something about it."

I let out a soft laugh and shake my head. "I am going to shower so I can be ready. Where are we going again?"

"To run some errands and I have a tattoo appointment that I don't want to cancel so I wanted to see if you would go with me?"

"Oh, a tattoo? Mm, yes! What are you getting?" I ask, as I get up from the bed and walk toward the bathroom.

"You'll see," he says and winks at me.

I step into the bathroom and close the door behind me. Hopping into the shower I turn the water as cold as it will go.

After an hour or so we are finally in the truck heading out of the house. Zac Brown Band plays on the radio. Jake is wearing a black Columbia shirt that hugs his forearms perfectly and dark denim jeans that give him a more professional but still casual look. His beard is majestic and it looks so shiny today, you would think he added some treatment to it. His hand is resting on my thigh and mine is placed right on top of his. Since he didn't tell me what else we were doing, I opted for a pink maxi dress that flows around my curves accented with a jean jacket in case it gets chilly later. My curls are cooperating today, holding a loose pattern that is my favorite. Since the accident, I haven't wanted to wear my contacts, so I have my oversized glasses on.

We stop at a few places. The UPS Store to return something, and a nursery to pick up a couple of new plants that he ordered. Then Tractor Supply for feed for his girls and the pharmacy to pick up some medication for Jake's dad. We are delivering the prescription to his dad at their car garage since he needs to check in over there anyway. I am still awestruck at the fact that he teaches full-time, coaches, and also owns his own business. This car shop, which I had not seen before, is one of the things Jake always dreamed of having. A place in which he could tinker with cars but also fix his own stuff if needed. An outlet, and he made it come true.

I am equally nervous and excited to see Jake's dad again but he assures me that there is nothing to be worried about. He liked me then, and he will like me now. We pull up to the garage and I see a living image of older Jake walking towards us. He looks just like he did ten years ago but somehow lighter. Jake mentioned that his parents got a divorce shortly after his injury and while it took them a while to be amicable, it clearly was for the best.

"Hi, Mr. Clarke," I say, giving him my hand to shake.

He takes it using it to pull me towards him, straight into his arms for a hug. "What a treat it is to see you, Allison."

"Please call me Allie," I say when he lets go of me.

"If you call me Joe," he bites back.

"Mr. Joe is the best I can do," I say smiling.

He adds, "Sounds good to me, Allie. Come on in lovebirds, I am sure Jake has questions and you can be nosy and walk around. See if you can keep yourself out of trouble."

Jake and his dad have a long conversation, mostly about work, so I stay busy reading a book on my Kindle. I don't go anywhere without it in case of situations like this, in which I have a longer waiting time than I expected.

After a while, they say their goodbyes, and Jake and I walk back through the garage toward the truck. On our way out we see a guy working on something that appears to be a race car. The paint is shiny blue and it is a two-door with a cage inside of it. Jake and his brother Derek used to race go-karts growing up, and because his dad worked on them. I am sure he still gets jobs from them. Word of mouth goes far in Baker Oaks, and after being part of the racing community for so long, people trust them.

"What's up, Thiago," Jake says and the guy under the hood turns his face towards him. He puts the tool he was using on the ground and walks towards us wiping his hand on a towel. He shakes Jake's hand into some sort of man salute that ends in a sideways hug and then he looks at me.

This guy has to be at least 6'5' and built like a fucking machine. He is covered in tattoos and his dark coffee eyes are intimidating. He looks like a man that you don't want to fuck with but then, he smiles, and he looks every bit of trouble that I am sure he is. "And who do we have here?" he says, offering me his hand.

"Hi, I'm Allie. I'm friends with Jake," I say as he shakes my hand and raises an eyebrow.

"Friend, huh? I have never met any *girl*friends of this knucklehead. My name is Santiago but everyone calls me Thiago." He brings my hand to his mouth and plants a kiss on it.

I can pick out an accent in the way he talks but I don't know from what language so I ask, "Portuguese or Spanish?"

He smiles and says "Spanish."

"Mucho gusto, Santiago." *Nice to meet you, Santiago* I say.

"El placer es todo mio." *The pleasure is mine.* He pivots to face Jake and tells him, "I like this one. Keep her, bro."

"I'm trying man, I'm trying," Jake says looking at me. He turns back to Thiago and raises his eyebrows while adding, "Hey, we're actually on our way to see your girl."

"Roe is not my girl man," Thiago says.

"Funny that you knew exactly who I was talking about, especially since she is not *your* girl and all." Jake snaps back. Savage Jake is my favorite. I love that he keeps zero things hidden unless he has to. He also has no problem letting you know how things are, even when you don't want to hear them.

"She did some tattoos for me, and we train together. That doesn't make her my girl, but keep laughing, I know how it is. Say hi to her for me," Thiago says to Jake, winking at me. Jake gives him the side eye and we all laugh. We say our goodbyes and make our way to the truck.

On our way to the tattoo place, Jake seems tense and I don't know why. It can't be because of the interaction we had with his friend, but something is definitely bothering him. I reach to turn the music up higher but Jake's hand reaches mine first and puts it down. He then turns the volume knob to the left, silencing the radio completely. I turn my face to look at him expecting to find him looking at me, but instead, he is looking ahead like nothing is happening. Completely ignoring my gaze on him, which is unusual. I can tell that something is wrong.

"What's going on?" I ask. He takes a deep breath, opens his mouth like he is going to say something, and then closes back up. Jaw tense, he could probably snap something in half with the way his teeth are clenching. He pulls over to a parking lot in a small strip on 6th Street. Puts the truck in park and after a deep breath, he speaks.

"What are we doing, Allie?" he asks with concern in his eyes.

"You said you were going to get a tattoo so that is what I was assuming we were doing," I say.

"What are *we* doing? Not here but in general. What is *this*? I know I said I would take whatever you could give me but I need to know before I get my hopes up. You damn sure have made it seem like you were right where you belong next to me but then you called yourself my friend. Is this how you treat all your friends, Allie? Kissing them until they lose their minds?"

Whoa, this took a turn. "Jake." His name is the only thing that comes out of my mouth.

"Don't *Jake* me, Allie. Answer the question, because I need to know before I set myself up to lose every single bit of sanity I have left. I'll take you as my fuck buddy if that's what you want, but I need you to lay it out right now so I can plan accordingly," he deadpans. His gaze is dark and serious and it is the first time that I see the true hurt behind his eyes and his words.

"I don't have fuck buddies, Jake. Never have, never will. I can't separate feelings from sex which is why I have never been able to sleep with anyone else since you." Now I'm pissed. "And to answer your question, I don't know what the fuck we are doing. I've been telling you since the moment you dragged me to your house from the airport. I usually don't stay more than six months in each place. We have been dancing around the fact that Baker Oaks is not my home. Am I enjoying every single day that I am with you? Absolutely. Do I want to think about what would happen in a few months? Nope, I sure don't. Do I want to introduce myself as your friend? Also sure don't, but what the fuck do I say? Huh? Oh hi, I'm Allie, Jake's old girlfriend who left forever ago. Enlighten me, Jake."

We are both practically hyperventilating and I can see his resolve breaking, this is not what I wanted. In fact, this is exactly what I wanted to avoid because I knew better. Jake doesn't do shit halfway, he is an all-in-or-nothing kinda guy.

We sit in the middle of this parking lot, surrounded by cars and people who are oblivious to the fire building inside of this truck. My ears feel hot and I have a feeling both of us could combust with just one spark. The sun is getting lower behind us, letting golden light shine through the window, right to Jake's eyes, making his skin look more like melted caramel than anything else, and because of the light that I can see the first tear rolling down his face. He wipes it off, taking a deep breath before talking again.

"I know that. I am sorry I snapped at you but hearing you introduce yourself as *my friend* hurt me worse than I thought it would." He rubs his face and continues, "I know we haven't talked about what will happen and selfishly, I don't want to because I really want to keep you here, with me, forever. However, I know that you have big wings and I am not going to be the one to clip them. I also have been avoiding the conversation and I should not have called you my fuck buddy. But *fuck, Allie,* I want to be more than just a friend. My heart doesn't race for friends the way it does for you. My fingers are constantly twitching, wanting to touch you, and only you. You are front and center in my mind, all the damn time. No friend of mine does that."

I swear you can hear the *thump* of our heartbeats filing the silence of the truck.

"Please don't make me call you that," he finishes with a low voice that sounds so close to a plea it breaks my heart which is why I don't think before the next words come out of my mouth, because how could I?

"So, is this you asking me to be your girlfriend, Jacob?" I raise my eyebrows.

"I'm done asking," he says, "You are mine, and everyone else should know that too."

"Okay," I say and before I can say anything else he seals my mouth with a kiss, and man oh man, what a kiss. Tender lips with ravenous teeth that bite straight into my lower lip. His tongue swipes against them after the initial sting with a soothing touch. This kiss is not tentative, it contains every, single, little bit of his possessiveness. Claiming me wholly, and I love it. I open my mouth for him, allowing him better access, and that fuels the beast even more. His hand goes behind my head, pulling me closer to him and I moan right into his lips. He swallows my cries and then starts to slow the kiss, finishing with a few pecks on my lips. Foreheads together, nose touching, and breathing heavy we sit in silence. This moment we are wrapped in reminding us that beyond the scorching kiss, we can also sense the way the other feels by just being here with each other.

"Please don't demote me to the friend zone again. Has a friend ever kissed you like that? Has a friend ever pulled those delicious sounds out of you with just a kiss?" He closes his eyes and takes a deep breath. "You are my friend but you are so much more than that, Honey. You always will be."

I can't deny him this so I just nod and pray that we will get some sort of clarity on what the fuck we are going to do in the next couple of months. "Okay, boyfriend, let's get out of here before we get a ticket for indecency." He smiles and jumps out of the truck, rushing to my side of the door to open it for me.

CHAPTER TWENTY-NINE

Jake

THEN

Epiphany, Taylor Swift

"Can you explain more about the injuries?" I ask Dr. Brandon for the third time since he has been here today. "I need to know exactly what I can and cannot do and when the next time I can train will be," I add. Something tells me that I am not going to like what they have to say considering both doctors and the nurses look as if they were going to tell me someone died.

"Jake. Your injuries are not to be taken lightly. You will need to keep your leg in a brace for four weeks and then do physical therapy for eight to twelve weeks more. We would like to keep you here for another week to run more tests and keep an eye on your healing. Right now, other than in a wheelchair and on the bed, you should not be moving much. Your ACL was destroyed and we had to replace it with a piece of your muscle. Your recovery will be lengthy but you should be able to make good progress and be back walking in three months. Running maybe in six," he says. "As for football, I am sorry to have to tell you but other than recreational I don't think you will be able to play ever again."

I throw the tray of food next to me onto the ground across from my hospital bed the minute he confirms my worst fear. No more football which also means no scholarship either and my world just got deeper into the shit storm. "Jake," the doctor says, touching my *good* leg. I should be grateful, I should because it could've ended worse, but this shit right here just fucked with everything.

"Don't *Jake* me, doc. Just go. Please. Unless you have some sort of miraculous cure to get me back on track for my scholarship, then leave." They walk out and that's the exact moment I start to feel how deep of a hole that this injury will leave me in. Who am I now without football? What am I going to do now?

It's 5:00 pm when I open my eyes again. I have been in and out of sleep all day since talking to the doctors this morning. My parents have both messaged me but I can't pick up the phone to talk to either of them. I want to go back to sleep but the smell of vanilla hits me dead in the face. Looking around for the origin, I find Allie sitting on a chair in the corner with her nose in a book. She must have come in when I was sleeping and didn't wake me up. She is wearing one of those long dresses that cover her whole body and gives her an ethereal look. My angel. Mine. I drink her in before I make any noise. Looking at her peacefully reading, with her legs under her, bottom lip between her teeth, and eyebrows pinched in a frown, I wonder how I got this lucky and how the hell am I going to keep her now that I have nothing to offer her. Nothing to promise her.

"Hola, beautiful." I startle her but she quickly sets her book aside and looks at me with nothing but pure joy in her eyes.

"God, how happy I am that I get to hear you call me that again. Hey, handsome." Untwisting her feet from under her, she walks towards me with a showstopper smile and my heart breaks a little more knowing that I don't get to keep her forever. *She deserves so much more than I will ever be able to give her.*

She sits on the bed next to me, leaning forward and giving me a soft kiss on my lips. So damn sweet and perfect. Thinking about ending things with her is killing me but I need to let her go when I have nothing to offer her other than my potential. Her family will never accept me if I can't provide their daughter the life she deserves.

"What's on your mind, handsome? I can practically hear the gears turning up there." Her fingertips are feather light on my forehead, resting magically on my temple, showing me more love than I have ever felt from anyone else before.

"I got some news from the doctors."

"Oh yeah? Care to share?" she says, grabbing onto one of my hands and placing it between hers. Her warmth reaches my heart, giving me the courage to tell her what I need to. I tell her everything, from the diagnosis to the outcome, and how I can never play again. What I don't tell her is how I know that now I am not enough for her. I am holding on to the love that she has to give me with every ounce of willpower I have and praying to God I find a way out of this mess without losing her in the process.

PASSPO

CHAPTER THIRTY

Allie

NOW

Back to You, Selena Gomez

"So Allie, how do you know this knucklehead?" Roe asks, prepping for Jake's tattoo.

We walked into the tattoo shop after the whole '*we are more than friends*' conversation in the truck. The place is small but it has that cozy feel that a lot of businesses in Baker Oaks have. When you walk through the clear glass door, instead of a doorbell to announce your arrival you hear a wind chime made of different-sized sea shells. To the left of the entrance, there is a natural wood-colored entryway table with crocheted items and a book of flash designs for you to pick from. It has real tattoos that I am guessing she has done and some illustrations of other ones. Everything from tiny tattoos to full sleeves and colorful designs. There is also a picture of her completely dressed in a riding uniform next to a motorcycle and another one of her smiling next to a dog that might be a golden retriever, basically her size. Towards the back, there are different tables and floating shelves with plants as well as some photographs of tattoos on the walls. The whole place screams bohemian but when you see her, this 5'2, blue-eyed, blonde-haired, beauty covered in tattoos, wearing overalls and vans, you wonder where the bohemian comes from.

"We went to high school together, kind of," I reply. She offered me a glass of wine as soon as we walked in and it's the same peachy Moscato I had at Jake's. Maybe this is a new brand that everyone loves, but I will not complain, especially not when it is this good. "I went to Baker High my senior year and we knew each other then." *Loved each other* is what I want to say. "I came back for work and fate would have it that we would meet again now."

Jake is looking at me from the tattoo chair with what I can only describe as love in his eyes. I am pretty sure this man loves me, the same way that I have loved him for the past ten years. I don't know who I was fooling when I thought I could just move on from this, from him. But maybe I never fooled anyone, and my heart has just been hiding in my chest secretly waiting for my brain to catch up. Jake's shirt is off, showing all his tattoos that are usually hiding under his clothes.

A broken heart across his chest with birds taking the halves away is displayed front and center. An owl, some racing ones, and a heartbeat that slowly dies down to a flat line. I want to ask him about them. Other than the racing ones that he got the minute he turned eighteen to give tribute to his dad and brother, I don't know the meaning of them. Before it felt intrusive to even ask, especially considering that they are not out for the world to see. He let *me* in though and that right there means the world to *me*.

"Mmm, so high school sweethearts rekindling their love? How second-chance-romance of you," Roe blabs and we both laugh.

Jake looks confused casting his eyes between the two of us sarcastically adding, "You two already have a secret language, great."

We continue laughing and eventually, Roe adds, "It's a book thing, and judging by her reaction, she reads the same type of books I do. I like this one, keep her."

Jake replies to her but without taking his eyes off me, "I'm trying Roe, I'm trying."

Same reply he gave the guy earlier so I say that, "You know, the guy from earlier, what was his name? Oh yes, Santiago, he said the same thing." Roe immediately tenses as she hears the name and I guess I got it right and my suspicions are true. There is definitely something going on there.

Jake smirks as he says "Yeah Roe, Thiago said the same thing, you two must be connected on a deeper level." Jake is not done with his sentence when Roe slaps his arm harshly, placing the disinfecting pad she is using to clean the site where she will apply the tattoo, making Jake stop his train of thought and stare at the little pixie tattoo artist. It is all fun and games until that moment and then she is all serious business.

He has a large owl on his right upper arm that has black and blue outlines. He said he is adding more color to it to give it more depth and to add hidden items because one day, he will have a whole sleeve. Roe places the new color scheme over it and nods and smiles, she gets up and pulls a cart near her stool. There is a large mirror across from where they are sitting giving me a direct view of what she is doing on his arm, even though I am sitting on the opposite end of the room.

"Do you mind music, Allie?" Roe asks and when I shake my head and pull my Kindle out of my bag to show her what I plan on doing, she smiles and grabs her phone, turning on some sort of rock music. She moves the stool near him and puts the tattoo gun to his skin. The sharp buzzing sound hums under the music playing while Jake closes his eyes and lays back on the chair, leaving me mesmerized by the whole aura of this moment for too long.

About an hour later the owl is done. It looks perfect. The colors carry shade, contrast, and highlights making it look almost three dimensional. She used some techniques on the eyes that make it seem like the owl's gaze follows you wherever you are. His skin is red around the edges of the owl and even bleeding some places but the smile he has plastered on his face is worth a million bucks.

Jake pays for the tattoo and hugs Roe. She punches him on the not-tattooed arm and mentions stopping by later at a place called Saddlers. I walk towards her to say goodbye too and she gives me the biggest hug I have ever received from a non-Latin stranger. "Come by later, first drink is on me," she says as she waves goodbye.

By the time we are out of the tattoo shop, it's getting darker. The sky shows shades of orange, pink, and purple in the most breathtaking sunset I've seen in a while. The air around us is crisp and not that humid, making me shiver slightly as we walk to the truck. Jake grabs my hand and pulls me to him, wraps me in his arms, and guides me past his truck.

"Where are we going now?" I ask quietly, comfortable in the warmth of his arms.

He kisses the top of my head and says, "To dinner, unless you want to go to the house first and get dressed in warmer clothing, the temperature seems to have dropped."

"You don't have to worry about me, Jake. If you are hungry, we can go to dinner first," I say nonchalantly, even though we both know that I could use some jeans or a jacket. I look up to see his face and find him smiling down at me with nothing but love in his eyes.

"Let *me* worry about you, Honey. Let me take care of you, let me show you how you occupy the front of my mind always. It is all I've wanted to do for the past ten years. I finally have you, let me do my job." He says calmly like he is not shaking my world with his words. He is going to be the cause of my death with his attention to detail and words. He rubs my arms and tilts our bodies turning around towards the truck. "Let's go home and you can change. We'll go to dinner after."

Home, there is that word again, tugging at my heartstrings and pulling me closer and closer to him. I barely survived leaving him once, and I don't know if I could do it again. I don't think I should either.

Jake

THEN

Chasing Cars, Snow Patrol

"You are not helping me with this," I snap. Allie is currently standing in front of me holding a bag full of toiletries in one hand while looking like a damn snack. Her dark leggings are molded to her legs as if they were painted on her. Her hair is wild, in a loose bun at the top of her head that she calls a *pineapple*. It is my favorite way she wears her curls. Wild and free, barely tamed by a hair tie, just like her. She has on one of my shirts that she stole from my closet and it could swallow her whole but she has it tied in a knot right above her navel. Her curves are on display for the world to see and I just want to scream *mine*. Instead, I am sitting in a wheelchair shaking my head because my gorgeous, generous, kind, and devoted girlfriend told the nurses she was going to help me shower.

"Jake, you smell. It is time for a shower and you can't stand up for long. Let me help you."

"I said no. I am not letting you reduce yourself to this. I can do it or a nurse can. Just go and I'll figure it out," I say, crossing my arms across my chest. They took the IV off earlier today and it feels like freedom.

Allie stomps her feet around me and pushes the wheelchair towards the bathroom. "I don't give a fuck about what you said,

Jake. I am doing this whether you like it or not." This infuriating girl will end me with her attitude.

She rolls me to the shower and locks the chair. Placing the bag of toiletries down, she takes off her white tennis shoes, that are covered in doodles everywhere, and steps onto the shower. She turns the water on, as hot as it will go, and then steps back out walking toward the door and locking it. Walking back to me with determination in her eyes, she stops right in front of me and puts her hands out so I can hold them. That I do, and she tries her best to help me stand up, but it is a futile attempt. I smirk, shaking my head. This girl. I push myself up from the wheelchair and drag my body to the chair inside of the shower.

"Take the gown off," she says with her bossy voice, and my dick twitches in my pants. What I would give to take the bossiness out of her right here and right now. There is no time for that so I just take the hospital gown off and throw it on the side. She steps in the shower, fully clothed without a care in the world, and drops to her knees right in front of me. *Jesus Christ.* I growl between my teeth when she pulls my boxers down my legs and tosses them out of the shower too. Seeing her kneeling in front of me has me bothered and hot and my dick standing in attention. She looks at it and laughs.

"What's so funny?" I ask raising an eyebrow

"The fact that I literally told you I was going to bathe you but your little friend over here just wants to play," she says pointing at my dick like she didn't just call it little.

"There is nothing little about it."

"You are right, but I need to keep it light and airy, or else I am going to end up sitting on it instead of helping you get clean."

Another hiss and twitch with those words. I want her to sit on it too. Maybe I will help her find a seat right on my dick and show her how much I can still do. Even with this fucked up situation. Before I can turn any of those fantasies into reality, she grabs a washcloth adding water to it, and then some soap.

She starts washing my feet and my legs. Lathering every single inch of skin with soap while being careful not to let my left leg get wet. The steam from the shower feels amazing but the sight of Allie at my feet, cleaning me is giving me mixed feelings. I am in between wanting to love her more for this and being completely mortified that she is doing this. To any other guy, this might be castrating but I am trying to see it for what it is, an act of love.

"One, Four, Three," I whisper with tears falling silently down my cheeks.

"What was that?" she says without stopping scrubbing every part of me, rising from her knees to wash my back and chest.

"I said One, Four, Three."

"What does that mean?" she asks, setting the sponge down. She grabs the shampoo bottle, squirts some on her hand, and stands behind me pulling my head backward gently. She kisses my forehead, smiling at me, and tells me to close my eyes. Following her directions and letting her lather the minty shampoo onto my hair, her fingers massaging in soft circles.

I finally speak again, "It means I love you. 'I' has one letter. 'Love' has four and 'you' has three. My mom used to say it to us all the time when we were little." I leave out the part in which she told me that when I found the one, the woman I could never see myself without, that I would use those three numbers to tell her I loved her.

"Son, sometimes you love people more than life itself and 'I love yous' just become everyday occurrences. Anyone can say those three words but not everyone will know the meaning of those three numbers. Save them for the special person that will hopefully cherish your heart the way I cherish yours."

She told me that once and I never thought at eighteen, in a hospital shower, I was going to say them for the first time. "One, Four, Three," I repeat.

I assume she grabs the shower head because there is warm water running over my hair and forehead as she rubs her fingers aiding the water in rinsing the suds off. She is as thorough as she was putting the soap on me. Every piece of my skin gets touched by the hard droplets of warm water from the shower head and by the fingertips of an angel disguised as a Latina firecracker who stole my heart.

"One, Four, Three, Two," she says and my heart almost gives out at the sound of those numbers.

"Wh-wh-what?" I stutter.

Turning off the water and grabbing a towel that she wraps around my head, drying my hair, cheeks, and neck she says, "If One, Four, Three, means I love you, then One, Four, Three, Two means I love you too, and I sure do." She gives me a quick peck on my lips. She finishes drying off my body, tenderly and meticulously until I am as clean as I will ever be again. She officially left a permanent mark on my heart and it breaks even more at the thought of having to let her go because this gem of a girl, no, not a girl, woman, deserves the world. Sadly I cannot give it to her anymore.

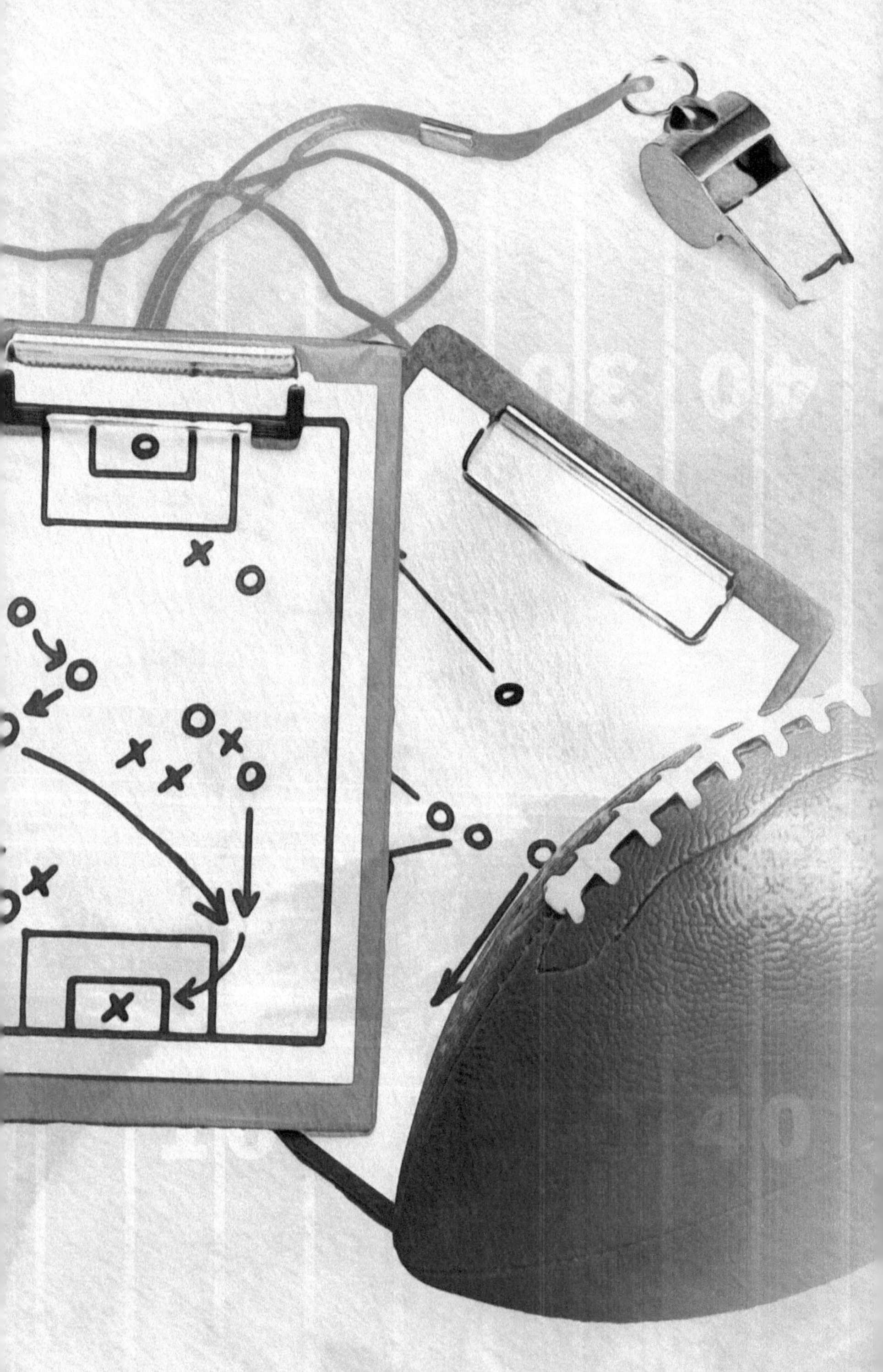

CHAPTER THIRTY-TWO

Jake

NOW

Shivers, Ed Sheeran

Going back to the house to let Allie change clothes pays off when I see her walk out of the room looking like she came out of my fucking dreams. The girl is absolutely stunning without putting in much effort. Her bouncy curls that frame her face with light caramel highlights that make her honey eyes pop. I wonder if she knows that the reason I call her honey is not only because she is as sweet as they come but also because her eyes always reminded me of exactly that, honey. She could be wearing my shirt and a messy bun and she still makes my heart stop. I kind of prefer her like that, natural and free. However, she is walking towards me smiling widely, knowing exactly what she is doing to me. I swear she did this shit on purpose. She catches me ogling her and that makes her sway her hips even more.

"If you didn't want to go out, baby, you could have just said so. Because the way you look right now is making me want to do many things to you and none of them can be done in public," I practically hiss. She is wearing dark jeans that are what I think people call high waisted. They stop right in the middle of her belly, hugging her curves beautifully. She has on a deep red sweater tucked in the front of her jeans, it's loose in the back which probably leaves her ass up to the imagination of whoever might look. That doesn't really help because, with those thighs and her curves, everyone knows that her ass is delicious, too. She has some low black boots with heels, making her legs look longer and her steps deadlier.

Instead of replying to my statement, Allie stops dead in her tracks and gives a little spin showing me the whole outfit from all angles. Her long hair falls to her back and damn it, I was right. The sweater is loose on the back making everyone question what's underneath it. "You like?" she says with a smirk and that is all it takes for me to lose my cool.

I get up from the couch and stride towards her, practically growling. Her eyes turn from mischievous to full of lust in a blink and when I reach her and pull her to me, she gasps. That little sound is going to be my undoing. I grab her neck with both hands and lower my lips to her without touching them. The air is thick between us and her breathing is fast. Her skin is like velvet under my fingers and her sweet vanilla scent engulfs me in a battle because all I want to do is show her exactly what she is doing to me. I'm close to saying *fuck it* and staying here but I want to take this woman out. *My woman.* I want everyone in this town to know that I am taken. I want everyone to see who I belong to. Who I've always belonged to.

"If you are going to kiss me, go ahead and do it, Jake," she says, almost panting, and now it is my turn to smile.

"Two can play this game baby. It's very difficult to see you looking like a damn goddess and not take your clothes off right here and right now, but I have plans for us tonight."

She licks her lips making me lose my train of thought, but I clear my throat and continue, "I am going to kiss you, Honey. But I am letting my heart settle down before I do, because the kiss I want to give you will lead to more kisses. More kisses in more places. We don't have time for that." Raking my eyes all over here, showing her my exact meaning.

She shivers under my gaze and her lips part in a small plea. I give in and touch her smooth lips with mine. Her burgundy lipstick looks like it could be sticky, but when my lips touch hers, it is like she has no lipstick at all. *Just like magic,* I think and maybe she is a witch because the spell that I've been under since the day I met her could only be explained by that.

"Let's go, baby. We have places to be." Pulling her by her hand, I walk her out of the house before I decide to lock her up and throw away the key, with me inside of her.

Dinner was great at our local Italian spot, La Cucina de Pepa. I know Allie has a weak side for carbs so Italian sounded like a good idea and I was right. That girl ate twice her weight in pasta and bread and I couldn't erase the smile from my face. We had an easy conversation, as usual, and we shared a bottle of wine that paired perfectly with the pasta. I still can't stop smiling every time I look at her. We're walking downtown, hand in hand, smiling like I haven't smiled in years.

We make it to our last stop of the night, Saddlers, the local bar. Partying is not my scene but Nick is celebrating his birthday tonight and I couldn't miss it. Stepping into the bar the walkway is dark and somewhat sticky, it takes a little extra effort to walk but not so much that would make you cringe to be here. The place is packed, per usual on a Saturday night, it's always popular with the line dance lessons they offer. The air is thick with sweat and smoke, maybe from vapes or from cigarettes, who knows.

Allie is walking in front of me pulling my hand and guiding *me* through the place like this is not the first time she's been here. Commanding the place with her presence. All I do is follow her closely, covering her back and marking my territory by eyeing everyone who glances our way. I don't know how she looks this confident in places like this but then she is nervous when nobody's watching. She shows her confidence to everyone else but saves her more vulnerable self for me. I love this version of her but I adore her other one too. She turns to look at me asking something but I can't hear her voice over the loud country song playing. I pull her closer to me and she yelps, giggling and raising her arms around my neck.

"What was that?" I whisper in her ear and I can feel the goosebumps crawling under my hands from the sound of my words. Always so responsive to me.

"I said, lead the way now because I don't know where your friends are."

I spin her around quickly in my arms and step in front of her to guide the way. Her arms are wrapped around my chest, leaving not even an inch of space between us. I see Nick's table in the back. I continue pushing through the crowd, nodding to the people I know who are waving or shouting my name. Some are people I grew up with, others are students' parents. I will never get used to hearing *Mr. Clarke* out at a bar. Nick has a couple of tables surrounded by people and drinks. Some of them we went to high school with and some are work friends. As I approach the table, Nick raises his glass towards me and everyone else turns their faces around to see us.

After we say our hellos, Nick hugs Allie like he hasn't seen her in ten years - which he hasn't - but she doesn't get the same treatment from Natalie, his wife. She is cordial but less affectionate and I wonder if it's because she and Tasha got close over the years. Speaking of Tasha, she is sitting at the corner table, farthest from where we are standing. Allie waves at her excitedly, but Tasha's returning wave is barely polite. Before this can turn into a disaster, I pull Allie away from the gathering towards the bar so we can order some drinks.

Seeing all of them after so long is kind of strange. Almost like my brain can't process that they all aged. In my mind, they are all still seniors, joking around in the hallways or partying like there is no tomorrow. I was surprised to be pulled into Nick's arms like long-time friends, especially since I got the cold shoulder from Natalie and Tasha who I thought would be more excited to see me. We used to be close but maybe me leaving everyone behind caused more problems than I had imagined.

Jake pulls me with him to get drinks and I see the tattoo girl from earlier behind the bar. She spots us and comes over to us, placing two napkins in front of us and flashing a wide smile.

"Long time no see lovebirds. What can I get you?" Roe asks.

"The usual for me," Jake replies.

"Mm, surprise me," I add.

She lifts her eyebrows at me and rubs her hands with a mischievous smile.

A few minutes later she comes back with our drinks and gives me a flight of little drinks. I have six small glasses each with different colors and consistencies. Some are bubbly, some creamy. I am sure my eyes go beyond wide when I see this, earning me a laugh from Jake and a smile from Roe.

"My brain is too chaotic to pick just one drink. I choose drinks from customer's vibes and my first-timers get a flight so I can get an idea of what they like. After this, I'll never get your drink wrong."

"She's right," Jake says, sipping on some dark-color concoction that I am sure has whiskey in it.

"You are insane." I sass and roll my eyes playfully.

"Maybe but it works. Go ahead," she adds. She places her rag next to her, and props her elbows on top of the counter and her chin on top of her fists. Intently staring at me while I take my first sip.

All the drinks are different and three of them are so bitter that I have to chug them to finish them. One is thick and sweet with an espresso undertone which I could have as an afternoon drink but absolutely not while out with friends. All four drinks must have been heavy on the alcohol though because I am already tipsy. The last two are my favorites. One is mild in taste but crisp on my tongue. I want to say 'apple something'. It also has some bubbles and I wonder what it is because I have never tasted a drink that felt like I was biting on a fresh apple.

Roe smiles at my expression saying, "I knew you were a fruit girly. You will love the last one too." And she is right. The last drink is flat but it tastes like passion fruit or guava. I can't pinpoint which one exactly but it brings back memories of going to my parents' country during summer break and having treats and fresh juice that taste very similar. After I am finished with all of them, Roe takes the tray and returns with a full glass of the last drink. I offer some to Jake and he takes a small sip. His eyes open wide and he laughs.

"What did I miss?" I ask, confused. Jake just leans in, brings his index finger under my chin, and lifts my face so my lips are directly in front of his. He licks my lower lip and then brings his hand behind my head pulling me closer to him. Closing his mouth on mine he kisses me deeply. He usually saves these kisses for the bedroom but he is unhinged right now. He sucks on my tongue and goes back to licking my lips. I stop the kiss because I am two seconds away from climbing him like a tree. He smiles, pulls his wallet out, and pays Roe.

"Finish your drink, Honey," he says. I pick up my glass, bring it to my lips, and start drinking. He leans in closer and whispers to my ear, "Hurry up and finish so we can go home, because that right there tastes just like your pussy and I didn't get my fill just from tasting it on your lips." I practically choke on my drink but he continues, "You are enjoying it so much that I just want to stick my fingers in you until you come all around them and then have you suck them clean. So, like I said, hurry up because we have things to do."

With that, I feel my thighs clench involuntarily. I get up quickly, completely flushed, not sure why those filthy words turned me on the way they did, I ask Jake, "Is that a threat?"

"A promise, beautiful." He winks.

I try to walk toward the door but before we can leave the bar, I am being pulled onto the dance floor by my hands. Roe stepped out from behind the bar area and is currently pulling me and another girl to the dance floor. The instructors at the bar are teaching the dance for Ed Sheeran's *Shivers,* but I already know it. I love dancing and sometimes I watch videos online and try to learn them. It's really the only reason I'm on social media.

Since I already know the dance, I can add different moves or give it more flare. Instead of cross-step, I dip and shake my hips in the same direction. Instead of the one spin, I can do a double pirouette and land on cue, and of course when the song says 'shivers,' I shake or drop my head forward and throw it back. After the whole dance floor practices a few times, the instructors let us know that the song will play again and I am practically jumping with excitement.

I look around and find Jake, eyes blazing and locked on mine. I point at him and jump right on beat, shaking my hips in a circular motion. In no time, I am completely lost in the music. Swaying my hips, shaking my body, hands on my hair, and spinning fast. The whole room disappears. I'm not focused on anything except for the way I feel while dancing and the way I feel with Jake's gaze fixed on me. He has not looked away at all. The song is almost over. Smiling at him, I take my moves up another notch, dipping lower, shaking harder, smiling wider, and shimmying as if I were in a dance competition.

The song ends and I hear applause. I clap too without realizing that I am dead center in the middle of the dance floor and people are just clapping around me and a few other girls. Roe and her friend run to me, giving me hugs and high-fives but my eyes go back to Jake. How could I not when he is looking at me like I am dessert? He has big bad wolf vibes and he could eat me if he wanted to.

"Girl, that was impressive. I didn't know you could dance like that," Roe says.

"I love dancing, Roe. The more we hang out you'll see it's practically second nature to me," I add, eyes still on Jake.

"Well, come back any time and we can dance some more." We give each other hugs.

And then, Jake is right behind me, holding my hips and pulling me flush against his erection. He sways gently and I do the same, I lift my hands and grab his neck. His mouth dips right to my ear when he says, "You have thirty seconds to walk out of here with me or I am about to take your sexy ass in the bathroom and show you exactly how much I want you." I laugh at his raspy tone but nod and walk us out of the bar. He speeds all the way home and then he fulfills his promise.

CHEER

CHAPTER THIRTY-THREE

Allie

THEN

Fingers Crossed, Elijah Woods

Jake has physical therapy today and I want to go with him. He has been going for weeks now and you can finally see the progress. He tries harder when I am there which is part of the reason I try not to miss going, but some days his appointments are in the morning and I just can't swing it. School is still school and even though I stopped skipping it, my mind is still not completely focused, even when I'm there. My last-period teacher is the most understanding and usually lets me leave so I can make it in time to Jake's sessions as long as I complete my assignments.

Jake has a variety of sessions at Brooks, the rehabilitation facility. He likes some of them and others he hates. The flexibility training with Mark is his least favorite and he has an hour-long session today. Last time he left almost in tears with Mark accusing him of not trying hard enough. He is a tough-love kind of therapist but I don't think that is working with Jake's state of mind right now.

I walk in the front door and Lila, the receptionist, greets me by my first name and tells me where they are working today. I smile and wave at her and the other staff that I find on my way to Jake. I am about to open the door to room 3B when I hear Mark's voice coming through the door.

"Jake, you need to breathe. Your leg won't move unless you give it oxygen."

"Don't tell me to breathe when you don't know how much this shit hurts. It feels like my leg will snap in half." Jake practically growls at him. I can tell he is in a mood just by the way his voice carries, and who can blame him? He has gone through hell these past few weeks and he is still not completely healed.

"I do know what it is like, but that is beside the fact that you are in charge of your recovery and right now you are only giving me thirty percent. I need at least eighty today, Jake."

"Oh, you know? Do you know what it's like to have everything gone in the blink of an eye due to an injury? My willingness to work goes beyond what I can physically endure. You manhandling patients doesn't give you an insight on what it is like."

"We can have the conversation on how much I know or don't know after you do ten more reps—end of discussion. I am not your psychologist. Different type of therapy here."

"Fucking Jerk," I hear Jake mumble, and then grunt which leads me to believe this bickering back and forth is over so I finally step inside the room. Mark doesn't seem surprised to see me but Jake does. I don't understand why, he knows I try to make every afternoon appointment . I didn't mention that I was coming today but it still shouldn't be a surprise.

He finishes his session, Mark helps him back into the wheelchair and pushes him out into the yard. I walk by him but we are both quiet. This is not the comfortable silence that we are both used to, this is more of a ticking-time-bomb silence. Any amount of pressure will set it off. And the worst part? I have no clue what happened.

After Mark leaves, I wait a few minutes to ask what is happening. But before I can say anything, Jake says my name in a sad whisper. Now my heart's already breaking by just hearing the emotion in his voice.

"What is it, Jake?" I ask, holding his hand and practically kneeling in front of him.

He can't even look me in the eyes before he starts talking, "We need to talk, Allie."

Allie, not honey, not baby, *Allie.*

"Did you accept Stanford yet?" he asks without hesitation.

Stanford? What the fuck? Is this what's wrong? "No, I have not. I am considering declining and just taking UF's acceptance."

"Why?" he deadpans, this time looking at me straight in my eyes. Finding deeper parts of me that only he can reach with just a look. He's frowning right at me and his eyes are carrying so many emotions. The empath in me immediately feels my heart constricting. Sadness, hopelessness, shame. I have never seen him look like that before and my gut is telling me that I won't like where this conversation goes.

"Because I want to be close to you, especially now. I am going to school to be a teacher, I can teach anywhere, even if it's here in Baker." I answer his question, really hoping not to break apart, before letting him tell me where his mind is at.

"What about Teach for America? What about traveling to see the world? How is staying here letting you do that?"

"I am not dying here, babe. I can still do that. *We* can still do that. You just have an injury, Jake. Your life is not over, but with me staying here and going to UF, I can help if needed."

"I'm not going to college!" Jake snaps at me in a voice that I've never heard from him before. A mix of anger and frustration.

"What? Why?"asking completely dumbfounded at his statement. "You might not be able to play but you can still go to school."

"How, huh? Or did you forget that I had a scholarship?" Breathing heavily, rubbing his eyes, and pausing for a second before he continues, "They just sent me the email last night saying that I can still go, but I would have to pay for it. I can't afford that."

"Oh, I didn't think about that." I try to hold his hands, but he is quick to snatch them from me.

"Yeah, not everyone is the two percent, Allie," he bites back.

"That's not fair, Jake. You know that's not how I think," I add, holding back my tears.

"Exactly! You don't even have to think about how the rest of the world pays for shit. Not everyone has a rich daddy who can save them from real-life responsibilities."

"Jake," I snap at him, "I know you are hurting and I am so sorry you got that email but please don't be mean. This is not who you are."

"Well, maybe I am. Maybe this is the new me," he continues, "I've officially lost everything, Allie. *Everything.*"

"You haven't lost me, Jake. You still have me."

He laughs and I cannot take the whiplash I'm getting from his reactions. I get closer to him and try to hold his hands again, this time he lets me.

"You need a whole man, Allie, not a crippled one that can't even go to college. I will never be able to give you the life you deserve. The life you need."

"You are all I need. You don't need to go to college. There are trade schools. There are so many options." I'm not able to control my tears this time. They are slowly trickling down my cheeks but I am not able to stop them. I wonder what the people around us think is happening. Do they think he is sick or do they know he is breaking me apart word by word? Do they know he is taking every piece that is keeping me together? Can they hear it? Because pain like this should be seen, heard, and felt. These words that he is delivering casually have the power to start a fire.

"You may think that now but when all your family is partying abroad and we can't go because I make nothing, it won't be enough. When you want to spend hundreds of dollars on a purse and you have to budget, it won't be enough."

"Jake, you will be enough!"

"I WON'T!" he screams, not even looking around to see who might be watching. Not caring one bit about how he is breaking my soul. "How can you say that I will always be enough when you haven't even loved anyone before? No one had even fucked you before me, Allie, and you want to tell me that I will be enough, above everything else. I think it sounds delusional and one of us needs to be rational here." He lands another blow.

"But I love you, Jake. Please—" sob, "please—" sob, "don't—" sob.

Interrupting me he continues, "We are young and it was great while it lasted but I think we are through. Don't beg. It's not a good look on you. There is no point in even keeping this going. Go home, email Stanford and tell them yes. Fly there and forget about me. Forget about this town, and live your dreams."

"Jake, stop it, please," I say between another sob. "I love you and I know you love me too," the tears are everywhere; I am done trying to control them at this point. "We can figure this out, babe." I'm wiping my face as much as I can without hurting my skin.

"Maybe, but you deserve more and I am not going to be the placeholder while you figure it out. This life is enough for me, but it will never be enough for you or your family. It's done. We are done." He stares at me while I hold in the rest of my sobs with both my hands, blinking rapidly, not even knowing what else to say. I am ready to beg him, again, not to do this when he says, "Go home, there is nothing else for you here."

I can't hold it in anymore, so I run away from him. I run away from this place. I run until I make it to my SUV, and drive as fast as I can go. I drive for what seems like hours, listening to songs that help keep the tears from falling because what else is there to do? Letting my tears run freely, gripping the steering wheel as tight as I can, I see the sunlight turn into dusk. The sky looks exactly as I feel, turning my desperation into darkness along with the light.

Eventually, the gas light turns on, signaling to me that life goes on, no matter how broken I feel. I make it home and go straight to my room. In the darkness I find comfort and let myself cry until there are no more tears left.

CHAPTER THIRTY-FOUR

Allie

NOW

Champagne Problems, Taylor Swift

Mondays are usually my favorite day of the week. It is like a fresh start. My little reminder that not everything is doomed and you get a do-over. I know many full-time working people love Fridays because of the weekends but have you ever worked with kids? By Fridays, you are exhausted and I find it to be the same in this professional development job. Today is a special kind of Monday because I am working at Baker Elementary this week to train their staff in a new multi-modal reading program. I never went to Baker Elementary since I didn't grow up here but so many of the people I met in high school did.

Jake had to be at work early so he already left and I didn't even get a chance to tell him that I was working right in town. Last week I took some time off and worked from home so maybe he just assumed it would be the same this week. He usually is very on top of asking me about work, but Saturday was so busy with errands, tattoos, and Nick's birthday. Yesterday, Jake spent most of the day with Nick making up for leaving his birthday celebration early, so I barely got to see him. I can't wait to see him tonight and tell him all about my day.

I leave the room and find the coffee pot on, a bagel by the toaster, and a note from Jake telling me to have a good day and to toast the bagel. I adore the way that he cares for me, even when he's not here. These little details are the things that stayed with me even when I wanted to forget it all. Taking my cup of coffee back to the room, I finish getting dressed. A loose above-the-knee dress with a dainty flower pattern and bubble sleeves is the winner for today. My curls are down, and for the first time since I've been back in Florida, they are somewhat tamed. I add a clip on the back to take some of them off my face. Going back out into the kitchen, I pour myself more coffee into a to-go cup, finish the bagel that I left on the counter, and head to work.

"Hi, I'm Ms. Z. I'm here for some meetings with Mr. Ryan today," I tell Lisa, according to the nameplate on her desk. I'm smiling and looking around trying not to look as nervous as I am right now. No matter how much I do my job, I still get nervous when I start with a new school or new teachers and today I get to do both. Mr. Ryan walks into the yellow-painted front office and takes me back to the teachers' workplace.

He explains that they often do Professional Learning Communities (PLCs) in the lead teacher's classroom and asks if I am comfortable with running them on my own. Nothing new for me so I am happy to follow along. PLCs are my favorite way to share tidbits with teachers because they have the meetings already planned. When I taught, I hated losing planning time in weekly meetings. So I love it when I get to work with teachers during those times instead of adding to their schedules with extra meeting days.

This new program I am presenting today is one of my favorites that my company offers. It gives the teachers data on the students' progress, every week. Things like fluency and vocabulary acquisition, which are so hard to assess in a full classroom, are assessed weekly on this program. Having a team working together makes a huge impact in students' progress. I couldn't have imagined having this much support when I was in the classroom.

My day goes fast and before I know it, it's 2:00 pm and I only have one more grade level to attend. I am meeting with the second grade last and I am pumped. Second grade was my favorite grade level to teach, so I cannot wait to share with these teachers all the tools at their disposal with this program. I love knowing they will be able to take the kids to the next level, ready for deeper multi-syllabic words and comprehension.

Looking at the map, I search for Mrs. Clarke's room. Room 212 on the right. It has been so easy to navigate because the floor plans of this school are almost the same as the high school. I haven't set foot in those halls since I was seventeen but I could never forget them.

I find her classroom empty, yet I still walk in and start setting up my small station. I love bringing multiple samples with me to the first meetings to get a feel for what the teachers may or may not like. I bring pens and stickers with me too because who doesn't love free swag? I continue setting up and grab my phone to shoot Jake a text.

He doesn't often reply right away. I have a feeling that he is all in with his students, the same way that he is all in with me and all in with everything that he does. I have never met a person more present than him.

> **Future Husband:** The offensive line is off today so my practice will be shorter. I'll see you soon. 143

I freeze looking at the numbers on that text. He has not only told me he loves me but then he goes and writes 143 in there? Like that won't make me have palpitations. Like I will be able to breathe easy afterward. There is no doubt in my mind that I love him. I always have and I always will but do I reply with the numbers too? Knowing what they mean to him?

At some point, I have to let go of my fears and finally give in to my heart. Stop punishing myself for the past and embrace the future. We are both adults now and if we want to make this work, we should. It all starts with a step, even if it's not small and it takes every single inch I have to give at this moment but I take it. I take it and I grab the opportunity to love this man wholly, the way I've wanted to for a decade.

> **Me:** 1432

While placing my phone down, I hear steps and look up to see Tasha, right in front of me. Her gorgeous blonde hair looks pristine right now in loose curls. She has on a black dress that fits her incredibly and white tennis shoes, accented with a jean jacket. *I am obsessed with this outfit.* I plan on telling her just that but when I get up and smile at her, her blue eyes turn icy as she walks towards me and takes a seat at the desk. I turn around to face her, confusion in my eyes but before I can say anything she opens up her journal and a pen and says, "I'm listening, get started."

"Hi, Tasha! I didn't know you were a teacher! How cool."

"You never knew what anyone else wanted to do with their lives other than you and Cara. So are you really surprised that you didn't know I wanted to teach?" Her tone is harsh and I don't understand why. She is talking to me like you would talk to the mean socialite that took the job you wanted without deserving it.

She stares me down, leaving me no choice but to apologize. "I'm sorry, high school was such a blur, sometimes I forget details. Take your name, for example, I completely forgot your last name is Clarke," I say.

"Oh, it wasn't when we knew each other." She continues sneering before adding, "I took my husband's last name and it was a bigger hassle to change it when we divorced. The kids were already used to calling me Mrs. Clarke so I kept it."

"Neat! I mean, not about the divorce but about you being able to keep it. I am sorry about the divorce though."

"Yeah right, I'm sure it opened the door wide open for you to crush his soul. *Again,*" she bites.

And until then, I had not put two and two together.

I gasp and she smiles, "Oh you poor thing, you didn't know? I guess he *can* keep secrets from you after all. Here I thought I was the only collateral damage from your fucked up love story."

"Wh- wh- what are you talking about?" I am aghast by her words and the delivery. My train of thought is completely lost and if Tasha notices she doesn't care because she continues.

"Jake. He was a wreck after you left. We all saw him lose himself. He did end up in college but he fucked his way through it. Women, alcohol, parties, you name it. He even stopped going to football games. One day, he finally snapped out of it and we all started seeing the Jake we knew come back to us," she continues with her voice getting more irritated. "You see, we all knew and loved him before you came and destroyed him. You were a wrecking ball in his life and smashed everything in your path, but he eventually got over you or so we all thought."

We stare at each other for another minute but she continues not letting me get a word in. "I will skip the way we fell in love with each other because I do believe he loved me, in his own broken way. But there was no competing with you in his heart. He tried, oh how he tried, but it was almost like he was looking for you in empty places. Like he was lonely even with people around him because you took his heart, dropped it, stomped on it, and never gave it back. Eventually, I got tired of living in your shadow. I got tired of competing with a ghost."

She takes a breath and when I think she is done she adds, "You did a number on him, Allie, and I never thought it could be mended. Seeing him with you again on Saturday proved me wrong. He was just too broken for anyone *but* you. So yeah, your love story—" she says with air quotes "—fucked more than just the two of you. I hope you know that. And if you didn't, I am damn glad to be the one to tell you."

That is what it takes for the tears to start falling, and for me to lose every single word I know other than, "Excuse me." Somehow, between broken sobs, I make it to the bathroom with my heart breaking all over again.

CHAPTER THIRTY-FIVE

Jake

THEN

Heart Like Yours, Willamette Stone

The minute Allie left, my tears started falling. I was beyond cruel, but how else would I get her to understand that I am not good enough anymore? Before this injury, I didn't have much to offer, but at least I had potential. How do I let her waste her heart on a man that I don't even *like* anymore? A man that I don't recognize anymore. Mark found me in the garden, still crying, an hour later, and called my mom. The fact that I am eighteen, and these doctors still call my parents is beyond me.

As I lay in bed thinking about today, and how I managed to fuck my whole life in these past weeks. I went from having everything to being completely detached from it all. I just want to go to sleep and wake up when this is all over. Before I attempt to do that, I make the mistake of looking at my phone. I see a line of texts and missed calls. This damn town that can't mind their own business. Everyone is so nosy. It annoys the hell out of me. I don't have time for this now, nor do I want to deal with it, so I click the button on the side of my phone, turn that shit off, and go to sleep.

A week passes before I attempt to deal with real life. I go to physical therapy and back to the house. I don't answer the door for anyone, and I am pretty sure my parents argue about me every single day. I can hear their muffled arguments behind closed doors, but honestly, I don't care anymore.

I thought my life had meaning beyond football and my friends, but that was true only before Allie. Thinking about never seeing her again might be breaking me more than anything else, but I managed to mess that up too. There is no way I can fix the words that I said to her. I can't just patch it up with an apology and call it a day.

My phone buzzes on my nightstand, so I pick it up and see a text thread with Nick, Cole, and Billy.

Nick: Dude, stop moping and just call her.

Cole: If I have to hear Cara saying that she will kill you again, I might cut your balls off myself. Allie is heartbroken bro and she doesn't deserve it. You should see her, she is like a shell.

Nick: Honestly, you don't deserve this shit either. Whatever happened, fix it.

Billy: I still don't know what you did to fuck up the best thing that has ever happened to you. We could all see how lost you were in her so I know that it wasn't anything dumb like cheating.

Cole: No, it was worse. He told her that she didn't know what she wanted and that he was done with her.

Nick: WTF

Billy: Why?!

Cole: Who knows, that's all Cara has told me.

Nick: We can see that everyone read the messages, asshole. Just reply or answer the damn phone.

I don't know why I finally decided to reply today. Why not all of the other hundreds of messages I have? I had no problems ignoring everything else. Maybe it is seeing that even the boys think that Allie is not okay. I knew Cara was pissed. She let me know herself as soon as I'm sure Allie called her, and every day after.

> **Me:** I will text Allie. Get off my back.

> **Cole:** DO NOT TEXT HER MAN. You wanna be dead? Go to her. Show your face and apologize like the man you are. This ain't you, we all know it, it's time for her to know it too.

> **Me:** And if she brushes me off?

> **Nick:** Then you show her every minute of every day how you feel about her until she forgives your ass. I would do the same for Natalie. When you know, you know man.

When you know you know. And damn it, if I don't already know. I knew the moment I met her that she was special, and the more I got to know her, the more I wanted to know the real her. I am so out of her league, but she still gave me a chance. She gave *us* a chance, and now I am not missing any chances and letting her go.

She said she wanted to figure out where we go from here, and maybe I should let her. Maybe, this once, I get to be selfish and take what she is offering. I would have to find a way for her to live her dreams still. You can't cover up a firefly and pretend they can shine just as brightly. I refuse to be the shadow that covers her light.

I pull my body from the bed, using my arms, to get on the chair. I wheel myself to the bathroom to take a shower, wash all the funk away, and head to my girl's house, to try and get her back.

CHAPTER THIRTY-SIX

Allie

NOW

The Last Time (Taylor's Version), Taylor Swift ft. Gary Lightbody & Drunk Me, Mitchell Tenpenny

By the grace of everything that is above, I was able to finish my meetings. After my crying session, I returned to her classroom and pushed through the worst training session of my career. Tasha's smirk at the end was not lost on me, she took pleasure in making me uncomfortable. She took pleasure in seeing me cry at work. I never thought of her as cruel, but according to her, I never thought of her at all.

Jake was married, is all I can think about on the way to his house. Funny how I called this place home in my head, multiple times, but now it is suddenly *his* house. Do I even know this man? Why would he hide something like this from me? *Breathe, Allie, breathe.*

I am determined to not let my emotions drive my reactions more than they already have. Yes, I was surprised, and still am, but I am sure there is a reason why he didn't tell me. Of course, I didn't expect him to be celibate, but the fact that he didn't even mention that he was married before does bother me. I am not going to act like a seventeen-year-old right now, and I will talk to him about this.

After arriving at the house, I take a shower, wash my hair, and put on comfortable clothes. There is something about washing my hair after a day of feeling like the world hates me, that makes it feel less heavy. Right now, I need to remove all the weight I can off my shoulders before I talk to Jake.

I have been sitting on the couch, trying to read, but not being able to make any progress for a couple hours, when the door opens and Jake walks through. Jake, with his perfect smile that can light up a room. He holds a couple of grocery bags in his hands, places them on top of a table, and walks straight to me. He always does this, and lets everything go as soon as he sees me. He makes me feel like nothing else matters but me. Like I am all he can see, and that nothing else is as important as having me in his arms, as soon as he can, for as often as he can. Then why, oh why, did he keep this from me?

The second his hands touch mine, and he truly looks in my eyes, he can see right through the fake smile I am wearing. His eyebrows scrunch in a frown. His gaze darkens and he asks, "What's wrong?" He's waiting for my reply, and searching my eyes, as he sits next to me without dropping my hand. He shows me patience with his silence. He shows me that he would wait for ages if needed, for me to tell him what is on my mind.

"I went to work on-site today. We didn't get a chance to talk yesterday, so it slipped my mind to tell you."

"Okay? Are you hurting? Was it too soon to go back to work?" he says worriedly.

"No, not really. They assigned me to Baker Elementary. I spent all day working with the teachers there." I pause when I notice the color leaving his face before adding, "With *all* of them."

He breathes heavily and closes his eyes. I can see his throat bobbing as he swallows. His body immediately tenses, he opens his eyes, and says, "You talked to Tasha didn't you?"

"I did. Jake, why didn't you tell me? I was so blindsided by that information, and that wasn't even the worst of it."

"What did she do? I was trying to avoid leaving you alone with her at all costs. It is part of the reason I pulled you away from the crew on Saturday."

"You still didn't answer my question, Jake. Why? Why didn't you tell me?" I ask, my voice breaking as the first tear falls.

"God, baby, please don't cry," he says, and I swear I can hear the panic in his voice. His hand comes up, wiping my tears away, and keeping it right on my cheek. This just makes me even more upset, so I shake my face away from him.

"Do not make this about me, Jake."

"Allie," he sighs.

"Don't *Allie* me, either. I asked a simple question." My tone is anything but friendly. I am done dancing around this. I want answers, and he is purposely trying not to give them to me. *I hate that*. It is almost like the lie is worse now. Omission and now evasion.

"When was a good time to tell you that I got married, Allie?" He pauses briefly and I assume he is done, but he continues, "You walked back into my life, and it was both like no time had passed, and like a century had gone by between the last time I saw you and now. When should I have brought that up? Sometime in between me losing you, and you coming back to me? How about the moment I saw you at the airport? Or how about when I practically showed you how fucking gone for you I am? I never stopped loving you. Trust me, I tried, but I failed at that, too."

His voice turned thunderous and shaky at the same time. Like he is holding on to every ounce of restraint he can. He is showing me his pain, but you can tell that he did not want to go there. Like the gentleman he is, he is putting me first again, and letting me in.

"Jake," I try to whisper but it comes out more stern than I hoped for. It sounds like I'm upset when in reality, I am hurting. I am hurting for me, but also for him. For this beautiful man, that has loved me for years, even when he didn't want to. Even when he shouldn't have. I thought my actions only affected him for a few years, but maybe they did more than that. Clearly, it's been so much longer, apparently the whole time we were apart. I owe him at the very least to listen to him now. I stay quiet while letting him gather himself and continue. He doesn't though. The man who keeps talking is not *my* Jake, but a very angry version of him.

"At first, I tried to get you back. I was hurt when you first left. And I didn't even attempt to ask you to stay. Then, I was pissed. I drank. I partied. I fucking did it all, to try to get you out of my mind, all while still recovering from the injury. I didn't come home some days. I didn't eat. I was a wreck, because how are you supposed to move on from the love of your life?" he sighs, "I finished college and started teaching here. I found purpose again, but I was numb if I wasn't coaching or in the classroom."

"One day, the boys and I got drunk at Sadler's. When I woke up the next day, there was a blonde in my bed, and all I wanted was to see caramel skin and soft curves there. I didn't remember shit, but every message on my phone said how glad they were that I was finally enjoying myself. That blonde, as you might guess, was Tasha. That one night turned into another one, and another night turned into more."

"I don't want the details on how you fell in love with someone else, Jake," I snap back.

"What the fuck was I supposed to do, Allie? Wait? For what? For you to finally show up again? Because I fucking waited, Allie. I waited for years before I let my guard down again. I waited for years before I realized that you told me you were better off without me, and you meant it. I am not going to sit here and apologize for attempting to move on!" he shouts.

"I DON'T WANT YOU TO APOLOGIZE!" I practically scream at him, getting up from the couch, stomping into his bedroom, and slamming the door. I start moving all my stuff that I can find into a pile. Tears falling down my face. I am shaking, unable to control my breath. If I don't get myself in check, I will be useless soon. I take a moment, close my eyes, and practice my breathing. In, *one, two, three, four. Out, one, two, three, four, hold.*

Jake walks into the room, and I snap my eyes open. Closing the door behind him he says, "I am not done with this conversation, Allie. Do you want to know why I never told you? Buckle up, because you're about to find out. I am tired of not sharing every part of me with you, and I am tired of waiting for you to be brave enough to share every part of you with me. So I'll go first. I'll be brave enough. I will put my heart on the line again. I will lay it all out, and then, you can scream at me if you want. Even though you have no reason to."

With that, he sits on the edge of his bed and pats the spot next to him. I sit beside him but as far away as I can be without falling off the bed. He wants me to sit here and listen to his love story with someone else. Fine, but I don't have to be near him while he does. I wipe my eyes and look at him, "Go ahead," I say.

"In the beginning, I didn't date Tasha, I fucked her. I fucked her the same way that I fucked many women after you. I used her the same I did them, to try to fill the void you left. It wasn't fair to them and I wasn't the man that I had been, but I lost sight of who I was when my lifeline was taken away from me. I justified the way that I used her by saying I was trying to get over you. One day, she called me out on my bullshit. I felt like an asshole, so I told her I was done with the mindless sex and that I wanted to take her out on a date. So we went. She was kind of fun. She was funny, kind, and sassy. Which I am sure you know. She was entertaining too. After a few dates, we fell into a comfortable friendship of sorts."

He pauses and looks at me. Then gets up and leaves the room. Leaving me in ominous silence. *Who does that?!* He comes back holding a glass of wine in one hand, and a beer in the other one. He hands me the wine and sets his beer on a coaster on the nightstand. The room has warm lighting that usually makes it feel cozy, but right now, it feels threatening. Unwelcoming. He removes his shoes, sits across from me on the bed, and grabs his beer.

After a swig of his beer, he continues, "I never really thought of her as my girlfriend. Every time I thought I could let my guard down and call her that, your name would come to mind and I couldn't do it. After months of stringing her along, she finally snapped and asked me to label things. She cried and I would've done almost anything to make her stop because, at that point, I did care about her. I guess in the midst of it all, I started healing my wounds. I told her I was serious about her, and we moved in together. She didn't want to live in this house, so I moved in with her and rented this house out. At some point, it became bearable to share my everyday life with her, so I married her."

I am looking at him sharing all of this, and I can tell he is hurting. This hurts him but it hurts me too. It's like seeing him fall in love with someone who is not me. The pieces of my heart I thought were glued back together, crumbled all at once. Like a sand castle being washed away by a wave.

"We had a routine. Wake up, work, come home, eat dinner, fuck, go to sleep. Every. Single. Day. We would hang out with Nick and Natalie, and some of the other guys, but that was it. We shared no interests. We had no long conversations. No new topics to discuss. Eventually, it became a chore. Living with her felt like a job, so I drank to try to feel something. I drank every night just so I could tolerate her because even though she was a good woman, she was not you. I don't think I ever even loved her, and I am sure she knew it too."

"One day after work, she found me drinking, and tried to kiss me hello but I turned my face. I could barely even look at her at this point, let alone kiss her. She ran crying to the room, and when I went to try to stop her, the words that came out of my mouth were, *Allie, wait.*"

I gasped, loudly. Covering my mouth to try to contain my sobs and my surprise, I look at him. He is crying too. Barely noticeable but you can see he is torn. He is not looking at me anymore but at the bottle in his hand.

"I didn't have it in me to go after her. I didn't deserve her forgiveness, not after that. It was then that I realized that I had become everything that I said I would never be, and she deserved better. She thought that maybe I was cheating on her, but what she didn't know was that I'd never chosen her. I had always been in love with you, since the first moment I saw you, and there was never room for anything else. There was never room for anyone else. Because she thought something was going on, she grabbed my phone and looked for your name. She couldn't find a contact, but she found you in the texts that I never deleted. She saw that your number was saved on my phone as *Future Wife*, and lost it. She packed my stuff and kicked me out. We got divorced a few months later."

I keep crying silently. Listening to this man bare his soul to me. Listening to how much I *actually* fucked his life up, beyond what I ever considered and probably beyond repair. He seems to be done, and because I don't know how to stop pouring salt over wounds, I say "I still don't know how we could be doing whatever this is when you kept something like that from me!"

"You are one to talk about keeping things hidden!" he yells and I flinch. "I'm sorry Allie, but fuck! How can you in good conscience say that to me, huh? At least you asked and I answered, When will I get my answers? When will you finally tell me what drove you away from me? What did I do that was so unforgivable that you had to disappear from my life and leave me with nothing but dust."

We stare at each other but I just shake my head and look down. He moves towards me and lifts my chin with his finger.

"Look at me, Honey. Please be honest with me. Just tell me what I did," he says with the most broken tone I have ever heard before.

"You didn't do anything, Jake."

"Then why the fuck did you leave me?! If I wasn't enough, if this town wasn't enough, why did you come back? Why did you let me open my heart and my life up to you again? If you were just planning on packing your bags and never looking back again, you are more cruel than I thought you were." He gets up and walks away from me.

Seeing him walk away is heartbreaking. Mind-altering. I am panicking so I yell, "I DID IT FOR YOU!"

He stops but doesn't turn his body and between sobs, I add, "I left because I loved you. Everything that I did after the day I last saw you, I did it for you!"

CHEER

CHAPTER THIRTY-SEVEN

Allie

THEN

Afterglow, Taylor Swift

Have you ever walked through life feeling like you lost all purpose? Like suddenly everything that you thought mattered, doesn't anymore? My mom tells me every day how worried she is about me. I barely eat, I don't sleep, and with the amount of times that I cry each day you would think I would've run out of tears by now, but they keep coming. Cara is ready to kill Jake, but she is worried that it might hurt me more.

My room smells like death. Containers of leftovers are piled everywhere. I won't even let Rosalia come in and clean. If I could just close my eyes and sleep until my heart stops hurting, I would. If I wasn't terrified of the way my dad would react, I would ask for something to take this pain away.

There is a firm knock on my door but before I can yell to leave me alone, the last person that I am expecting walks in, my dad. I sit up and stare at him in a daze, wondering what in the actual fuck is he doing here. He usually doesn't step one foot in any of our rooms. It's almost like we are beneath him, and other than my mom, we are undeserving of his time. This is his world, and we are all just living in it. He makes sure we feel it, too. He does something even more surprising, and sits on my bed, looking at me with tender eyes.

"Hola, mi niña." *Hi, my girl.*

"Bendición papi," *Blessings Daddy,* I reply–such a Dominican thing to say but it means so much to my parents. They take pride in knowing that their kids keep the traditions, even if sometimes it's just a word.

"I wanted to come in and check on you. Your mom is really worried about you. She said you haven't even left your room. That's not like you, mi niña."

This is the second time he calls me his girl and he usually doesn't talk to me like that unless he is trying to sugarcoat something.

"I'm just going through a lot right now, Papi. I'll be okay though. Te lo prometo." *I promise.*

"Why don't you tell me what's going on?" he says.

"Because it is about Jake, Papi. I know you hate him, and I don't want to add more to that feeling."

"I want to know what's bothering you. Just tell me. Chances are, what I am thinking is worse than what he did, so tell me."

So I do. I tell him everything. I tell him about how much I love Jake. I tell my dad about how Jake makes me feel and how he treats me. I tell dad about Jake's injury and how he lost his scholarship. I tell him about how it broke my heart knowing that Jake wouldn't be able to attend college. I tell him about how Jake broke my heart.

Dad lets me finish without uttering a word, also unlike him. Once I am done showing him all my cards, he rubs his face and looks down. I can see he has something to tell me and I have never seen him hesitate to share, so this must be important.

"What is it?" I ask.

"Allie, what do you want with this boy?" he asks.

"Honestly, Papi? I thought he was the one. I thought we were going to be together forever, but apparently, he didn't feel the same way," in between sobs I continue, "I only want what's best for him though. I wish he could continue with whatever is left in his life without feeling like he lost it all."

"What if I tell you that there is a way that he can still go to college? I can't promise you he will be able to move on with everything else, but at least he can have that. I know his family can't afford it and he won't let them go into debt."

"How do you know that?"

"Just know that I do," he replies.

"What do you mean there is a way?"

"What if I pay for his college tuition, full ride? He won't have to worry about any college expenses, not even housing or food."

"You would do that?" I ask astounded.

"Si, mi niña." *Yes, my girl.*

"Papi, that would mean the world to me! I can't wait to tell him!" I sit up and practically jolt in excitement, but his expression falters. Confused, I ask him, "What is it? This is great news!"

"The thing is Allie, I don't want you to tell him. My one rule with this is that you don't talk to him again. He hurt you, sweetie, and I don't ever want to see you like this again, or your mom worrying as much as she has these past days."

"Dad, I *will* tell him. How could I not?"

"Then he won't get anything. If you want him to get this, it will be anonymous and you won't see him again. If you break that promise, he will lose the money," he adds like he did not just pour more water over the quicksand.

"Is this you making me choose, Dad? Are you making me choose between him having a future or being with me?"

"I guess I am," he says without any ounce of remorse. "The decision is ultimately yours. Let me know by the end of the week."

With that, he stands up and walks out of my room. Leaving me more shattered than when he found me.

I have been thinking about dad's proposal for the past few days. I have not left my room much and I have zero reasons to leave the house, meaning that all of my time has gone to thinking. My heart wants to tell him to fuck off, but my brain is thinking about what this could mean for Jake and his family. For Jake and his future. Because of his whole *'don't tell anyone about this'* bullshit, I can't even talk to Cara about it. I can't even talk to Jake at all.

My mom came in a while ago and asked me to get dressed and come downstairs. She said it all in Spanish, in her *'I mean business'* voice, and I am not playing with that. She is such a gentle soul so when she is serious and uses that tone, nobody wants to find out what will happen if you don't obey. So here I am, getting out of the pajamas I've lived in since who knows when.

My hair is wet, pulled up in a messy bun. I put on some jean shorts and a tee shirt that is too big for me but extra comfortable. She just said to be out of pajamas, she didn't specify what to wear, so comfortable clothes it is. I head downstairs, straight to the kitchen to get some of Rosalia's snacks before meeting my mom. I am assuming she is either in the studio or in her library.

My mom is a huge snob for books and I am sure that is where I got my love for them too. My dad builds her a library everywhere we move without exception. He hires people to just pack her books and ship them to wherever we are going next. If my mom says she needs an extra room for books, he makes it happen. He may be a dick to us but he sure makes my mom feel like the queen she is.

I find her exactly where I thought she would be—crossing the French doors into a sunlit Florida room, or sunroom as most people call it, with floor-to-ceiling bookshelves. They are full of incredible books, some that I never want to read, and some that I am dying to read. She has a whole system on how I can check out books. She writes her rating in the top corner, the main tropes for the book and the age she thinks is appropriate for me to read. She has a whole shelf full of 'Eighteen or Twenty-One Plus' books that I am salivating over reading but she won't budge. "*I want you to experience real relationships, Allie, before you read about all of these,*" she always says. I know that most of them are spicy books but it is not that much different than health class or what happens at parties, or at least I don't think so.

She sits on a recliner, facing the doors, with her back to the large windows. She has a blanket over her legs and she's sipping on her coffee with a book open on her lap. Across from her, there is a large lounging chair–*wait, there is someone there.* When I take a better look, I find Jake sitting in the chair. Leg propped up and his wheelchair next to him. He is looking down at what seems to be a book.

They are both so lost in whatever they are reading, that they don't notice me standing there completely blown away by what I am seeing. I clear my throat, signaling to them that there's someone here and Jake startles. My mom, on the other hand, doesn't even look up from her book. She sips her coffee one more time, closes her book, places it on the table next to her, and gets up from the recliner. She walks towards me, coffee in hand, and a gloomy look on her face.

She kisses me on the cheek and whispers, "I hope you make the right choice." She walks away with my thoughts and closes the double doors.

Looking at Jake, I see the torment in his eyes. Why is he the one looking like *that* when I am the one carrying the weight of the world on my shoulders? Then I remember that the main reason I have been crying and heartbroken did not start with my dad's proposal but with Jake breaking my heart. Now I am mad all over again.

"What are you doing here, Jake?"

"Can we talk?" he asks with his puppy eyes. How can you even say no to that?

However, I don't reply and just stare at him, waiting. He points to the recliner my mom was sitting in, and I take a seat. "I'm listening," I say.

"Allie, I don't even know where to start. There are no excuses for how I acted and the things I said to you the other day. I've been sick to my stomach thinking about it."

"Uh-huh."

"I wish I could say that I can't believe I said those things to you, but I can. I was a complete asshole to you and you didn't deserve that. But I have been hurting a lot. It's not an excuse for how I treated you, but pain clouded my judgment. You know I love you, more than words can even describe. I am just going through a lot right now and I thought I was doing the honorable thing by letting you go." Tears are streaming down his face but he continues, "The only thing that I did was break both our hearts in the process. I came here today to apologize and to beg you to take me back."

Silence. Deafening silence. Heartbreaking silence. Earth-shattering silence. I've been praying for these words to come, but now with the decision I have to make, I'm not sure I want to hear them anymore. Now I am in the spot I never wanted to be in. Choosing him or choosing my heart. I can't have both. If I tell him right now that I love him and that we will conquer all the challenges of life, what will happen to him? Will he be able to follow what's left of his dreams? If I tell him that I am done, then he gets his future, but he doesn't get *me*. Tears fall down my face now.

"Oh Allie, please don't cry. Don't cry anymore for me, please. Please let me back in, Honey. I love you and I will do everything I can to show you, every day, for the rest of my life and in whatever comes next."

At that moment, I finally get clarity. There is never going to be a winner here. We lose either way. But I can't be selfish. I can't let this good man lose everything he has always worked for. He deserves the world, even if I am not in it.

"Jake, sorry won't fix it. Just telling me you apologize is not going to change things, it will not erase the things that you said."

"I know, Honey, I know. But I will die trying to show you how much I didn't mean it. I will prove to you over and over again how much you mean to me. You are all I need, let me show you that I can be exactly what you need, too." He sounds desperate. Broken. Sad.

Looking up, past Jake, through the glass doors, I see my dad. He is standing, leaning on the counter, wearing a dark suit with his eyes focused on me. The minute he sees me staring back at him, he raises an eyebrow, and I know what he is wondering.

What are you going to do, Allie?

I take a breath, close my eyes briefly, and when I look back at him nod. To let him know with that small gesture, that I'll do what he says, as long as he can keep his end of the deal. Un contrato con el diablo. *A deal with the devil.*

"I know you are hurting, Jake. I can see it, I can feel it. I'm not going to lie, what you said to me hurt, and it still does, but it opened my eyes to some things that I do believe were true. I still have a lot of life to live. I also don't think I want to settle in Baker. I want to travel and explore. I want to meet different people. I am not ready to just stay here and live happily ever after." Now it's his turn to look stunned.

If I am about to break his heart, I need to do it in a way that won't give him any hope. I don't want to hurt him, but I need to destroy him, to save him. To give him a future.

"I don't blame you for what you said, I might need to thank you for it. I was willing to let an opportunity like Stanford pass by because I didn't want to leave you, but honestly, this might be what we both need. A clean slate and a fresh start. I love you and I always will but I think this is goodbye." I get up before he can see the tears about to burst from my eyes. I don't know how I was able to hold it in for that long.

Opening the doors, without looking back, I say, "Have a nice life, Jake. It was great having you in mine." Then I run, straight to my dad.

He is waiting and when he sees me, he extends his arms and wraps me up in a hug. We walk outside towards his car. He opens the back door and lets me in, quickly closing the door, and leaving Jake outside, looking absolutely destroyed.

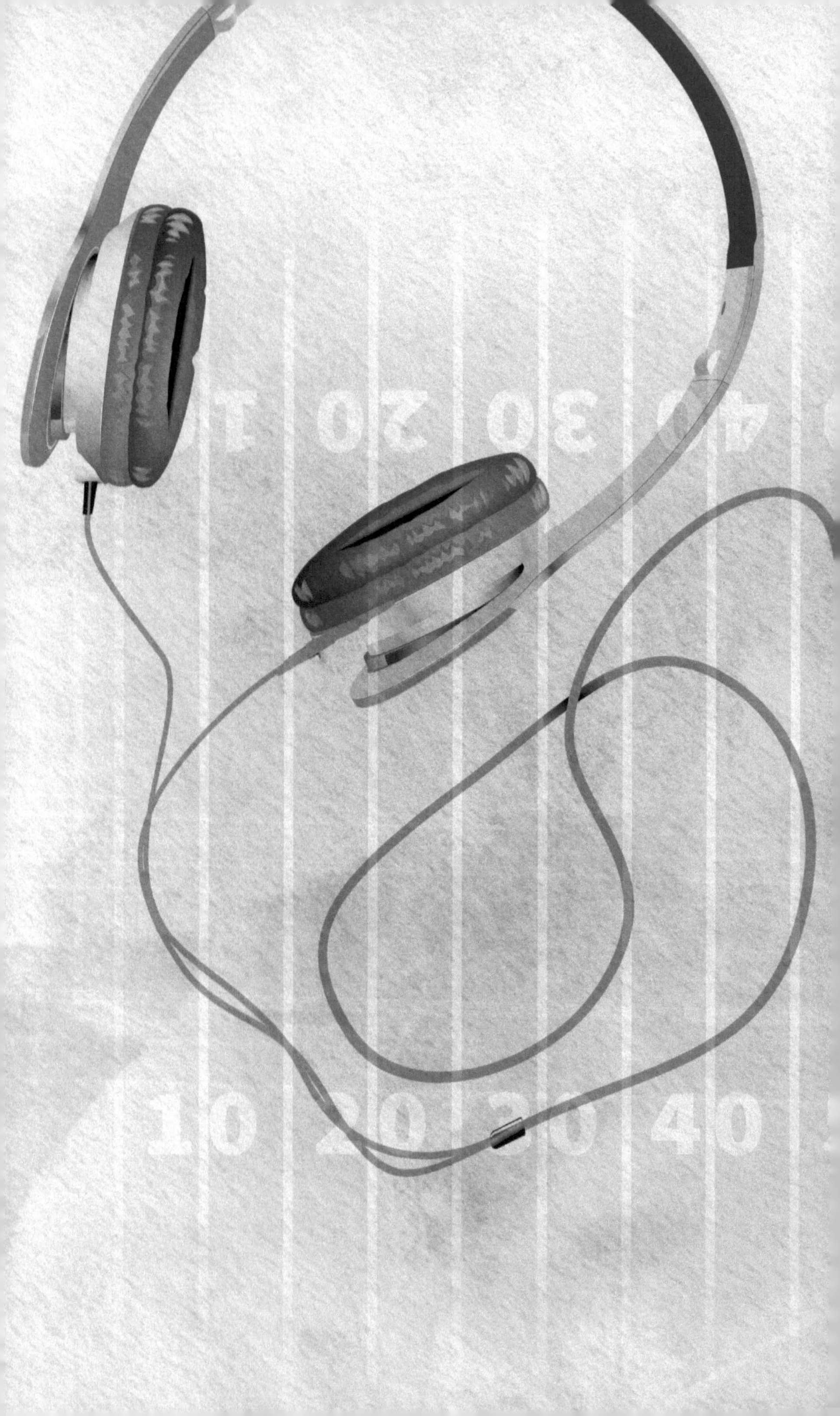

Part Four

MAYBE NEXT TIME, JAMIE MILLER

I THOUGHT YOU WERE IT,
I THOUGHT WE WERE MEANT TO BE.
MAYBE IN ANOTHER LIFE,
YOU'D BE MINE.

PASSPO

Allie

NOW

I Almost Do (Taylor's Version), Taylor Swift

"So yeah, Jake, I did it for you. Maybe at some point in the past few years, I could've reached out again. My dad is trying to make amends for that ultimatum he gave me because after that, he lost me, too. It was never easy to even think about how differently that could've gone. I actually imagined that you were married and had the children you always wanted. Living in your precious town, with a deserving woman. I never thought I would find you single and willing to give me another chance. Willing to fall in love with me again." I sob.

He gets up and walks towards me, wrapping me in his arms. Wrapping me up in him. His hand goes to my head as I lay it right on his chest, and let it all out.

"Shh, Honey, I got you. Let it all out. I am right here," he continues, using a soothing voice and gentle caresses. I let the tears fall and my heart pours out all the angst, fear, and secrets that it has been holding for so long.

"You silly girl, you thought I was willing to fall in love with you again? I never fell out of love, Allie. That was the main issue with everyone else but not with me. I found love in you once, and it never let me go. I belong to you, my Honey, wholeheartedly. There is no love without you in the equation. I fell for you the moment I first saw you, and you, my love, caught me. There is no more falling after you hit solid ground."

He kisses the top of my head then grabs my face with both his hands and pushes me back so he can see me. So I can see *him*. Looking me right in my eyes he says, "You are my solid ground, Honey. Don't let another earthquake break that from us." With that, he kisses me. He kisses like he always does, gentle at first, and then ravenous. Like if the time he has with me is inconsistent, and he won't waste a single moment playing it safe.

His lips go beyond my lips, to my neck, to my collarbone, and my ear. He kisses, licks, and nips like I am dessert and he has a sweet tooth. He starts pulling my dress up and continues to kiss me, on my chest, right below my bra, going down towards my belly button. We should stop to finish the conversation, but I can't seem to gather the strength to make him. "Jake, I—"

"Honey, you can tell me what you want, or I can show you exactly what you need," he says, stopping halfway to my navel and looking up at me with pure lust in his eyes. "Let me show you how well I know you. Let me show you that you are exactly who I want and who I have always needed." His fingers move up to palm my breast. His eyes not leaving mine, he pulls my bra down and takes my nipple in between his index finger and thumb. Rubbing slowly and then pinching hard, he elicits a moan from me. I arch my back and close my eyes, and I swear I can feel his smirk. I shimmy under him and that is all the confirmation he needs before he lowers his head and devours me.

His fingers are teasing and pulling, rubbing, and pinching at my nipples. His tongue is deep in my pussy, licking and teasing my clit.

"Look at you," he rasps, "so fucking wet for me." He lowers his hand from one of my breasts and pushes two fingers into me. He continues licking and rubbing, and I continue squirming.

"More," I whisper.

"So demanding," he snaps back.

He uses his free hand to angle me up, putting his arm under my ass, tilting me more towards his face. The sounds coming out of me are indecent and that seems to fuel him even more. When he curves his fingers inside of me and bites right on my sensitive clit, I lose all control I have and I crash into pleasure. Heat floods over my body and pools in my belly. My skin is tingling with goosebumps everywhere. I shake under him and he doesn't relent. He continues until I am limp against his mouth.

He looks up, undoing his jeans, never taking his eyes off of me for one moment. "God damn, Allie," he says before his mouth is clashing against mine. I can taste myself on him, tangy and somewhat sweet. He smirks against my mouth, almost like he knows what I'm thinking. I want to roll my eyes at him, but instead, he grabs me and flips us over, with me straddling him. My pussy sliding right onto his dick. "Fuck," he growls while looking at me, intensively, passionately.

He can sense I am going to say something about my body. I hate this position because he can see all my curves, soft or not. He can see how my breasts sag and how many stretch marks I have. It makes me self-conscious but with his eyes heating the more he looks at me, it makes me hesitate before I say anything else.

This man has never said anything negative about my body and he looks at me like there is nothing else he would rather look at, like there's no one else. He makes me feel desired and that gives me a funny feeling, all over my body. I put my ankles under his ass, using his muscles for leverage. My hands start to grip his headboard for balance, but he wraps his arm around my back, unclasps my bra, and slides it down off my arms. Forcing my hands to let go of the headboard so he can remove the bra completely. I balance on my knees and gasp when he touches my nipples.

Touching them and fluttering his fingers to my back, he applies pressure, pulling me to him. He can see the hesitation in my eyes. He knows what I am thinking, and what I am feeling before I can even reply. "Allie, unless the words coming out of your mouth are going to be positive about your fantastic curves, your smooth skin, or your delicious ass, save them. You. Are. Fucking. Perfect," he says dragging a nipple into his mouth. Letting it go with a popping noise he adds, "Perfect and *mine*."

Our mouths clash against each other. Licking, sucking, desperate. Silently saying 'sorry and I forgive you'. I start moving with the same rhythm that he set. Matching his cadence, the way my heart is matching his. I push his chest down earning me a scowl and his eyebrows to raise. "My turn, Jake. Let *me* show you how much I want *you*."

"Yes, ma'am," he says, licking his lips.

And I do. I ride him like I am unhinged. My pussy is as wet as it has ever been. I can feel the slickness making filthy, perfect sounds, causing the most delicious friction. He brings his hands to my ass and squeezes hard, making me shiver and moan. "So fucking responsive to me, baby," he says and I show him exactly how responsive I can be.

I increase my tempo, moving to a new rhythm I've never felt before. Showing him how much I want him.

"Eyes on me, Honey. Look at me while you ride my dick."

I do just as he says, letting out a small moan and licking my lips. My eyes on him, his hands on my body, and the way he feels inside of me is too much. "Jake, I—" he knows exactly what I need and places a finger on my clit. Applying the right amount of pressure, making the pool building in my stomach, grow and burn so good at the same time. He can tell I am almost there and with his other hand, pinches my nipple. I am done for. I let out a moan and a gasp when I feel myself contract against him.

I close my eyes, lost in pleasure when I hear him say, "Look at me, Honey, watch me come undone for you." And that he does. I can feel him come inside of me. Filling me up. Making a mess of both of us, not letting go of my eyes for one second.

Our breath catches, our rhythm slows, he pulls me to him and I collapse on top of him. Sated and filled, in more ways than one.

He kisses my cheek, flips me back over, and tells me, "Stay there." He stands up and walks to the bathroom. Comes back out with a small wet rag and a victorious smile.

"Hi," I whisper.

"Hi, back at you. Lay on your back, Honey." I obey, looking at him, wondering what on earth he is doing. He kisses me softly and uses the rag to wipe down every inch of my skin, cleaning up the mess we made together, and my heart flutters. I am not sure why I didn't let him show me before how he could take care of me, but I am tired of letting this man put himself last. I am ready to put him first. If he lets me.

CHAPTER THIRTY-NINE

Allie

NOW

The Alcott, The National Ft. Taylor Swift

I want to get dressed so we can finish the conversation we started but he won't let me. He tells me he needs to go put the groceries away. After a while, he comes back with a bottle of wine, a tray of snacks, and a few beers. He places the food on the bed while I wrap my body in the sheets. I feel completely self-conscious about my naked body, but wearing my clothes doesn't feel right either. Like always, he seems to read my thoughts and notices when I put an arm across my chest. He lowers his body and hands me one of his tee shirts. I put it on and it immediately feels like he is hugging me. His scent enthralls me and it is the best feeling in the world. "Thank you."

"I should be thanking you. I love seeing you wear my clothes. I don't think I will ever get tired of it."

"I love wearing your shirts. Since I was a little girl, I always looked at magazines and movies of girls wearing their husbands' or boyfriends' shirts, but I always thought that was only for smaller girls, not for me. Until you. Makes me feel like I fit, somewhere."

"You just needed to find the right person for you, Honey. You fit right here, with me. You don't need to make yourself smaller, to find comfort in things that you want. You are just the right amount of everything," he says. Making my heart melt even more.

All the anger that I felt when this evening started is gone. My eyes hurt from crying, but I feel content. I feel safe. All I want to do is clear the air and figure out where we go from here. I grab a piece of - *wait, are these potatoes? when did he make these?*, a very crunchy potato skin with cheese and bacon, no sour cream. I take a bite, close my eyes and practically moan at how delicious these are. A little cold but still perfect.

Jake chuckles, "Was I right on getting those, huh?"

"First of all, where did they come from? Second of all, is this a whole plate of just potatoes? Third of all, no sour cream! You are speaking my love language here."

At that, he laughs a little harder and I can see his shoulders relax. "I got them at Publix, when I saw all the types of potatoes they had as sides, I had to get them."

"You don't even like potatoes, Jake."

"But you do."

This man. Who wrote him? Because in real life, they don't come like this. They don't say the perfect thing exactly at the right time. I finish a couple more potatoes and keep drinking the peachy wine that I have come to love. There's a small silence and I know that means one of us is gathering the courage to speak, to ask the hard questions. With questions come answers, and I am not sure if I am ready for them. Not to give them, and not to hear them.

"Allie, I don't want to keep dancing around this. Can we just talk about, well, everything?"

I nod, placing my glass down on the side table. I sit criss-cross, pull my hair up, and tie it with the Invisibobble that never leaves my wrist. I swallow, take a deep breath, and ask, "What do you want to know?"

"No, no, no," he says, shaking his head and his hands. "We are clearing up the whole marriage thing first and then, we can talk about the decision you made, for me, without my input." I sigh and he continues, "What do *you* want to know?"

"Do you love her?" I ask without holding anything back.

"No. Plain and simple. I don't think I ever did. I did care about her though, and I have felt like the shittiest human for years, after what I put her through," he answers honestly.

"How long ago were you guys married and why, when I was probing, asking if I was going to run into someone, you didn't even mention it?" Wow, I really came on strong, holding nothing back.

He chugs his beer and tosses it into the trash bin, landing it right in the middle. He does a little celebration shrug and says, "I was twenty-two when I first got together with her, right after your birthday. We got married the following year and we were divorced by twenty-four," he swallows before he continues, "Everyone in this town knows about our history Allie. About hers and mine. And yours and mine. Very few people will bring it up. Natalie might have, but I know Nick talked to her so I wasn't worried. The two of them are inseparable. I know I hurt Tasha and Natalie was the friend she confided in, so that affected the way she feels about you and me."

Taking a deep breath he finishes, "And Allie, how was I supposed to tell you '*Hey, by the way, I was married to one of your old friends and we might run into her in town*'. I just got you back. Haven't you realized by now that I am willing to do whatever it takes for just another day with you? Hell, for another minute with you? I would give it all up."

"I love you," I say before I can stop it from coming out of my mouth, but what is the point in keeping it in now?

He holds my face with both hands and kisses my lips tenderly. "You have no fucking idea how long I've wondered if you still loved me."

"I never stopped. I loved you then and I love you now, Jake."

"Yeah, but how was I supposed to know? You disappeared on me, Allie."

"I HAD TO," I shout, frustrated again. "Your future was thrust in my hands, Jake. Everything else was already taken from you and I had the chance to give you something back, so I took it."

Putting space between us, he shakes his head and closes his eyes. I can see his jaw clenching and his shoulders rising again. I am losing him, again.

"What was I supposed to do?!"

"You should have asked *me!* You should have let me make that decision with you. I don't care that your dad said you couldn't tell me but you were supposed to trust me. We could've figured something out."

"You had just dumped me Jake. I don't know if you have any idea of how broken I was. For weeks, I barely ate, I was hardly surviving. Then my dad made that proposal and I just wanted to make sure you didn't lose everything," I say, exasperated.

"But I did lose everything, Allie. I lost it all. Yes, I have a career now but I have been numb for years. You were hardly surviving for weeks? I have been in survival mode for ten years. This isn't living, this is barely getting by. You took my life with you when you left. I didn't know I was barely living until you came back, and suddenly the colors are brighter, the grass is greener, the sun is warmer, and the days are longer. You do that to me."

He lets out a big breath and rubbing his eyes he says, "I was just being. I wasn't living. I missed you so damn much, it was fundamental. Not only did my heart miss you but my soul did too. I got a glimpse of what it was like living as a whole when I found you, and then you left and I was only a shell of myself. I can see it even clearer now."

He truly loves me. This sweet, kind, caring man truly loves me. Still. Even after everything. Even after the time that has passed. He loves me. I'm not sure why I am so surprised, he shows me every day how much I mean to him. With his touch, kisses, and longing stares. With the coffee he makes just for me in the mornings. The random texts with songs that remind him of me. The way he cradles me at night. His never-ending patience. He shows me every day.

"I do have a question," he says. He looks unsure like whatever he is about to say might throw us into the fire again. I don't think I can deal with the whiplash of emotions but I'd rather get this over with.

"You left that day and never came back. You didn't finish school, you never replied to my texts and calls. Your social media disappeared, eventually. Your family moved. It was like you never existed, but then, you texted me from the same number, so I know your phone number was always the same. You never blocked me because the text messages went through and so did the phone calls, at least until the last time I tried. It seemed like you just forgot about me."

"I didn't forget about you, Jake. That would be impossible. You also made it really hard to even attempt to move on with all your calls."

"But you never even answered the phone," he says in a defeated voice.

"I know," I reply. I stand up quickly and ask him to give me a second. I go back to the spare room and find one of my suitcases. At the bottom, there is an envelope that I bring with me everywhere I go. Since I travel for work, I don't own much. I have some stuff at Cara's and some stuff with my parents, but everything I own is usually with me. Including this envelope. I grab it from the suitcase and bring it back to Jake's room, handing it to him.

"What is this?" he asks.

I reply with the only answer I have and probably the one he was least expecting, "The whole truth."

CHAPTER FORTY

Allie

THEN

Stick Season, Noah Kahan

It's been months since I left Baker Oaks. My parents were able to get the school to use the credits I had, to finish my transcript and I just didn't walk at graduation. My dad sent me to Europe, to spend the rest of the school year and the summer with my Tia and her family. We traveled, we ate, we cried, we laughed. I was able to spend time with her little ones and, overall, clear my head.

I left Baker Oaks and erased everything about my life there, except Cara. I messaged her to let her know where I was going. And even though I deleted social media and turned off my phone, she knew that I would be back in time to start college with her. We also email now and then, which is nice. She only mentioned Jake a handful of times, but eventually, she got the gist and stopped.

I am ready to go back to the States tomorrow but something in me is not entirely sure I will be okay when I get back. I don't want to go anywhere near Baker Oaks, but I do have to face regular life eventually.

I grab my phone, which I haven't used in months. I have around fifty missed calls and a couple of voice messages, all from Jake. I don't want to deal with this. I don't want to remember the life I thought we could have. I just want to forget it all and start over. I delete the call log and open the voice message list.

There are four messages from him, not a lot compared to the amount of calls he left. But I'm sure they are all about the same thing. I don't want to hear his voice again. I try to swipe left on the first message to delete it, but instead, I accidentally click the play button and his voice comes through my speakers.

Allie, answer the damn phone. I know you are upset and I know I fucked up, but you have to know I didn't mean any of it. You know me better than this, Honey. Is there anything I can do to show you that I meant my apology? I know you said 'Sorry doesn't fix it', but you need to let me try and fix it.

Beep.

His voice may torment me from now on. He sounds miserable. He sounds broken. *I did that, I broke him.* There is no going back from this feeling of guilt so I might as well listen to the rest of his messages.

It's been a month, Allie. I have tried to give you space. Your brothers won't tell me anything. They say they don't know what happened. I saw your mom, too, by the way. She smiled at me casually, like I was a stranger, and walked past me. Did she forget about me too, Allie?

Beep.

There are some sobs in between words and hearing him cry breaks me in half. My tears start falling too.

I guess I never meant the same to you as what you meant to me because if you loved me, at least half as much as I love you, being away from me would be destroying you. Just like it is destroying me.

Beep.

It is destroying me, Jake. You have no idea.

Do you know what it is like to lose the one thread of hope you have? I went to check your Instagram and it was gone. Your Facebook is gone. There is not one piece of you left anywhere. Except, you are everywhere here. I am sitting on the bench on 6th Street right now. If I close my eyes, I can almost feel you sitting next to me, just like all those times we would sit here before. If I pay close attention, I can almost hear your laugh. I can almost see your hair flowing against your face. If I truly wanted to, I bet I could even smell you. Your sweet tropical scent. But when I open my eyes, you are not here. Did I imagine it all? Did I imagine what we had, huh? Or did you trick me? Are you that good of a liar, Allie? Did you make it all up? Were you ever even here? Because if you were—

Beep.

The message cuts off but he doesn't call again. I know that because the last message he left was a week after that one. He sounds sad, yes, but more than anything, he sounds angry. I don't think I have heard his voice like that, ever. Knowing that I caused him that much pain makes this situation worse. What would happen if I called him right now and told him the truth? Could I call my dad's bluff?

Somehow I wish I could tell him the way that I feel. I wish I could talk to someone, anyone, about what it feels like to be burning inside. My life went up in flames. It looks perfectly fine from the outside, but the truth is, nothing will ever be the same. I will never be the same.

I have one more message from him, and I don't know if I should listen to it. Tears are still falling. I let out little gasps in between. If I don't gather myself soon, I might end up having bigger issues. My anxiety has been barely hanging on to sanity and I can't let myself spiral anymore than I have. One last message, it can't be worse than the rest.

I got a scholarship, Allie. I don't know how, but UF called and said that my tuition and living expenses would be covered for a whole degree. I decided to change tracks a little though. I am picking a degree that I can use here in Baker. Maybe coach one day. But you know the worst part of all? I can't even be happy about this because the one person I want to tell, the one I want to celebrate with, to cry with, to talk to, won't answer the phone. I get it. You don't want to be with me anymore, but you are my friend. I really could use my friend right now. Maybe I was never the one for you, and I can learn to respect that but don't take my friend away from me too. Please call me back.

Beep.

I wish I could do something about this pain. It is torture. Plain and simple.

That night I cried myself to sleep. I replayed his voicemails over and over again until I had memorized every word, every pause, every sob he left in them. I promised myself that I wouldn't reach out and I wouldn't find out more about him, but if he is going to be leaving me messages, maybe I should listen to them. And keep a part of him with me forever. I delete all the other messages I have, so my voicemail doesn't get full.

It is now time to head to the airport. My family drives me and after the usual hugs and tears, we say goodbye and see you later. Walking through the airport, I feel like a zombie. I am sure I look like one too. There was a crater-sized hole in my chest that won't go away and now refuses to be ignored.

I find my gate and right next to it there is a small kiosk that sells the usual. Candy, books, key chains, and swag with *'Thank you for visiting Switzerland'* everywhere. There is also a box with journals that have things written on the cover. I walk toward them to check them out. I was wrong, these are not journals, they are letter kits. I don't know who writes letters anymore but they are adorable, and calling my name. I buy a couple of them and sit down while I wait for my flight to start boarding.

I stare at the clear plastic bag holding the letter kits and I suddenly get the urge to open one and write. I want to write Jake a letter. A letter I will never send but a letter with the answers to his questions. I grab a Tül pen from my purse. Those always live there because they are my favorite, making it easy to start this idea before it becomes another thing I don't want to follow through on. Placing the open kit on my lap, I grab the first piece of paper, lay it flat on top of the clipboard included and write.

CHAPTER FORTY-ONE

Allie

THEN

Little Do You Know, Alex & Sierra

Dear Jake,

I don't even know what this will end up being like. What the words that I write will end up meaning to me. I know exactly what they'll mean to you, nothing because you will never see them. I listened to your voice messages and I don't know what hurts more. Hearing your voice or knowing that I was the cause of the pain. I know that nothing makes sense to you now, but in five years when you have a successful career, and you're able to provide for your family the way you always wanted, you'll appreciate it. Hell, in five years I'm not even sure you will even remember me. You might be going around town and barely remember that once upon a time, you loved a girl who loved you back. Because whether you want to believe it or not, I love you. I love you so fucking much.

I know that is the reason this hurts so much. My heart opened up to you, completely. Wholly. It beats solely for you, but you are not here and it hurts. I know this is my fault. I know I made my bed and now I have to lie on it. It just fucking hurts. so damn much. I miss every single thing about you. I miss talking to you. I miss sharing lazy moments with you. I miss your mouth on mine and your hands on my body. I miss you and I have a feeling, I will spend the rest of my life missing you.

I hope you never forget that. I hope you never forget that you are my favorite person in the world even when I won't be able to see you ever again.

143.

Allie

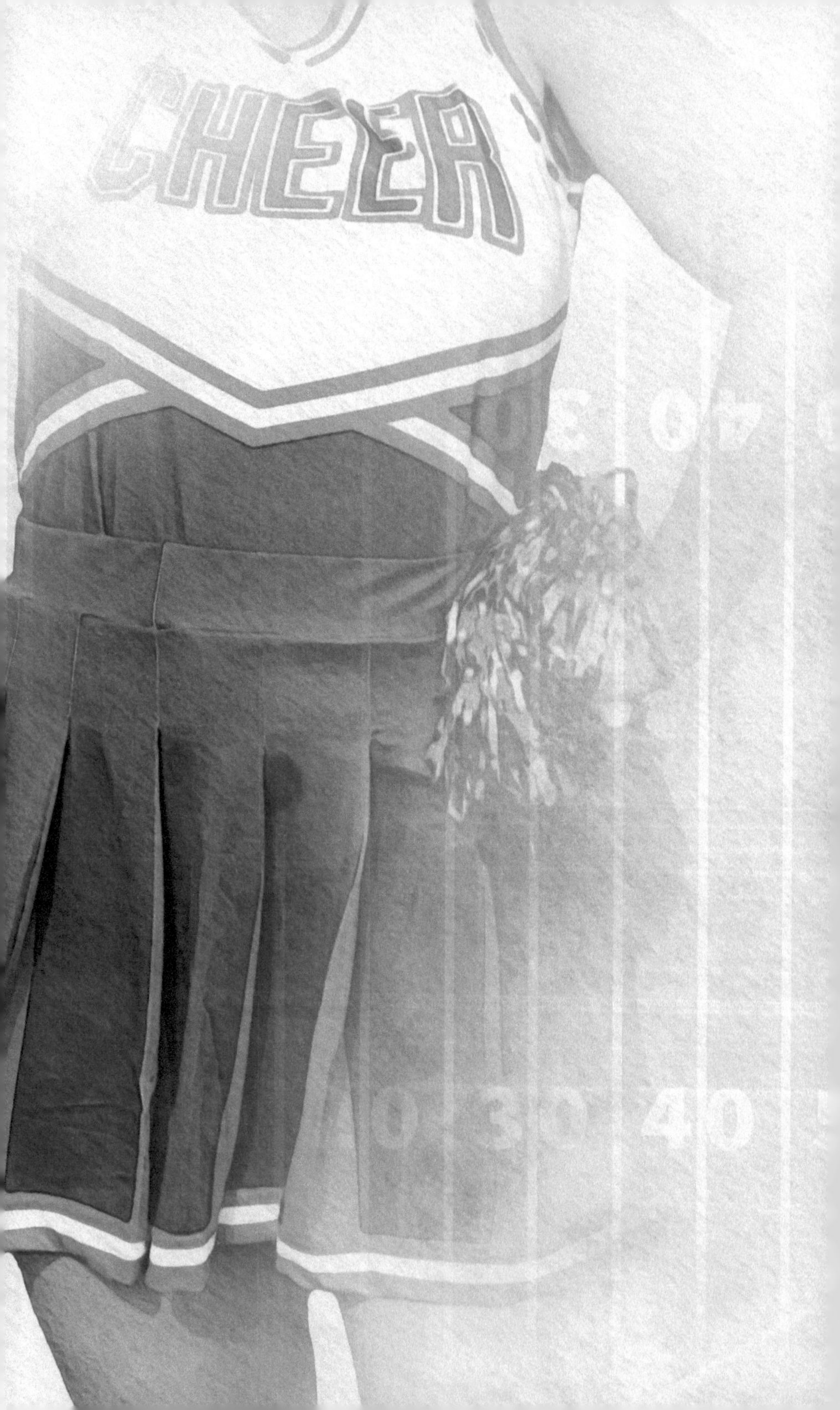

CHAPTER FORTY-TWO

Allie

THEN

See you later (ten years), Jenna Raine

> **Future Husband:** I saw in Cara's stories that you are back in the states. Answer the damn phone Allie.

> **Future Husband:** It is not beyond me to come and hunt you down. We need to talk.

> **Future Husband:** I will never get tired of calling you. I will do it every day if it means that at some point you will answer the fucking phone.

> **Future Husband:** I'm patient. I will wait.

> **Future Husband:** I will wait for you. I'll be right here.

CHEER

CHAPTER FORTY-THREE

Allie

THEN

(18 YEARS OLD)

Tee Shirt, Birdy

Dear Jake,

You called again. Ten missed calls this past week. You left three messages. You told me about your life and about how much you miss me. You told me about running into Cara and how awkward it was. You told me to take care of her because she broke up with Cole. You told me you loved me. Past tense. You didn't say you still do and that hurt. I deserve it, I guess. I deserve everything you are throwing my way and I should just take it. I should just ignore your calls or block your number but I can't seem to be able to do it.

Classes start next week. I will get my degree in Early Childhood Education. I don't think I will ever want to teach older kids, so I am going to opt for the safe choice. Cara will do the same with a minor in Special Education. She said and I quote 'It takes a weirdo to work with the highest special needs, and I happen to be that weirdo.'

Speaking of Cara. I don't think she is hurting like you think she is. Or at least she doesn't seem like it. She seems okay like she made peace with their decision.

Will we ever get to that point? Will we ever be at peace with each other? Will I ever forgive myself?

Time will only tell I guess. In the meantime, I am keeping your messages so I can replay them every morning. I have one of your T-shirts and I sleep in it almost every night. Waking up with you surrounding me and listening to your voice, even if it's sad, gives me hope that maybe one day I will find a love like ours again. If I don't, at least I was lucky enough to experience it once. How magical it was.

143.

Allie

CHAPTER FORTY-FOUR

Jake

THEN

(20 YEARS OLD)

All I want, Kodaline

"Hola, this is Allie. You know what comes next. Leave me a message or send me a text. I probably won't call back but I'll know you love me. Bye!"

"When you are done recording your message, hang up or press pound for more options. Beep!"

Happy Birthday Allie. Nineteen. How has it been over a year since the last time I saw you? I know I said in my last call that I wasn't going to call again. Well, I guess that makes me a liar. The Gators won tonight. I should be happy for my friends playing, I should. But I'm not. I miss playing and I hate being on the sidelines.

You know what I hate the most though? How much I still fucking love you. I don't want to love you anymore. I don't want to keep living with the thought that you might show up and tell me that it was all a nightmare. It doesn't matter how fucking mad at you I am, if I could see you just one more time, I would die happily, I'm sure.

Why did you fucking leave me, Allie? If you loved me, why did you leave me? If you truly loved me, why did you take my heart away with you? I might as well have died on that field because being without you is not fucking living.

Somehow I have to be a supportive friend. I have to go be the life of the party. Be the good friend I have always been, but I don't know who that is anymore. I guess he left with you.

Beep.

CHAPTER FORTY-FIVE

Allie

THEN

(20 YEARS OLD)

Big Girls Don't Cry, Fergie

Dear Jake,

I fucking hate missing you. I hate missing you more than I hate the series of text messages that you send I get them all by the way The nice ones in which you promise to wait for me. The hard ones in which you tell me how much I fucked up your life. Do you want an update, Jake? Or do you only call when you are drunk and lonely? Do you even miss me or do you miss the ghost of me? You don't even know me anymore. I am tired of fighting this, Jake. The more we hold on... The more calls you make and messages you send, the more it continues to hurt You need to let me go. You need to move on. You will be a catch for whoever gets you. You are every girl's dream boyfriend You will be someone's dream husband one day, but that won't ever happen unless you let it You need to let me go. You need to forget about me. I won't be able to forget you, Jake but I sure am trying to find some happiness, too. I am tired of crying and hurting. I even started therapy because I couldn't continue going through life like this, a shell of who I was. Utterly broken and shattered into tiny pieces that exist everywhere but within me. I have to put my big girl pants on and stop crying over something that neither of us can change. I will forever love you though. I hope you know that since I won't ever get to tell you again.

143.
Allie

CHAPTER FORTY-SIX

Jake

THEN

(22 YEARS OLD)

21, Gracie Abrams

"Hola, this is Allie. You know what comes next. Leave a message or send me a text. I probably won't call back but I'll know you love me. Bye!"

"When you are done recording your message, hang up or press pound for more options. Beep!"

Twenty-one, huh? I guess you are finally old enough to be considered a real adult. I wish I could say I wasn't thinking of you last night, but I was. I was thinking about you out drinking, without me. I was thinking about what you were wearing. I was thinking about what you were drinking. If you were happy while out celebrating with your friends, and then I didn't even have to imagine it. Cara's Instagram showed me exactly how happy you are.

In every single picture, you look blissfully happy. You look at ease and full of life, just like you used to look right here in my arms. I hate it as much as I hate being away from you. I hate that someone else might be putting that smile on your face. I hate that I am still so far away from you, that I don't know what your life is anymore.

Are you still funny, kind, and smart? Do you still like dancing in the dark? Do you still read? Do you still love that espresso bean coffee that drove me crazy with energy? Are you ignoring me because *it hurts or are you ignoring me because I never meant anything to you?*

I really want to wish that every drink you have tonight reminds you of me. I would be lying if I said that I wish that you were as miserable as I am, but the truth is that I just wish you the best. Would I want to be the one making you smile? Do I wish I was the one buying you your first legal drinks and dancing with you, even if I didn't want to? Yes, I do but that doesn't change the fact that I am glad you are happy, even if it is not with me.

I finally see it now. Love, true love, should not hold you back, ever, even if that means holding your heart back. It's not about forgetting you, that won't ever happen, it's about knowing that I just want you to be happy. I can spend my time wishing for unfulfillable promises or I can use my wishes to hope you get the best life that you can. If there's anyone that deserves to be happy, it's you, my love.

You probably think I am pathetic. Calling you and leaving messages. I would think I am pathetic, too and as much as it kills me to say this, I think this will be the last time I call you. I can't keep doing this to myself. At some point, I have to face the fact that you moved on. That you are better off without me and that you and I don't belong anymore. At some point, I have to push forward.

I think this is that point.

I never wanted anything else for you, other than you being the happiest version of yourself that you can be. It seems like you got that now. I do feel fucking lucky to have gotten you in my life once. Some people spend a lifetime looking for something an ounce of what we had, and I got to experience it fully, wholeheartedly, and all in for a while.

I love you Allie and I always will.
Goodbye, Honey.

CHEER

CHAPTER FORTY-SEVEN

Allie

THEN

(23 YEARS OLD)

Forget Me (Cover), Celina Sharma

Dear Jake,

Its been two years since the last time you called I haven't heard your voice since and I just realized it. It took me a while to figure out the small changes I felt and the fact that your calls stopped. I still missed you everyday but I wasn't mad anymore. This feeling of acceptance happened in the same way that we fell in love. Little details at a time, and then all at once. At first, I realized you didn't call for a year when it was my twenty second birthday and I didn't get a message from you. It bothered me but not as much as I thought it would, so I let it go. I didn't write again either and I didn't question it. After all, maybe you were ready to move on which is exactly what I asked for.

This summer, Cara came back from visiting her parents and said that some of your friends were talking shit about me because of what I did to you, like I had a choice. Then she said that you stopped them and said that it wasn't worth it and I was torn. Destroyed, again. That's when I realized that it had been two years without hearing from you. I thought that I was okay with it all, but hearing that you thought talking about me wasn't worth it hurt. A lot. I would be okay with you moving on, with you not picking up the phone anymore. It would be easy to understand why you hate me or why you would never want to see me again.

What I don't understand is, how could you say what we had wasn't worth anything? Did I mean nothing to you that you have to even stop all talk about me? Cara said that you didn't ask, not even once, about me? Is this true? Was I not a crucial part of your life, like you were to me?

Move on all you want but forgetting me? Erasing me? That fucking hurts because I sure as hell can't erase you. I guess its time for me to try and do the same but wish me luck because I can't seem to even move on. Not when everything comes back to you.

Allie

CHAPTER FORTY-EIGHT

Allie

NOW

Time To Be Your 21, Alexz Johnson

"You didn't write 143 on the last letter," Jake says, wiping the tears off his face. He read them all, *twice*. He read every single letter, every unhinged comment and thought I had about us for years. Every tear. Every heartbreak.

He went through all the emotions as well. Little by little and then all at once. Right now I can't tell if he is heartbroken or if he is upset. Either way, seeing him crying on his bed, with my letters strewn all over, might be the most hurtful image in my brain.

"You know I never stopped loving you, but I was completely torn that day." My hands are slimy from clenching my fists while he was reading. I laid all my cards on the table. The truth never spoken was finally shared. Now the ball is in his court.

"I think I remember that day. Cara was hanging out with us for the first time in a while. Everyone was drinking and grilling her about so much, then your name came up. I had to shut the conversation down because I wasn't going to let anyone talk shit about you, but also because it was like a slap to the face. I hadn't brought up your name in a long time so I was able to pretend you didn't exist. I was able to pretend I was going to be able to stay married to my brand new wife and live a happy life." Sighing with relief and complete calmness in his eyes. "I knew in that moment, what I know now, Allie."

"And what is that, Jake?"

"I thought it was as clear as day but I guess I need to put it into words. I love you, Honey. I always have, and I always will. There was never anyone else that could replace you or make me forget you. The question is, are you ready to let me love you?"

I let out a sob and you can see the surprise in his face when this happens. He comes closer to me, putting one hand on my face and moving a ringlet behind my ear. His forehead lands on mine. I close my eyes, more tears fall. Tears that he wipes away with his thumb, tenderly. I don't deserve his never ending patience. I don't deserve him.

"Shh, it's okay. I'm not going anywhere," he coos.

I move until I am straddling his lap. His hand instantly going to my ass while he pulls my neck forward with the other one. He peppers kisses on my lips. Delicate kisses like he is afraid he might break me. His eyes are closed, his eyelashes brush his cheeks. His nose touches mine and he is holding on to me for dear life. Not rushing this moment, we shut out everything else that may be happening, leaving only the two of us in existence. He sighs and I can almost hear my own heart shattering like glass.

He is afraid. He is afraid of letting me in all the way. He is afraid I might break his heart again, and who can blame him?

He wraps his arms around me, bringing me closer to him. He holds me tight in his embrace. A warm hug I never want to escape again. He lays us both down, climbing on top of me, and kissing me softly. When I try to deepen the kiss he won't let me in, instead he lifts slightly, whispering against my lips, "Let's go to sleep, Honey. We can continue this conversation tomorrow. Right now, we need to let it rest." He kisses my forehead and lays down beside me. Pulling me flush against his chest, fitting perfectly behind me, murmuring, "I love you."

The next morning comes roughly. I am in a daze and he is rushing to get out the door. We overslept big time. He is flustered, I can see it in the reddish tone on his cheeks and how his movements are abrupt and all over the place.

"Hey," I whisper. My voice is rough and dry, so I clear my throat. "I'm sorry you are running late."

"Why are you sorry, baby?" he asks, taking a second to stop and look at me. I have on one of his shirts and nothing else. My bare legs are showing and my hair, I'm sure, is a rat's nest. I know he is late but he is still taking his time, drinking me in from head to toes. He smirks and I roll my eyes.

"Eyes up here, Jakey." We both laugh. The tension fleeting the air, helping us relax a little. "I should've set an alarm or been mindful of my word vomit last night."

"I wanted to hear all of it. I needed to know, Honey. I do have to go, or I'm going to be later than I already am. I can't cancel practice today. We have a big game Friday so the boys need me. But I do want us to continue the conversation from last night."

I nod, letting him know that I understand and that it is okay. "I'll be here when you come home."

"Please be." He jogs towards me, bag in hand, and drops a kiss on my lips. A quick soft peck before he turns around and walks towards the door. The house suddenly seems smaller with him almost out of it. I wave at him and he winks. "See you later, Allie."

I haven't checked my email, but I planned to work from here today. My meetings at this assignment are getting less demanding so I am waiting for them to let me know my next one. Usually, when I start having more days where I work from home, it's a true indicator that my time is up, and I am being sent somewhere else soon. But for the first time in my career, I don't want to be on the move.

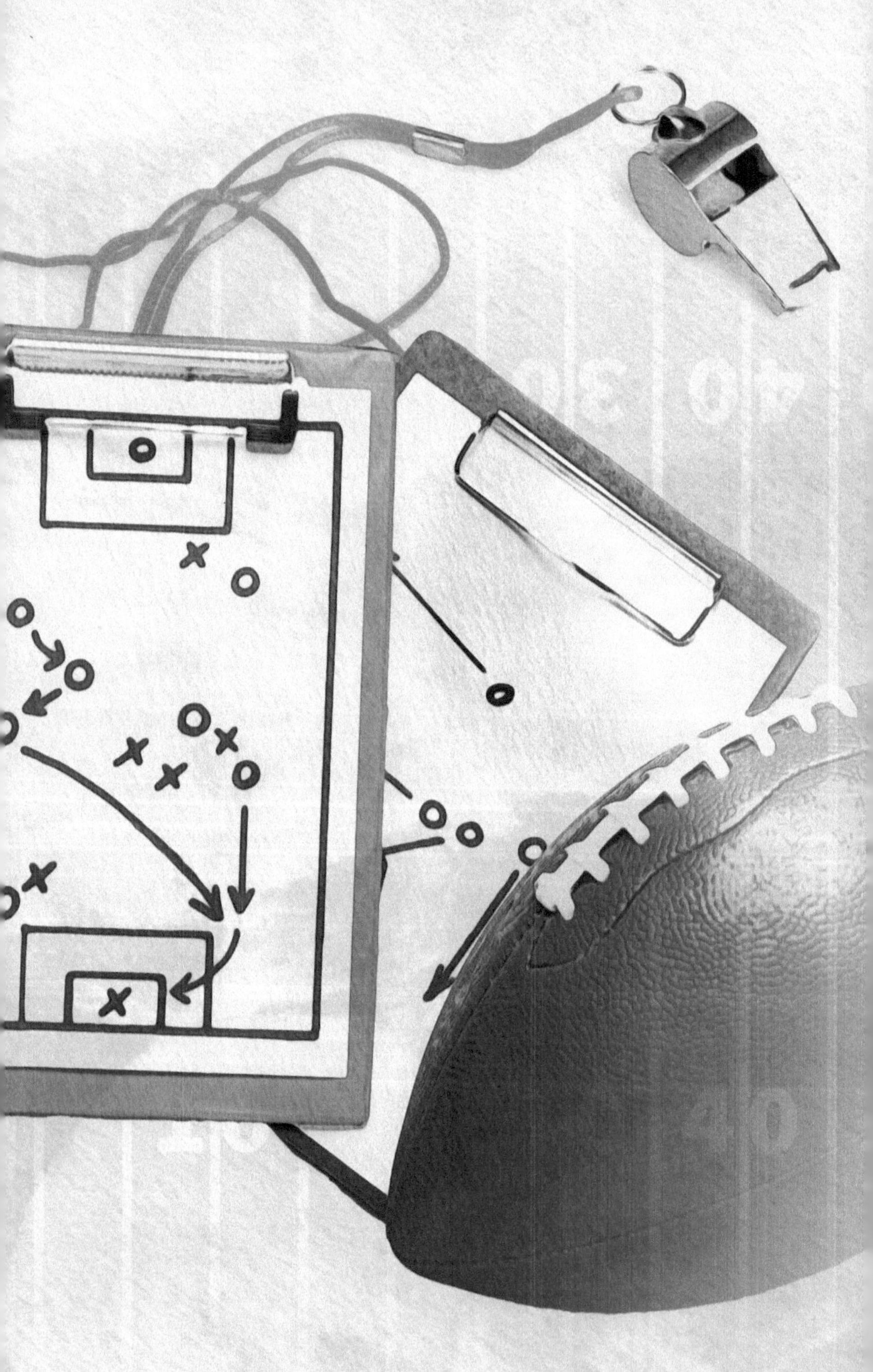

CHAPTER FORTY-NINE

Jake

NOW

Anyone, Justin Bieber

I love teaching. I love my job with every ounce of my body but more than anything, I love the kids. I especially enjoy teaching the same guys I coach. Somehow it brings us closer together, making it a fulfilling profession. Some days I might be tired but I still enjoy being in my classroom. Today was not one of those days.

I am tired from not sleeping last night. *Who could have slept after that whole shitstorm of information?* On top of that, practice today was a disaster. Every player who cares is all in their head about the game Friday, and they all care. We haven't made it to State since I was playing, and we all know how that ended, with nobody playing and everyone losing. The team was on edge and playing like they've never been coached a day in their life.

Now, I am on my way home, to have this conversation that should've happened years ago. So much time lost when we could have just made that decision *together*. It is easier to say that now, of course, that we are mature, and have had time in between to reflect on all the dumb shit we did in our teens.

Walking into the house, my heart is beating fast and my hands are sweaty. I feel like a teenager walking to pick up my date for the first time. Except, I'm a grown-ass man, walking into my own house, where the love of my life waits for me, ready to discuss what might change the rest of our lives.

Sitting on the couch with her legs tucked under her, a book in her hand, and a blanket over her, Allie looks up when she hears me walk in. "Hey, handsome," she says with a grin, closing her book and placing it on the end table next to her wine glass.

"Hola, beautiful." I walk towards her, placing my bag on the ground, I sit on the couch by her side. I want to kiss her but I don't know if that is where we are at right now.

She must sense my hesitation because she untangles her legs from under her and comes near me, kissing me gently on the lips before whispering, "How was your day today?"

I fucking love this comfortable side of her. The Allie who is not worried about being herself. The one that waits for me to come home after we both go to work. The one that makes this house a home.

Kicking my shoes off my feet, I put them on the rustic coffee table in front of me, and tell her about my day. She listens attentively. Her hand on mine, rubbing small circles on the top. She seems at peace. I hope it is me who brings that to her.

"How about your day?" I ask without even knowing what she did today. Did she go back to the elementary school? Has she been home crying the whole time? Did she leave the house at all?

"It was fine, pretty normal. I was given some news though," she says with panic in her eyes.

"Oh really? What kind of news?"

"It depends," she says.

"On what?" Raising my eyebrow at her.

"On where we are going from here."

In that moment I realize that she is making quicker circles on my hand and shaking her leg. Both are signs that she is nervous about whatever she is about to tell me. My heart skips a beat, waiting for her to break my heart again. I can sense it.

"They are asking me to go to Atlanta to train at another school for a few weeks. My flight leaves on Friday around 10:00 pm. I think that means I'm going to miss your game."

"That's okay, there will be other games." I'm not sure where she is going with this. Is she leaving Friday and then never coming back? Or is she leaving for a few weeks and then coming back to me? "What are your plans for after that? Are you coming back to Baker?"

She looks at me with sadness in her eyes. Dropping my heart again, like it weighs nothing. She alone can destroy me without words. This is the moment I might lose her again.

"What are we doing here, Jake?" she asks after taking a deep breath.

There are no right answers here but I am ready to beg her to give us another chance to and not leave. I am laying all my cards on the table. I am not making the same mistake twice.

"I don't know but I want to fucking find out, Honey. I don't want to lie to you and tell you that I can drop you off at the airport and wish you well without feeling like my life slipped through my fingers, again. I want to be with you. Even if that means, packing my bags and following you wherever you go next. I am not willing to find out how to move on after I know exactly how you feel in my arms again."

"Jake, you are not quitting your job to come with me," she blurts out, crossing her arms over her chest.

"Well, I don't want you to leave my life, so my life will have to adapt to yours. I can do this with no issues, I just need to finish the school year. Then, I'm all yours. In the meantime, we need to try something out because I am not letting you go again. I refuse."

"Jake."

"Allie." I grab her arms, and pull her towards me. "I made this mistake once, Honey, I'm not making it again. I am willing to do whatever it takes to have you in my life."

"Jake, I don't want you to give your life up for me." Tears start falling down her face. Fuck, I hate seeing her cry but I swear she has an open faucet on her face the minute she has big emotions. She is like a cup that is always full. Full of love and passion so the minute another drop falls in it, she cries.

"Honey, don't you understand? There is no life without you. *That* was not living. I was barely existing. Hold on to me, hold on to us. For once, choose me. I know it is scary, and maybe this town won't be enough for you, but I love you more so I am willing to give it up."

"I always chose you. I made that decision because I was choosing your future."

"I know that's what you thought, baby, but my future was always you. So now I am begging you to let me be exactly that. If I am enough for you, if my love will be enough for you, then let me make the choice. Let me follow you and your dreams."

"What about your dreams?" she asks in between sobs.

"My dream has always been you," I say, unapologetically.

"I love you," she whispers.

"I love you too, baby. Now what?"

"Long distance until we can figure some things out? I don't want you leaving your school or Baker abruptly. We can FaceTime, we can talk on the phone, right?" I ask putting all my cards on the table.

"Yes, we will figure this out," he says as he holds my hand and kisses my knuckles gently before adding, "together." Reassuring me with more than words that we will be okay.

Say Don't Go (Taylor's Version), Taylor Swift

Jake couldn't bring me to the airport because the playoff game is tonight. The Sharks are playing The Commanders, the same team they played the night Jake got injured. I'm still in between cloud nine and terrified about trying this long-distance thing with Jake, but I love him and I am only fooling myself into thinking that I could move on from him, twice.

I took an Uber to the airport, the trunk loaded with my bags. Phone in hand, I look out the window, when I get a text message from Cara.

Cara: Why are you getting on that plane?

Me: Because I have to.

Cara: Says who?

Me: The fuck? My JOB!

Cara: You are telling me right now that you are picking your job over the love of your life? You were fucking miserable for years. Don't do that again, Allison.

Me: Don't Allison me. This has been my dream job my entire career.

Cara: But what is your dream? Not your dream job but your dream life?

Me: Idk

Cara: I think you do, you just don't want to admit it.

Me: oh but since you know me so well, friend, enlighten me.

Cara: For once in your fucking life Allie, put yourself first. I'm not telling you that I know what you want in life. You need to find it yourself, in you. You know the answer, you know it in your heart.

Me: I don't have a choice. I have to go to work.

Cara: Babe, you are a teacher. You can teach, literally anywhere. You also have more money than any adult would need at our age, just sitting in your bank account. Why don't you stop being the responsible one and for once in your life be the selfish one. Put yourself first.

Me: I'm not touching that money.

Cara: FML

Me: WHAT?!?!?!?!?

Cara: We all make mistakes. You need to let that shit go. Your dad is trying to make amends. Let him.

Cara: And fine, let him doesn't mean let him control your life because the independent bitch that you are now won't go backwards

Cara: Let him make amends though or at least try.

Cara: ☒

Me: K

She's not wrong though. Why am I going to this job? I do love my job, but do I love it more than I love Jake? No. Why am I putting him last again? I thought helping him have professional stability was what he wanted. But I was wrong. He just wants me to pick *him*. To put him first. And that's exactly what I am going to do.

I text Cara one more time.

> **Me:** Actually, fuck the job. Fuck responsibilities. I will figure that shit out.

> **Cara:** ☒ …

> **Me:** I'm going to show this man, exactly how much I love him.

> **Cara:** YASSSSSS QUEEN! Go. Fucking. Show. Him.

I put the phone in my bag, and tell the driver, "Sir, change of plans, let's turn around."

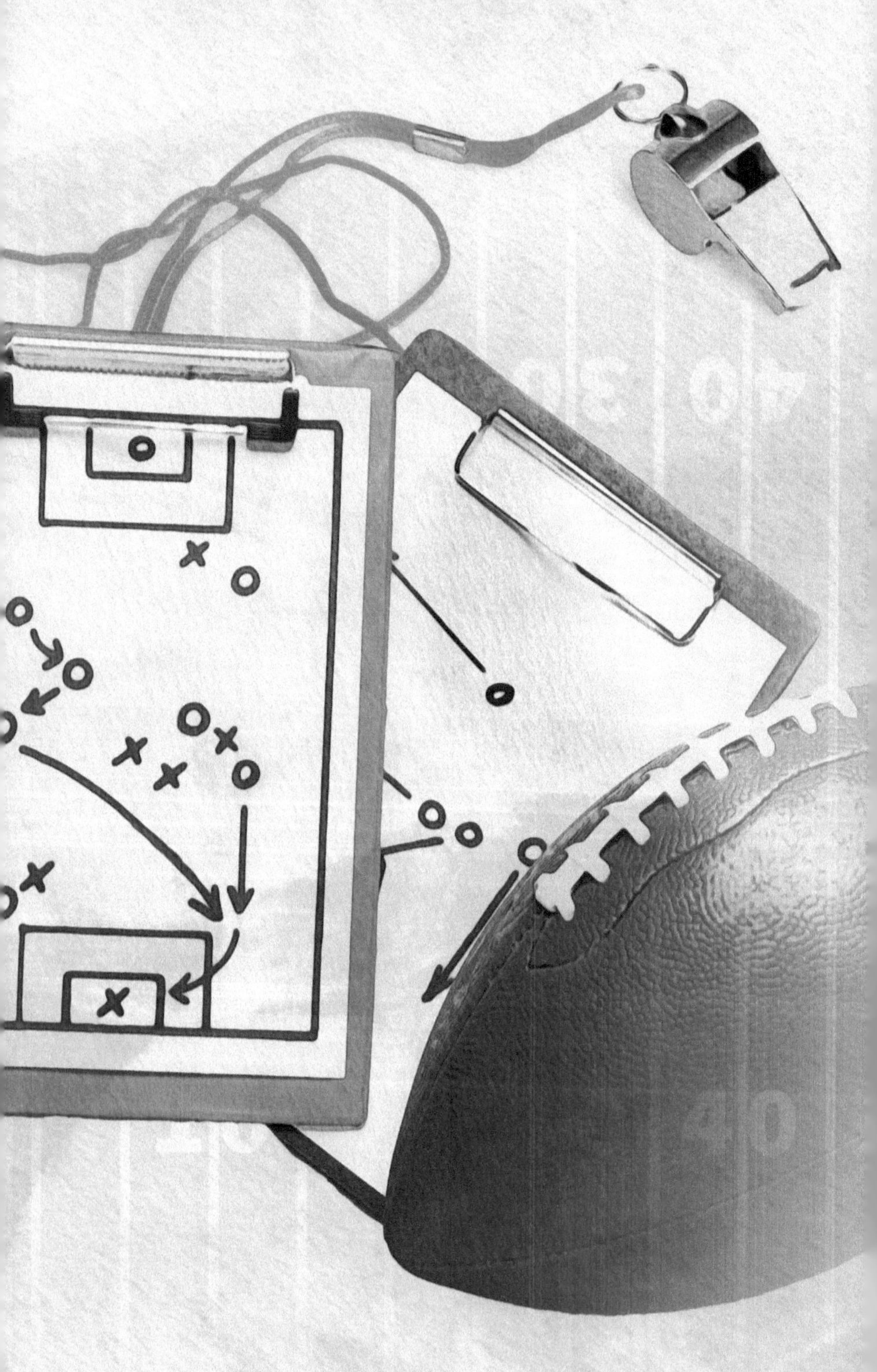

CHAPTER FIFTY-ONE

NOW

Take Me Home, Us the Duo

"TEN!"
"NINE!"
"EIGHT!"
The crowd is cheering as our running back steps away from the touchdown. We have been tied for the past five minutes and with the clock against us, this is the last chance we have to make a touchdown and win this game. This has been a hard game. The Commanders are good and they showed up to this game. But. So. Did. We.
"SEVEN!"
"SIX!"
The running back is almost there. Some of the other guys are running behind him, pushing everyone else away. Guarding him with his life. He doesn't dare look back. Five more steps and he will make it. A Commander is right behind him, practically breathing down his neck. I can feel the air in the stadium shift. I can see people on the edge of their seats.
"FIVE!"
"FOUR!"
"THREE!"

TOUCHDOWN! With three seconds left on the clock, he made it. He fucking did it. A touchdown. We won! We fucking won the game. The crowd goes wild. People are cheering, clapping, screaming, and crying. The Commanders are completely defeated. Their coaches are shaking their heads, throwing their hats down, and yelling at their players. I could never understand why coaches get so angry at kids when they lose. Yes, it is disappointing but they played a damn good game and at the end of the day, they are kids. They are going to beat themselves up enough.

Running towards the team, who are currently gathered at the end zone, I can't help but smile wide. We did it. They did it. They deserved this and they got it. They played well but more than that, they put in the time and effort to work through the things that needed improvement and this is their reward. All I can think about is how I can't wait to call Allie and tell her about this.

Walking back towards the locker room, I have to blink a couple of times and rub my face because I think I am hallucinating. Walking across the middle of the field is Allie, wearing a fucking Sharks Jersey, looking like a damn vision. Curls flowing in the wind, tights that hug her perfect legs, and the Sharks Jersey acting like a half-fitted dress around her curves. She is smiling big and when she sees that I notice her, she starts running towards me. *What on earth is she doing here?*

"Allie? Baby, what are you doing here?" I ask, completely dumbfounded and a little out of breath, both from running and because this woman takes my breath away every time I see her.

"I couldn't leave you again. I wanted to show you that I would be happy here. Baker is enough. You are enough. You always were and you will always be. I'm tired of fighting it. I love you and I don't want to go another day without you."

I kiss her. I kiss her and show her exactly what those words mean to me. Pulling her closer to me. Holding her head, breathing her in. When she lets out a little moan, I pull away, suddenly remembering that we are on a football field, and a high school football field at that. I kiss her nose, and her forehead, and look down smiling like a fool. An in-love fool.

"Jake, you guys won! I am so proud of you." Her hands holding my face and her eyes looking right into my soul. I nod and smile. I wouldn't want to celebrate with anyone but her right now. Or ever. For the rest of my life, she is the only thing I need. My only constant. Everything else can change.

"Do you feel on top of the world right now baby?" she asks with giddiness in her voice.

"With you by my side? I do," I reply. We don't say anything for a moment. Both just standing in this moment together. Taking it all in. Her hands are still holding my neck. The brightest smile on her face and her eyes glossy with emotion. Hope, happiness, *love*. It is all there.

"Take me home, Jake Clarke," she says.

"And where is home, Honey?"

"Home is wherever you are," she says and my world stops spinning. I am about to show this woman how she is *exactly* that. My home.

"I've been waiting a lifetime to hear you say that." I hold her hand and pull her straight into the parking lot. "Let's go home, Honey."

Allie

TWO YEARS LATER

Timeless, Taylor Swift

"You look stunning," Cara says, wiping her tears away. We have been waiting for this day for a year, but if we are both being honest, we have been dreaming about it since we were in high school. Today, I get to marry my best friend.

We are hosting a small ceremony in a venue by the river. Beautiful oak trees surround an open area of grass that is lit up with fairy lights. White chairs face forward to an arbor with beige and orange drapes right in front of the water. My dream venue with my dream man.

A lot has changed in the last couple of years. I officially moved to Baker and quit my job. I now work from home for a professional development company. I travel a few times a month, but not for more than a day or two. Jake is still coaching and teaching at Baker High. It has been a dream and although he asked me to marry him a few months after I moved in with him, we wanted to wait until I had a better relationship with my dad before we had our ceremony.

"Thank you, babe. I feel like a princess," I tell her. My dress is perfect. Exactly what I wanted. A cut that accentuates my body type perfectly with lace and beads making a floral pattern on the top. My hair is pulled to the side in a loose braid, with some curls framing my face, just like Jake loves it.

"You are a fucking queen. Feel like it!"

Walking down the aisle, Taylor Swift's Lover is playing in the background. With both my parents holding my hands, I walk towards the man who has always had my heart. He is smiling from ear to ear, in his black tuxedo with his best friends and my brothers by him. Tears fill his eyes, completely locked with mine. He looks at me the same way that he always has; like the world ceases to exist, like there is only me.

My mom walks me to him, giving him the usual spiel of, "Take care of my girl." His rough hands hold mine tenderly, the biggest oxymoron. He looks at me and mouths *hi*. We are lost in each other until we hear the officiant clear his throat and we both giggle looking at him.

"Now, Allie. It is your turn to share your vows with Jake," the officiant says. Going first was a good idea because I was already completely overwhelmed with my emotions and Allie hadn't even started. I know that she will kill me with her words, per usual. She looks nervous and it is the most adorable sight. Again, I'm glad because it helps me breathe easier to see a little of her nervous self come through this fucking vision of a woman in front of me. Talk about making my heart stop, with that dress, and her hair framing her face perfectly. Minutes away from being completely mine, from being my wife.

"Twelve years ago we were two kids who fell head over heels in love with each other. People thought we were going to be the ones who would stay together forever. Voted most likely to run away together. Unfortunately, mistakes were made and we were apart for too damn long. I don't want to keep beating around the bush on why or how, but I am so glad we found each other again."

"You were great for me then and you are pure perfection for me now. In the big gestures and in the little everyday things that make my heart skip a beat every time. The way you wake up early and quietly let me sleep longer. The way that you cook me breakfast and make me coffee the way I like it, when you don't even drink any. The way you always smile when you see me, like you missed me even if you just walk away for a second."

"We have built millions of memories. Laughing. Arguing. Crying. Sleepless nights. Months apart. Years together. New friendships gained. Old friendships lost. Broken pieces of each other being healed through love, hard work, and time."

"And we are still here, not only with a beautiful strong relationship but also ready to start the next chapter in our love story. And I wouldn't trade any single moment, especially if I get to keep calling you home."

"People ask me if I regret leaving my job and my lifestyle. Settling for the slow-paced, small-town life, but they don't know that my answer will never change, I will never regret *you*. I will never regret us. I don't have to miss home because *you* are my home and wherever *you* are is where I belong. The best decision that I have ever made, hands down, is choosing you. And I still can't believe I get to love you every day but even more, that you choose to love me too."

"You are my best friend and sometimes that means giving me reality checks and telling me hard truths and although I might not seem to appreciate it in the moment, I will be forever grateful for that. And for your faith in me even when I've lost all faith in myself. For loving me as I have changed from the naive cheerleader to the woman I am now. For you being my constant. For you being my rock. My listening ears. My favorite hug. The coziest pillow. And my laugh on the hardest days. So I guess what I am trying to say is thank you. Thank you for choosing me every day. For making me see the best parts of me through your eyes and for holding my hand while I fight the worst ones."

"And here I am, promising that I will. I will always love you on this journey even when the load gets heavy. Even when we turn gray, even when I get so mad that I don't want to, I promise I will. I promise that I will stand by you in parenting, business endeavors, and life decisions; even with deciding what's for dinner. I promise I will be the very best friend you could ever ask for. I promise that I will guard your heart with all that I have and then some more. But above all, I promise to choose you, unapologetically, through rough or smooth terrain, in sunshine, and rain, from sunrise to sunset, when we're happy and when we're mad, and everything in between, I will choose you. You know I am obsessed with love stories, but ours is my favorite forever and ever until wherever we end up."

"One Four Three, Jake."

The crowd is silent. She not only took my words away, but she took them from everyone else. This fucking woman is incredible and she is completely mine.

"Jake, you may now kiss your bride." The words that I have been waiting a lifetime to hear. I pull her to me in one swoop, hold her by the neck, dip her low, and kiss my wife.

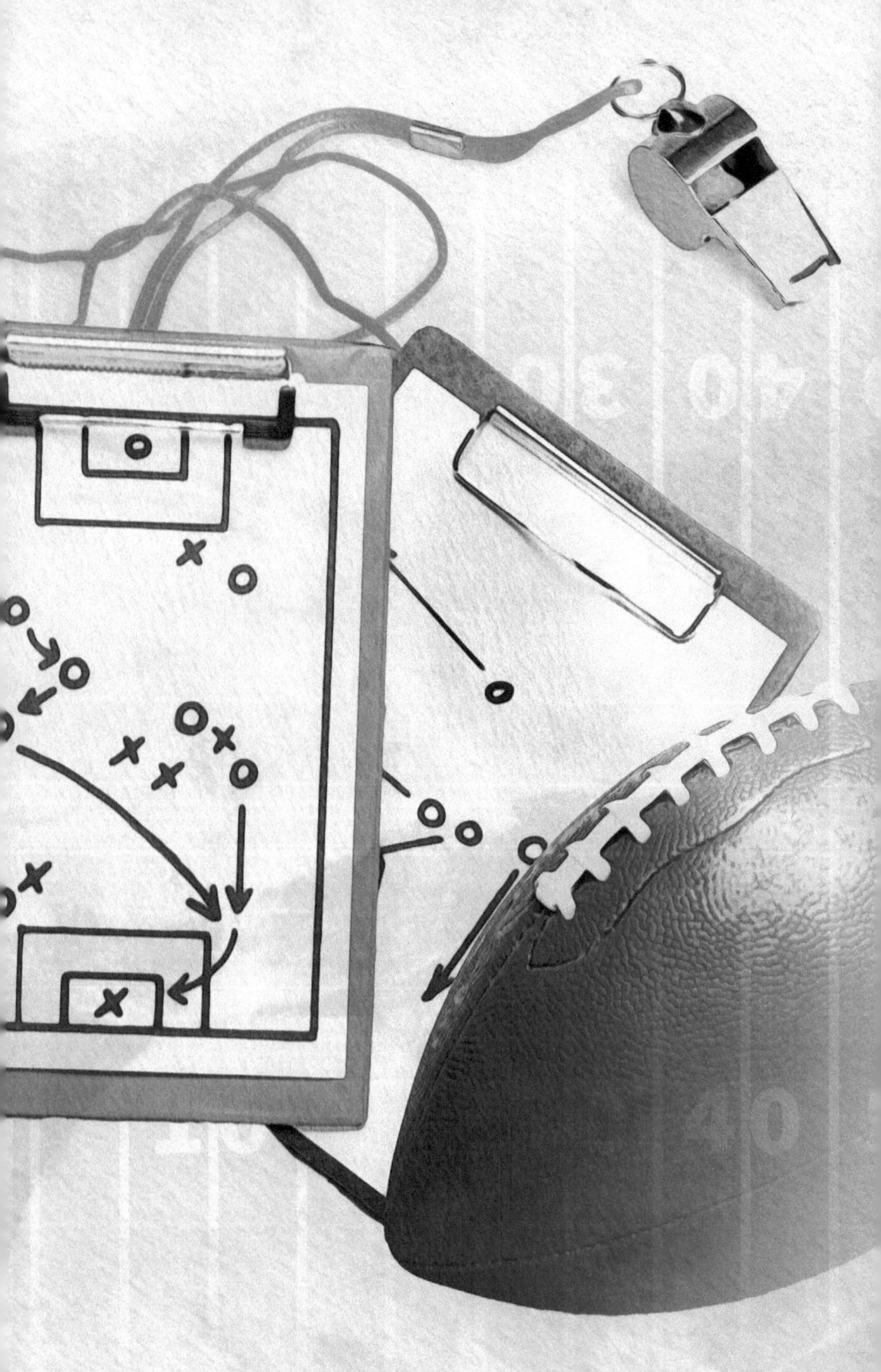

Jake

SIX YEARS LATER

Next Thing You Know, Jordan Davis

"Daddy?"

"Yes son," I say, pushing Nico on the swing while watching Allie sitting by the pool, sipping on her peach wine with our daughter sleeping on her chest. It's been one of those easy summer days at home. Cuddle time with the kids in bed, pancakes and eggs on the porch, and swimming for hours. Our little girl has been on a sleep regression for what seems like weeks now. If she's not on top of Allie she won't sleep so my girls have been cranky.

"Did you know the sun is a star?" he asks with pride in his voice.

"Really? I didn't know that," I reply, letting him share with me whatever fact he learned from one of the hundreds of books that he has read in his short life. The little boy always has a book in his hands, just like his mama.

"Yeap," he says, popping his p. He is a miniature version of Allie from the way he loves books to the way his words sound. My favorite is hearing him say his little words in Spanish that he's used to hearing his mama say or when he places emphasis on little things the same way she does– like the p at the end of words.

"Do you know why it's a star, Nico?"

"Because it's made of gas daddy, helium and *hadrogen*."

"Hydrogen?"

"Yeap, hydrogen," he adds, so confident in his answer that it makes my heart fill with pride.

"That's amazing buddy boy. Thank you for sharing that with me. Do you think we can go see what our girls are doing?"

"Sure thing, daddy." He jumps off the swing and runs towards his mom faster than I can keep up with him.

"Hi, Honey," I say, kissing her forehead and rubbing Milena's back.

"Jacob Clarke, I swear if you wake her up, I'm going to be K-I-L-L you," she says, staring at me with murderous eyes.

Nico giggles and we both look at him and he says, "Mamá you know I can spell. It's not very nice to tell daddy you will kill him." *This kid.*

Allie lifts her sunglasses to look at our too-smart-for-his-own-good little boy and raises her eyebrows so we both know immediately she means business.

"Uh oh," I say.

"Nicolas Clarke, te he dicho que no repitas palabras de adultos." *I've told you not to repeat grown up words.*

"Pero mamá—" *But mom...*

"Pero nada, stay out of grown-up conversations okay?"

"Sí mamá." *Yes, mami.* He gives her a side hug, being careful not to wake his sister up. "Puedo volver a jugar?" *Can I go back to play?*

She nods and he runs off to climb in his tree house. It never ceases to amaze me with the ease that our children speak both English and Spanish. Millie actually speaks mostly Spanish since she's only two and Allie stays home with her. My favorite is how they call her mamá, but they have never called me anything other than daddy. Well or any variation of that when the little one-year-olds were trying to call my name.

Milena is getting restless on top of Allie so I pick her up carefully not to wake her but still give her mama a break from being under the hold of this little nugget. I rest her against my chest and she wiggles until her head is deep into the crook of my neck. Her tiny fingers wrapped around the back of my head and her other hand rubs her eye. "Shh, shh, shh, it's okay, Millie baby. Daddy's here." I move her up and down while swaying back and forth until I can hear her breathing slow again and her fist falls against my chest. *Daddy's here, baby girl, you're safe.*

Allie sits up and looks at me with a soft smile while stretching her arms.

"Did you get any more sleep, Honey?"

"Maybe? I feel like I fell asleep too but everything is a blur. I need her to sleep, Jake. I don't know how much longer I can keep doing this," she says, immediately frowning. It takes her so long to admit she needs help so the fact that she is even voicing that is a huge thing for her.

"How can I help?"

She reaches over and places a hand on our daughter's unruly golden curls and looks at me with tears in her eyes.

"Hey, hey, hey, come here." I open my arm so she can tuck herself in next to me and she also buries her head in my neck. *Two peas in a pod.* Sometimes I wonder what they got from me but then I see Nico's chocolate eyes and all his questions about how things work and I can see myself in him. Or I see how excited Millie gets about sushi or about any food really, and I can also see myself in her.

"Honey, this will pass too. Just let me help."

"I'm just so tired, but I hate that she might wake you up when you have to work tomorrow."

"It's okay, I'm her parent too. Let me take this off your plate. Do you want me to sleep with her in the other room?"

"It's that horrible of me?" she says, wiping tears off her face and looking at me with tired eyes.

"No, Honey, it's not. You're tired, everyone gets tired. Let me take care of you. Let me take care of both of you," I say, kissing Millie's head and reaching to touch Allie's cheek.

"Why are you so good to me?"

"Because you deserve that and more, Honey. Now go. Go sleep, I'll take care of them."

The bright morning light woke me from the best night sleep I've had in a while. The bed is empty and Jake's side is still made. Walking out of our room, I go to try and find my family but the smell of coffee sparks my senses. *Coffee first, then family.*

I walk into the living room and find Jake in the recliner with Millie on his chest and Nico next to him. Both kids are asleep and Jake is watching something on the TV.

"Hey baby," I say and as soon as he hears me, he smiles big. Like he didn't spend all night with both of our kids. I can guarantee he ended up sleeping in that recliner with one child against his ribs and another over his chest.

"Good morning, beautiful. How did you sleep?" he asks with the biggest smile on his face.

"I slept great thanks to you. I don't even want to ask you about how your night was."

"Ask, Allie," he says but he has not stopped smiling at me.

"Jake, please don't make me ask. I feel terrible already."

"Honey, just trust me. Ask me about my night."

This man. "Okay Jake, how was your night?" I ask.

He gets up from the recliner, placing Millie on the couch and covering Nico with his dinosaur blanket. He wraps his arms around my waist and kisses my forehead.

"Look at me, Honey." So I look up and his eyes are practically smiling at me.

"I had a great night because I got to snuggle with the most perfect two year old little girl I have ever laid eyes on. She was awake for a couple hours last night and she was singing, and counting, and trying to brush my hair. She is so happy, Allie, and it's mostly because of you. She spends her days with her amazing mom who is not only raising her but teaching her, too. Her amazing mom that works endlessly to have our household running smoothly. Her amazing mom who has eyes just like hers. Then, when she finally fell asleep, Nico came out of his room because he had a nightmare and you know what he said?" He stops and takes a deep breath before continuing, "He said, 'Daddy, can I lay with you? All the monsters go away when I cuddle with you.' I get to be his safe space. I get to be the hero fighting the bad guys and his knight protecting the castle. This is more than I could have ever hoped for and I have it all with the one person I have always loved. So yeah, Honey, I had a great night doing the best job I've ever had."

With that he kisses my lips softly, tenderly, patiently. His lips caress more than my own. His lips are touching my soul. "I'm going to go take a shower. Go enjoy your coffee in peace. I'll take Nico to school, too." He walks to our room but before he goes in I notice that he's looking down the hall. watching our perfect angels sleeping soundly. .I can't believe I almost walked away from it all. I don't know how I could have ever thought that my life would ever be complete without him.

Acknowledgements

Oh my Gosh, thank you so much for reading my book. I have so many words that I wish I could say but more than anything, I just want to say thank you. Out of the millions of books out there, you took time to read mine and that means more than you know. Jake and Allie are close to my heart and you giving them a chance is filling my heart with love.

I want to take this opportunity to say thank you to everyone who made this book possible. Sure, I wrote it but so much more goes into creating a story and publishing. Way more than just having a story in your heart, even though that is the right place to start.

Thank you Joey for your never-ending belief in me. For being my solid rock and for not once asking me to close my computer when I was elbows deep in drafting or editing. Thank you for being my number one supporter and when I start to doubt myself you remind me how incredible I am.

To N. and M., because when you both heard I was writing a book, your little jumps and claps made me keep pushing to show you that you should always go after your dreams.

To Adriana for being more than a best friend and alpha reader. Thank you for proofreading tons of my words and changing all my "its" for "it's" when they were necessary. Thank you for hyping me up after I shared my unhinged ideas and for helping me be completely delusional.

To Jen and Crystal for willingly reading this book as it was being written and not letting me give up with your sweet comments.

To my beta readers. Jayné, your grammar corrections, sweet comments, and suggestions made this book better. Thank you for giving me feedback gently but also helping me make this book what it is today. Mikayla Hornedo, your whole author self, gave this baby book a try and gave me valuable feedback. I will never be able to repay you. Mandy, you beta read for so many big authors, the fact that you took time from your busy schedule meant the world to me too. Kelsey, your input was incredible and I loved your overall help in making this book even better. Thank you so much.

To Wonder and Wander Editing for dealing with the hardest part of writing and doing it graciously. Thank you for your never-ending work making sure this book was the best version of itself possible. Thank you for making me feel like I knew what I was doing even when you had to flip the order of my sentences so many times (my bilingual brain chaos). Sophie, you are an angel and more people need you in their lives.

To KBG, Kim, you already know the screams that came out of my body when I saw this illustrated cover. Thank you for making my dreams come true. You're one in a million!

To all the Arc readers who read and review my baby book. Thank you from the bottom of this indie author's heart. Thank you to all, especially to Colleen, Sarah and Beth.

To my author friends, Veronica, Nicole, Emily, Bella, Mikayla, and Rachel. Thank you for answering my million questions and for showing me that this job can be so rewarding but also challenging. Thank you for never making me feel like I was bothering you with all my comments and for walking me off the ledge, multiple times without even knowing it. Thank you for showing me that we all thrive better when we work together and there is room for everyone in the publishing world.

To my mom and brothers for always making me feel like I could do anything I set my mind to. Gracias de todo corazón.

To YOU reader, for giving me a chance and making my wildest dreams come true.

Last but not least, thank you, Joey, again. I hope when you read this, you see all the little and big parts of you in Jake and know that you are such an incredible husband, I had to find a way to share you with the world. Even if it's just in the form of a fictional character. You deserve the world babe, just like you have given the world to me.

Now off to cry in baby author tears and on to the next book.

143,

Ambar

About The Author

Ambar is a debut author of Small Town Romance Series: Baker Oaks. She writes multicultural romance that brings joy and butterflies to her readers. Ambar is a wife and mom of two who has been living in Florida since 2015, and who loves the small town where she currently lives.

Born and raised in the Dominican Republic, she embraces cultural differences and brings that to her books. When she is not writing, she is enjoying time with her family, traveling, and reading.

To learn more, scan her

Want more Baker Oaks?

Roe, 24

"Drop the doll and change it for Roe," I say, annoyed at the handsome man standing in front of me.

He smirks, showing me that perfect dimple, stretches his hand and says, "Santiago, nice to see you."

I don't even entertain the hand stretched in front of me before adding, "I'm not sure how men treat women where you are from but out here, we save the pet names for actual relationships. What do you want *Sunshine?" I ask sarcastically.*

"How about a Bud Light?" He asks taking the edge off his words.

Bud Light? I did not picture this guy drinking that at all. "Coming right up."

I walk towards my tap and fill a cup with beer, spilling some everywhere because even after years of pouring beer, I still make a mess. Before I turn back to him, I get an idea. I pour some whiskey, old good Old Rip Van Winkle, on the rocks in two short glasses.

Placing both drinks in front of him and looking him dead in the eyes I say, "Here, why don't you drink some whiskey, like a real man." And down one of the glasses in one gulp. "On the house." I wink at him and walk the opposite way, leaving the other one for him to enjoy.

TTOC coming fall 2024